Job

by Sean Longley

"Police officers go bad for two reasons:

They're bent for money or bent for the job"

Sir Robert Mark

Chapter 1

The boy cannot be more than ten years old. He runs, bending at the waist commando style and ducking through the branches into the hollow center of the bush. It is different inside. It is mottled green. Under water, with tendrils waving like weeds. Camouflage. Even the sounds and shouts of the footballers seem deadened and far away.

It takes a moment for his eyes to get use to the half-light, then seconds for him to take it in. One leg is crooked up at the knee, with the other twisted beneath her body. She is bone white, and for a moment he thinks that the bleached angles are branches. He starts, taking in the stained, damp hair plastered over the ruined face, the naked breasts and the ugly slash from sternum to genitals through which glimpses of blue and red glisten like oil in sunshine. He is fascinated, frozen in the moment until the sounds of Sunday wear their way through and he screams, backing out into the sunshine shutting his eyes tightly and calling for his mother.

The woman siting on the bench will be unable to explain why she knew that it was her child who was screaming, or what it was about the pitch that made her rise and run towards the source. She holds, calms and follows the trembling finger point through the gap into the hedge. A wave of sight and smell. A retch controlled and swallowed down as she comforts her son with one hand while she reaches into her pocket.

The first 999 call is made at 09:37, the news of the discovery falling into the undisturbed surface of a springtime Sunday morning. Ripples run. Voices rise and fall. A man in jogging gear takes the news to a group of men in hi-visibility vests. The second call. It is now 09:43. A calmer voice and a landline number that the call center operator can identify as coming from a council lock up on Peckham Rye. Ripples spread. Through the mothers and fathers, the dog walkers, the footballers, kite flyers and returning revelers across the Rye. Through the concrete and the clay of South London along buried wires. Crossing the city bouncing from mobile mast to mobile mast like Spiderman. 999 calls and responses. All the way to Lewisham Police Station and the Serious Crime Directorate. To the Duty Team Leader on

Sunday. To DCI Ken McGuiness, who is nursing a headache and a hope that an uncharacteristic outbreak of peace and goodwill might let him leave at the end of an eight hour shift and return to his pregnant wife.

The response is quick. It has to be. The Metropolitan Police always learns from its mistakes and prides itself on being the most educated force in England. The air shimmers blue and red. Sirens yelp and wail. Cordons are set up. Details are requested. Evidence and actions are recorded in the notebooks issued for that purpose. White suited forensic technicians sift the debris, collecting, collating and recording. The Forensic Medical Examiner arrives, fresh from the 19th hole as the cliché demands. He pronounces life extinct, which surprises nobody, given the caved in head and partial disemboweling. 11:23. She is officially dead, whoever she may be, and Sunday is officially ruined. The officials doing the ruining spread out in force. They clear the football pitches and the playgrounds. They confine the dog walkers and playpark families behind a frontier of plastic crime scene tape. By the time the ambulance arrives to collect the remains, even the ice cream van has thrown in the towel. Peckham Rye is abandoned to aftermath.

Tarmacking and traffic mean that the roads are as free flowing as a Scotsman's arteries. McGuiness is resigned, and stares out of the window. He checks his reflection as identical red brick streets amble past. He's not looking any younger. His hair is still black, but there are one or two grey hairs that have become more assertive as time and responsibility wear down his not exactly golden youthful looks. His scar still crosses his lower lip, and his nose is still broken. His face shows every second of his forty two years. He yawns. It is work's time being wasted and nobody is going home early today. DS Kath Stevens is driving. She is drumming her fingers on the wheel and looking more pissed off than the situation requires. It is not as if the deceased is going to come back to life if the senior investigating officer doesn't show up in an hour, and the prospect of finding a lunatic with a blood stained sword fleeing the scene wearing nothing but a tartan dressing gown are poor. He turns to look at her. He has worked with her before, and she has always been a safe pair of hands. Conscientious, and as neat and rounded as her schoolgirl handwriting. Thin rather than slim, late thirties. Heavy make up. A local girl, with an accent that occasionally gets on his tits. It's not that she's actually whining. It just sounds that way. He

wonders whether he should ask her what the problem is.
Decides against it. She's job. Job stays at work. She knows him
well enough not to be afraid to talk to him about anything that's
work related. Anything else and there's family, friends, and pets
or even, if you have more money than sense, professionals.
The car in front judders to a halt. Break lights glare red and
catch the dirt on the windscreen. It stipples her cheek and makes
her face look inflamed. She's not smiling as she says,

"I'm up the Bailey later this week."

A tremble in her voice makes her bleat slightly, and swallow to
catch herself.

"I'm not looking forward to it, guv, to be honest."

She's steadier, but still sounds worried. It's out of character for
her. She's been around the block a few times, and shouldn't be
getting the vapours about the prospect of answering a few
questions, even at London's most famous and imposing court.
It's not a case he was involved in himself. She'd been seconded to
a different team in one of the Met's periodic staffing crises. He
hadn't heard any rumours about this one going bad, although
that wouldn't be the sort of thing anyone would boast about. He
puts on his best senior officer's face.

"All you can do is tell the truth, Kath. We're only there to present
the evidence we gathered. It's down to the prosecution now it's
at Court. Are they saying that you put the thumb screws on some
poor, innocent defendant?"

Very reassuring. Just the right note of humour as well. A mental
pat on the back. Well done, chief inspector. You are a manager
and an investigator. The new face of the new Met.

"I wasn't even interviewing. I was exhibits officer.   There's no
reason for me to be there, really. Unless...."

This does get his attention. The exhibits officer's job is to
catalogue all the physical evidence. To record where things were
found, by whom and where; then make sure that everything gets
to court in a recognisable state. Not exactly controversial, unless

you really managed to screw things up and that's not her. She's the sort who irons and files her knickers. A little bit OCD.

"It's a shooting. The dead man was a dealer. He had a key to a flat in Docklands on him. There was money everywhere. All over the place. Piles of it. It took 6 of us a whole day to count and catalogue it, and I recorded every exhibit. Every seal number, where it was found, by whom and how much. When I went to check everything against the statements it came up five grand short. The statements say it's an Adidas sports bag with twenty five grand in it. My search book says twenty."

Her hands drum on the wheel convulsively. It's over the top, but probably just the way she is. She likes things neat. It's all a little bit Rain Man, and as she eases the car expertly through a gap in traffic he consoles himself with the thought that she is an excellent driver.

"I wouldn't worry about it, Kath. It's obviously a mistake. If that's the best the defence can come up with chances are your man will see the writing on the wall, plead it out and you'll all be in the pub by lunchtime. This sort of thing happens all the time. People cock things up. There's no conspiracy. If I had to answer questions about it, I'd be more than willing to give up the fact that I'd made a minor mistake in the filing. That should take the wind out of their sails. I'd be amazed if it came to that, though."

She smiles. And pulls the car off the main road onto a track that leads down hill into a car park. A white forensic tent has been put up. It covers the whole of the bush and surrounding area. Nothing is being left to chance. McGuiness and Stevens put on the full CSI kit of boiler suits, gloves and foot coverings before ducking inside the tent. He sees the dead woman. Not young. Her hair is dyed and her nails are painted a swimming pool blue, but there is an unmistakable sagging around the neck and jaw that even the catastrophic injuries to her head and face can't disguise. She's naked, so either the killer has been very forensically minded, washed the body elsewhere and dumped her on the Rye or it's a sex thing. Maybe it's both. Forensic TV has made everyone an expert. Either way, the solution isn't going to be found on Peckham Rye this morning. At least, not by him. The lads and lasses in the white boiler suits are there for that, and they are the experts. He's here getting the flavour and flying the flag. Never fear, citizens, the murder squad is here. On the scene and ready to protect the public. Playing their part in bringing out the dead.

***

The bus bellows and pants as it accelerates down hill. Father Anthony Mitchell sits in the center of the top deck and stares out of the window at London. He notices flashing lights. Blue and white cars, high visibility strips glinting like granite, and a huddle of policemen in a park. He wonders what could have caused this gathering. A brief thought. Gone and lost among the half familiar images of an English city. It has been a long time. He yawns, stretches and settles to watch London as the bus passes Peckham Rye.

Father Anthony waits. The arms of the chair are slightly too high, and he is forced to sit to attention or have his elbows pinned by his sides. An expanse of desk lies between him and the empty chair that will soon contain Bishop Mark Catesby. The office is a study in Spartan. A crucifix the only break in the walls' white emptiness. No ornaments. The desk is mahogany, as are the bookshelves that loom in from every side. The books are large, leather and gilt, patterns of green, black, red and gold repeating and endlessly reflecting off glass. The flat screen television and the ergonomic chair are incongruous. Functional and modern. The television is on, but mute. A red faced man talks enthusiastically about what rolling captions tell him is racing from Newmarket. Horses are being guided towards starting cages.

Bishop Catesby sits heavily. He opens a desk draw, withdraws a remote and points it at the screen without a word. The horses vanish and are replaced by an image that is so uncomfortably familiar that it makes Father Anthony's stomach contract. A white church, squat and box like with a stub of a tower. Three bricks thick and a silhouette of a bell against the vivid sky. Bougainvillea and palm trees. Red earth, stamped flat and hard, bordered on two sides by grey sheds and on the third by a set of four concrete steps rising to the church door.

A crowd has formed, milling belligerently around the square. The film is silent, but Father Anthony hears the distorted voices of transistor radios, vicious, inciting, haranguing the crowd. A chant begins, spreading until every mouth opens and closes in a rhythm reinforced by stamping feet and waving fists. The camera pans in a circle, settling on a jeep. Five European soldiers finger automatic weapons in nervous displacement. One is standing on the flat back of the vehicle. He lowers a light machine gun at the camera. A hand falls upon his arm and he raises the weapon back to safety. He pulls off his blue helmet and runs his fingers through blond hair. He sits, shrugging and lighting a cigarette. The camera zooms in on his face. His eyes are narrowed and his face is streaked with dust and sweat. He looks self conscious, aware that he is out of place and does not understand his surroundings. Reduced to an observer despite his gun. He hides his anxiety behind a cupped hand.

The camera moves back to the crowd. Machete blades flash silver blue above heads. They advance on the church, shout, stamp and retreat, narrowing the distance with each surge. The film distorts and reforms. Chaos. They are at the foot of the steps. The camera moves to the door, hazing and focusing. It opens inward, and a man walks into the sunlight. He is European, dressed in a cassock and dog collar. He carries a large wooden cross. He speaks to them; utterly serene as knives whirl wickedly inches from his face. It is impossible to read his lips. The camera is too far away and the footage is dirty with pixels. The cross shadows his face. The impression is confessional, intimate. The anger breaks over him. He kneels, crossing himself with his right hand as he holds the wooden crucifix in front of him. A haze of static, and when the film resumes the crowd are on their knees. The priest rises, makes the sign of the cross in the air and bows. He turns his back and withdraws to the church, closing the door. The camera's attention returns to the jeep. The blond soldier throws his cigarette over his shoulder and clasps his hands. His face is beatific.

Father Anthony falls into a stillness so profound he can feel his heart beating and the controlled rush of blood to his extremities. He closes his eyes and tries to force some reality into his memory. It was only a month ago, but all he can see is the footage. The soldiers. The mob. Everything is grainy and monochrome. Second hand. There was no physical reason for it. He hadn't been injured. Yet there it was, a part of his life that could have happened to someone else. Perhaps something had gone wrong and the intensity of the experience had just been misfiled. It could be rediscovered at any time. These things usually came to him by accident. Flotsam that surfaced without warning. The combination of a long lost bicycle lock or the results of a football match. The undiluted afternoon was there somewhere and there was no point in holding one's breath. It was in God's hands.

A cough. The Bishop is on his feet and has his hand extended. Father Anthony rises, mortified that his inattention could be mistaken for pride. Mark Catesby is too polished a politician to show any displeasure.

"Taken by a German aid worker on his mobile telephone. There's not a man in the world, be he Catholic, Muslim or even Church of England who hasn't seen it.
It couldn't come at a better time. Some among us have behaved very badly. We have what the politicians call an image problem"

His face contorts as his fingers claw exaggerated quotation marks.

"But this film. It's inspirational. I have to ask you Father. What happened?"

Father Anthony Mitchell's response has the fluency of practice.

"I really can't remember. I have prayed, but God hasn't found me worthy of taking into his confidence. I can remember some things, of course. The inside of the church. The people huddled around the altar. The certainty of my own death and my surprise at how tranquil I felt. I can even remember how the sunlight hurt my eyes so much when I came outside that I could hardly see the mob. I didn't even know that the soldiers were there. If I had, I would probably have tried to appeal to them. "

He slumps back into his uncomfortable chair. Spent. Expecting derision. Anger even. Disappointment for certain. He notices that there is a peculiar smell in the room. A mixture of leather, musk and must. He cannot decide whether this comes from the building itself, or if the Bishop has brought it with him. His eyes are drawn back to the television. The riders' shirts are vividly colourful and the horses beautifully sleek, their muscles as defined as Roman statues. A black horse is winning, and he finds himself willing it to stumble.

The Bishop coughs, and repeats himself with cleared throat volume.

'How do you see yourself serving the Church?"

He knows it has to be now. The asking may be uncomfortable and the chances of getting slim, but he lives in an age of miracles. He has seen the proof, and who knows whether a blessing will be repeated. He is humble. Hesitant. The voice of an invalid.

"I should like to go on retreat, your grace. My health is not good. I get these terrible headaches. It's like my skull is going to burst. I hoped that silence and contemplation…"

Bishop Catesby raises a hand, palm out like a traffic policeman. It brings Father Anthony to an obedient stop.

"I understand that you have been through a great deal." He gestures towards a fat manila folder on his desk, "and I don't mean just in Africa. I have to ask you one question, do you still have faith?"

The silence is broken by the sound of Bishop Catesby leafing through the file. The pages flick as his nails glint pinkly, their cuticles like crescent moons. Father Anthony nods. The question requires no verbal response.

"When you were found by the Bristol Ring Road in 1985 it was assumed that you had been the victim of a hit and run driver. You spent 7 months in a coma, before waking up and announcing to the surprised nursing staff that you wanted to see a priest. Everything that happened to you for the months that you lay in that bed was planned and performed upon you by others. Every action you took after waking up was catalogued and dissected by specialists who regarded your faith as evidence that you were suffering from some kind of mental illness. You had no idea of your name, where you came from or the events that brought you to the roadside and caused your injuries. Although you were chronologically at least in your early twenties, the only free will you were allowed to exercise was your choice of name. Why did you chose the name Anthony, father?"

"It was the name of the nurse who looked after me while I was in intensive care. Well, Antonia Mitchell. It is a tradition. Foundlings always take their carer's name. I used to visit her before I went to Africa, but she died."

Bishop Catesby purses his lips. The conversation is a journey. It has a destination. It would be less troublesome if he travelled with a companion rather than a prisoner. He lowers his voice. It is intimate. Companionable. Who could disagree?

"That tradition applies to infants, Anthony. To those abandoned innocents who need a name to write above a hospital cot. It was not given to you. You were an adult, even though you had no memory of your life before the accident. I have no doubt that Mrs Mitchell was flattered by your choice, but that is exactly what it was. A choice. You do believe that God involves himself in the lives of his children, don't you?"

Father Anthony nods. A trickle of pain meanders down his temple. It is mild, something he would hardly register were it not for the way the meeting was developing. It unsettles him.

"I do"

A statement of faith. Uncontroversial. What harm could come of that? The Bishop bares his teeth. An advocate's smile. He lays out his case.

"Well then. There you were. 1986. If you had even been to church before you came round you had no memory of it, yet when you had the chance you chose to take the name of St Anthony of Padua. The Patron Saint of lost things. The saint who could be relied upon to bring you home. And he did. You came home to the Church. It is as elegant as a mediaeval parable. "

The hand is raised again. The palm is pink, soft as prime steak. This is not to be a dialogue.

"You told the doctors that you saw your damnation as you lay in your coma. Instead of shrugging it off you came to the Church.

That is not a coincidence. You were called to what could make you whole. You needed the Church just as you are needed."

The palm becomes a point. Lord Kitchener seeking a recruit across a no mans land of polished wood. His skin gathers at the corner of his eyes. Laughter lines without humour, despite the lightness of voice and the half parody of the gesture. Father Anthony is horrified. He gasps. Surely they cannot mean to send him back.

"Your Grace. I can't go back there. There are so many things that I don't understand..."

He hears the catch in his voice and it fills him with disgust. He sounds like a child. He searches for the right phrase, one that would get across the horror he feels. Defeated, he opens his arms and surrenders. Bishop Catesby smiles. There is no need for unpleasantness.

"We aren't monsters, Anthony. Nobody expects you to go back. You probably have some form of post traumatic stress disorder, and we'll arrange for you to get the appropriate counseling. But you are needed. Not there, but here. London has changed a lot in the ten years you spent in Africa. There's a huge African community here, and as a Lingala and African French speaker you are in a unique position to reach out to them. There are some deeply unpleasant people purporting to cater for spiritual welfare among this diaspora. The police fished the mutilated body of a ten year old boy out of the Thames a few years ago. They believe he had been some kind of human sacrifice. The Church needs representatives who won't be reduced to irrelevant dispensers of Sunday morning wine and wafers. There's work to be done here that is every bit as vital as that which you have been doing for the last ten years. It wouldn't be dangerous. Compared to what you are used to, the life of the parish priest in England will be quite restful. Obviously, if you really need to get away we'll support that, but you could be making such an important difference to people's lives."
Father Anthony realises that this is a consultation. His views have been heard, taken into account and rejected in favour of a solution that was decided before he took his seat. He leaves as he arrived, a man about to take up the post of parish priest of St Stevens, Rotherhithe.

***

Germaine MacHeath stands on the path at the side of the football pitch waiting for the game to end so he can collect his brother and go for Sunday Lunch. The support isn't exactly twenty deep at the touchline, so although the pitch is about fifteen feet away, there's nothing stopping him losing himself in the beautiful game if he wanted to. But he doesn't. He's not a big football fan. Nominally Arsenal, but that's more of a cultural thing, growing up in Lewisham and with Ian Wright being a local boy. Knows enough to hold a conversation but never been to a game. Other interests.

He checks the time. Half an hour to go plus injury time, and only three minutes later than when he last looked. He swears to himself, then stamps his feet and hunches his shoulders into his coat. It's not exactly cold but the inactivity makes it feel that way. On the pitch he sees Danny trap the ball and make a run. He beats one defender before being bundled to the ground. There are shouts of outrage from the two girls who seem to be the entire home support. He thinks he recognises one of them. Short, light skinned girl with processed hair and gaps between her front teeth. Seen her around the area, he's sure. The other one is a tall blonde in black leggings, with a jacket that is either Prada or Deptford Market. She looks like the sort of university girl that made staying in education worthwhile. She notices him looking at her, then turns away and says something to her friend. He grins to himself, and checks the time again. Twenty seven minutes left. Germaine MacHeath. Stuck in the park that time forgot. There is nothing to do but try and catch the blonde girl's eye, but she is too far away. He is almost relieved when the police arrive and close the game down. "Thank goodness you are here, officer." There's a first time for everything.

It's a short drive from Peckham to Brockley. Fifteen minutes at most. Danny the student finds the bin liner his brother has forced him to sit on uncomfortable and degrading. His oppressor is unsympathetic, pointing out that it is hardly his fault that the police blocked all access to the changing rooms, and that not getting mud on the cream leather upholstery of his brother's Range Rover hardly makes him a latter day Rosa Parks. He's not even sitting in the back of the car.

"Is Damien going to be there?"

Danny looks a little nervous. It's not like he thinks that there's going to be trouble at the family Sunday lunch, but the memory of a thousand petty childhood pub garden acts of violence committed over crisps, coke and adult inattention is still strong. His brother laughs.

"I doubt it. Omen won't have time for Sunday with family when there are girls out there unstalked, with unlocked bedroom windows and pretty screams."
They both laugh. Danny was always all right when there were the two of them. Germaine has always been what his mother called "a big, strong boy". Cousin Damien only became a problem when his brother went away.

The MacHeath family home is a Victorian terraced house on a street that could be anywhere in South East London. It was a council house until their mother managed to buy it in the 1980's, stretching her nurse's pay until it almost broke to join the property owning democracy. Buying it properly had taken years of double shifts, repair bills, day care and being too tired to do anything but shuffle her way through cooking an evening meal. It was important that her boys ate home cooked food and not fried chicken. Eating together is what makes a proper family. The Range Rover glides to a stop outside, gleaming and out of place as a tank among the rows of red brick. The journey may change, and leather seats are a step up from bus passes, but the doorstep fumble for the key never does. The MacHeath boys let themselves in and are home.

The kitchen is full of steam and smells of cooking. Danny is light on his feet. A kiss for his mother filled with genuine warmth. One for his auntie with an equal measure of duty, then off up the stairs to shower. Germaine greets, goes to the fridge and helps himself to a can of lager. His mother has brought these in specially. Her tastes don't run to Stella Artois, a brand chosen because the adverts used to call it reassuringly expensive. No son of hers is going to drink like a tramp. Germaine takes a glass. His mother is the house. It is part of her; like the blue uniform and the Lewisham Hospital ID badge. She won't have him drinking from a can, and the house rules.

Barbara MacHeath and Sandra Anderson have been friends for longer than either of them wanted to remember. Back when she was Barbara Williams, and before she even met the man who would show her a good time and a clean pair of heels, keeping only one of his many promises in the process then leaving her with two sons and a family name that was almost Shakespeare. Meadow View Children's Home was in Catford, and although the residents came from a variety of backgrounds, they all knew they were Londoners. Sandra Anderson was short, skinny and mixed race. Six years old and small for her age. So far, so very usual, but you could tell that she was different as soon as she opened her mouth. Sandra Anderson had a broad, West Country accent. It was unfortunate for her that this was the year that "I've Got a Brand New Combine Harvester" was one of the biggest selling records in Britain. It wasn't that a difference this massive might have gone unnoticed without it, but the song gave her new housemates such a ready stock of nicknames and taunts that Bristol Social Services might as well have delivered a joke book.

Sandra's only piece of luck was that she was forced to share a room with Barbara Williams. If she had been less tearful and helpless, the now second youngest girl at Meadow View might have resented having to share her room more than she felt sorry for the new arrival. Even at the age of seven she possessed the glare that would become famous for sending the most determined prescription seeking drug addict fleeing from the Accident and Emergency Department. Nobody was going to bully her friend, and Sandra was her friend. She said so, and nobody was going to argue with her. Least of all the youngest girl. A combination of Barbara's protection and natural erosion meant that by Sandra's seventh birthday her accent was the same as everyone else's. The jokes dried up. It was just the nickname that stuck. No matter how many times she tried to tell her friends that Bristol was a city, just like London but smaller, she was a country girl with a wide selection of agricultural machinery and farm animals. She was "Country", and that was that. You only get to pick your own name if you are a drag queen or a Mexican wrestler.

The price of Barbara's friendship was that she was in charge. She would pick where they were going to go, what they wore and whom they liked and disliked. Grown up, and with children of their own, Barbara was still in charge, doling out the chicken and potatoes, and directing the conversation to how well her sons were doing. Danny's education needed extensive discussion, as did Germaine's successes in what he told them was music promotion, but seemed to Sandra to involve night clubs, a well known source of drugs and crime. Finally, her Damien gets a mention. Last on the list, even though he was three years older than Danny and only eight months younger than Germaine.

"I swear I saw Damien the other day, Country. I was on the 171 going through Peckham. He was on the square by the Pulse with a lovely looking light skinned girl. Is she his girlfriend? What's her name?"

Germaine smiles, and Sandra knows there is unkindness behind it before he opens his mouth.

"I can tell you who it isn't, Auntie, if you want?"

Danny is smiling too. As if he would have the nerve to be so disrespectful without his brother to hide behind. Germaine is off before she has the chance to reply, racing towards the punch line.

"She's not Jessica Ennis. She's too fast for Omen to catch."

The problem with being so light skinned is that she blushes like a white girl, even at her age. She can feel her cheeks heating up. It is so unfair. It is not as if Germaine hasn't been in trouble, although she is has far too much respect for his mother to mention it. Her voice catches and she stutters as she speaks. She always does when she has to defend her son. Wub, wub, wub, like a turkey. Country and her farm animals.

"That's not fair, Germaine. That girl lied, and the police covered up evidence that she had gone with lots of boys before. And don't call him Omen. It's horrible. His name is Damien, and he was just in the wrong place at the wrong time."

"True that, auntie. The wrong place is gang banging a thirteen year old girl, and the wrong time is just as you paint her knickers with your DNA."

Both boys laugh and touch fists across the table.

"Enough!"

The voice of authority. Laughter freezes and hangs in mid air like Wiley Coyote running off a cliff.

"If you boys can't behave yourself at the table, then you had better make a start on the washing up. Now say sorry to your auntie."

Muttering their apologies, Germaine and Danny clear the table and troop dutifully towards the sink. Their mother considers dishwashers to be a sign of immorality, and this is going to take some time.

Chapter 2

The sun is going down over Lewisham Market. On the seventh floor of Europe's largest police station picture windows open onto Legoland South London. Built to loom and show the world the blue gang runs the streets.

Team meeting of what the random name generator has decided is to be called Operation Grandville. Twenty officers, a whiteboard and DCI McGuiness, not exactly fresh from the autopsy and armed with the startling news that the woman in the bush has something that make her as recognizable as a celebrity, a criminal record.

"Ladies and gentlemen, you all know I'm Chief Inspector McGuiness. Operation Grandville concerns the murder of a lady we now know to be Jane Marie Canavan, whose body was found in a hollow hedge on Peckham Rye Common this morning. The pathologist reckons that either the blows to the head, of which there were at least three and as many as five, or the stab wounds to the abdomen were enough to kill her on their own. They were both inflicted very close to each other in time, so we are looking at a frenzied attack. Jane died violently, in fear and in pain.

She had had sex at some stage in the evening before her murder. There are no genital injuries, so while we cannot rule out that the two are completely unrelated, the identity of the person whose DNA has been recovered has to be a person of interest to this enquiry.

We haven't found her clothing, her handbag, her phone or any other identifying documents. She wasn't street homeless, her fingernails are well looked after and she was generally clean, so unless she was a nudist and an Amish, her phone, cards, bag and clothing are out there. Anyone found with any of these is to be arrested and I want all stations and officers in the Met area and in all surrounding forces alerted to the fact that we want to talk to this person and we are to have first call on any questioning, no matter what other offences have brought them to attention.

I am going to need a full background on her. All we know at present is that she is fifty one years old, and she was living in

Bridgend in South Wales when she was a teenager. She has one juvenile conviction for arson, which is how we were able to get an identification so quickly. I need to know what she was doing in London, how long she's been here, who her friends were and most importantly, all about her lifestyle. I am putting the two of you onto this and DS Wilson is in charge. I need a full camera check for all CCTV in the surrounding streets. At least a one mile radius, which takes us into Peckham and out as far as East Dulwich and Nunhead. She got to the Rye somehow. Let's find out how. The four of you are on this, reporting to Sergeant Peters. All local authority and private business cameras are to be fully investigated and all footage is to be secured. This is a vital enquiry and I do not want anything overlooked. DI Walsh is going to review all the notes the uniforms took of names and addresses of people on the Rye. He is in charge of all house-to-house enquiries and statement taking. He will be appointing one of you who is video interview trained to take a statement from the little lad who found her and his mother. This must be done sensitively, but we cannot afford to sit on our hands until he has forgotten all the details, so a bit of firmness may be required. The rest of you are under DI Walsh. He'll tell you where to go and who to interview. DS Stevens is exhibits officer, so anything you take is to be logged with her."

Delegation is the key to management, and it is all about management. Everyone knows what to do, and he is free to concentrate on what's important. The room hives about its business and he makes his exit to the Forensic Science Service labs in Lambeth. The exhibits taken during the post mortem need to be analyzed as soon as possible. The chain of evidence needs to be preserved, so that the defence cannot claim that whatever DNA the scientists may have found can't be shown to come from Jane Marie Canavan. Someone needs to take it, and as it is the most important part of the enquiry at the moment it should be him. As he pulls the car into the traffic, he calls home and is treacherously relieved to get an answerphone.

"Maxine, it's me. We've caught one and I have to do the lab run then get back to Lewisham for a briefing. Don't wait up."

He hesitates. Wonders if he should tell her that he loves her then decides against it. He's not a puppies, kittens, hearts and flowers sort of man, and a change of personality looks suspicious. The streetlights have begun to flicker on and it starts to rain, almost hard enough to stop the wipers squealing against the glass.

It takes all of ten minutes to book the exhibits into FSS storage. The shift is changing, and McGuiness waits in the car, hunched in the seat like he's undercover. It's irrational and he knows it. The chances of there being someone he knows outside the job here on a Sunday night are slim to none. He is trying not to think about his wife. The radio is on, and playing a selection of 80's hits that doesn't distract him. Quite the reverse. He slumps in his seat as the Jam launch into Eaton Rifles. Takes you back, this, he thinks. Back to Uni. Back to cramped bed-sits and roll ups. Back to when he first got to know Max, or Maxine Imogene Slade as she was then, although "got to know" might be a bit of an exaggeration.

He had seen her when his Dad dropped him off at the hall of residence for the first time. She was climbing the outside steps to the caretaker's flat. She was wearing black leggings and a Dennis the Menace mohair sweater that slipped off her shoulder to show the world that that gravity didn't touch her. His father had nudged him, pointed her out. "You'll have a good time here, son, right enough." He'd joined in the laughter, but they both knew that she was out of his league. Her clothes and the confident sway of her hips as she glided up the concrete stairwell marked her out as one of the cool kids. The ones who wouldn't give him the time of day at school and who went to the parties to which he was never invited. "Be yourself, son," went the parental advice in a family in which honesty was elevated above all. He had no talent for reinvention at that age, and it probably saved him from a lot of painful memories. The 1980's could be unforgiving for the follower of fashion.

She cropped up everywhere. Her room was on the same landing, making some form of contact inevitable. Her appearance in his tutorial group was practically accompanied by celestial light and a heavenly choir. It gave him the chance to get to know her from a distance. He found her accent entrancing. Flat vowels placed her in the South East and an inability to maintain them hinted at the privilege that her strident conviction emphatically rejected. Maxine Slade was on the side of the oppressed. She spoke up for the miners, CND and the Wapping strikers. She went to Stonehenge Festival. She wore black and white stripy tights. She smoked dope. The young McGuiness was so besotted by her that he was blind to the fact that his status as possibly the only genuinely working class student on the block was precisely what made her so unobtainable. He spent two painful years permanently on the verge of asking her out, although in all honesty even speaking to her outside the confines of a discussion about the English Civil War would have been unimaginable. Then she disappeared.

There was no such thing as a secret, and what happened to Maxine was common knowledge within days. She had lost it, taken acid and run out of the house to be found hitchhiking naked by the police. She was in hospital. She wasn't coming back. It was often repeated, and always with the gloating schadenfreude that only the downfall of a pretty, popular and intelligent girl can bring. Every time he heard it Ken was filled with a mixture of pity and resentment, with an undercurrent of excitement at the mental image of Maxine Slade in the raw that made him feel vaguely uncomfortable. He didn't defend her out loud, but he fought bloody battles for her reputation in his imagination.

He never forgot her. When he stopped being Kenny the student and became PC McGuiness he even ran her through the Police National Computer. It revealed a caution for possession of puff, and an address that was "live" in 1989. The trail was cold. She stayed with him as an ideal against which his actual girlfriends could never compare. He never collected photos of her or anything weird, but there was always a part of him that kept a shrine to Maxine Imogen Slade.

The only way from the top of the pedestal is down. Every couple will have tears and laughter, as they say, but Maxine off her meds was more than capable of giving the full emotional range in a single sentence. It would be out of order to blame her. They'd decided what to do together, so he had to take his own part of the responsibility on, but it didn't make it any better. It's only natural that he'd look for a shoulder to cry on, and naturally predictable what would happen once the crying was over.

Doctor Sarah Reed walks over to the car, opens the passenger door and gets in. Forensic scientist, expert witness and, he supposes, mistress. Girlfriend would be wrong. He's a married man. Lover offends him to the lapsed Catholic core. She's wearing a red woolen coat that makes him think of forests and the big bad wolf. She's almost as tall as he is, and if she's not quite young enough to be his daughter, she's a credible candidate for younger sister at twenty nine. The interior light reflects from her black hair for a second, and then she closes the door and leans across to kiss him on the mouth. It's not passionate. You would have to be watching them very closely to notice it go beyond a casual greeting and the street is empty. He turns his head away from her and drives.

Chapter 3

He only agreed to come to some student party because his brother asked and he had nothing better to do. It kills a few hours on a Sunday night before the really important business begins. It's unfortunate, really. Germaine likes a drink and a smoke as much as the next man, but he has to keep a clear head. He leans against a door and watches them dance. They are only a few years younger than him, but they could be from a different planet. He is thinking of wandering off and waiting for his ride in the nearest pub, when he sees her. She's not dancing and she's not part of the group who are smoking weed around the sofa. She leans against the door and she smiles as he looks her up and down, showing him her Hollywood orthodontistry. She's still got her jacket on, and with teeth like that, you know it really is Prada. She has swapped her leggings for a mini skirt. She's fit and she knows it.

Germaine MacHeath pushes himself away from the door and crosses the room to her. He can see she keeps the smile, and doesn't drop her eyes from his.

"Hello. I'm Germaine."

She gives him the smile. It is even better at close range, he thinks, a weapon of mass seduction.

"I know. You're Dan's big brother. Carla's told me all about you."

Dan. His little brother's secret student identity is safely stored for the future. He searches his memory for a Carla and comes up with a family name. Adams. Gappy Carla Adams. She had an older sister who was briefly queen of the shoplifters when they were at school.

"Not all bad I hope."

"Not all, no."

They smile again. He extends his hand and touches her upper arm. The room is close, pregnant with heat and the smells of sweat, hair, perfume and smoke of both varieties but her skin is cool. A mutual flinch. A jolt. Electricity arcs as he guides her towards the stairwell, away from the thunder of the bass and the rustle of conversation.

"What's your name then?"

"Polly"

He puts his hand on her hip as she leans against the wall. She doesn't pull away.

"So, Polly, what does a girl like you like to do when she's not studying?"

She shrugs, her hip moving against his hand,

"This and that. I like to eat. Restaurants. I love going out, dressing up."

She's keeping her voice flat and estuary, but the long vowel sound in "love" is unmistakably up market.

"So could I take you out for a meal, then?"

"Do you think you can afford me?"

He grins.

"Money isn't a problem."

He pulls her towards him, and she doesn't resist. She looks up into his face. The moment is so perfect that the urgent ringing from his inside pocket is almost inevitable.

"Yeah?"

"I'm outside Shanks. You coming?"

He takes out silver card holder and presses a business card into her hand.

"I've got to go. That's my driver. Places to be. You know. Call me though, and we'll get dressed up."

He kisses her. Both cheeks brushed and no saliva. He turns to look back at her as he leaves and notices she is slightly flushed.

**

North Greenwich, by Deptford Bridge railway station is South London's adultery capital. There are a lot of cheap hotels, and since the Olympic show jumpers packed up their dancing horses and left town in 2012, no real reason for wanting to stay in them. It's pushing ten o'clock and Ken McGuiness is thinking of how he can make his excuses and go home to his wife. The sex is fine. Great, even and he is surprised by how easy it is to deal with the guilt. It is just a physical thing, like a cigarette or an illicit trip to Greggs when Maxine put them both on one of her fad diets. No harm, no foul. It hardly feels like he's cheating. Lying next to Sarah, speaking to her. Talking about books, TV shows they liked and the things about work that piss them off seems so much more intimate. She is talking about work now, her worries about her job and the Forensic Science Service being sold off into the private sector. She is leaning on him, her arm across his chest, and he has to move her to get up.

"You are right", he says over his shoulder as he walks into the en suite, "it's a service not a bloody business. They'll be doing it to us next, then it won't be about who done it but who pays. Not what I signed up for. Either everyone matters or nobody does. It's not about prioritising the dead."

He turns the heat up until standing under the flow makes him wince. He shuts his eyes as the water soaks him from the head down and wonders why he says these things to her. "Everyone matters or nobody does." Where the fuck did that come from? He must have read it somewhere. Or possibly heard it on TV. It has something of the Dirty Harry about it. Admirable sentiments, true, but he has to concede that here doesn't feel like the time or the place for moralising. He wonders what would happen if this became his full time life for a second, before he turns the shower off emphatically and steps out onto the mat. Ken McGuiness checks his neck, shoulders and back in the mirror. He is careful, taking the time to wipe away the condensation. He knows the value of forensic evidence.

Back in the bedroom, he gets dressed in a hurry. There is rain on the windows, and the wind is lamenting faintly through the trickle vents. Sarah lies on top of the covers, and he catches himself comparing her with Maxine. Unfair. She's at least ten years younger and, most importantly, not pregnant. It is such a cliché he almost shudders. He is brisk when he speaks to her. Professional. A detective chief inspector not someone who is playing away while his wife is in the club.

"Sarah, that stuff I dropped off to the lab. It's the swabs from the woman whose body was dumped on Peckham Rye. You couldn't give the job a bit of a hurry up, could you?"

He smiles in a way that he hopes is winning. It is how he talked to her when she was someone he chatted to in the course of the working day. Fine in the reception room of her lab, but it sounds as wrong as a kazoo solo with her naked, sprawled on the bed and him half in and half out of his trousers. She doesn't look at him as she answers.

There is nothing in her voice that hints that she is upset, and McGuiness allows himself the luxury of telling himself that she knows the score as he rides the lift down. The rain has set in in earnest, bouncing off the pavement and running the gutters. He pulls up the collar of his coat and steps out into the night like a spy.

***

The SUV's suspension barely registers the potholes at the junction between Greenwich High Street and Blackheath Hill. The neon sign outside the Travelodge shatters into tiny blue dots in the raindrops on the side window. Germaine MacHeath sits in the front passenger seat. Ray "Sugar" Blake is driving. He's a big man, big enough to fill the driver's seat even though the car is huge. A reassuring presence when you are heading into bandit country, even though technically he's the one riding shotgun. Speaking of which:

"You got something for me, Shugs?"

The big man grunts. Nods at the glove box. A handgun. It's safe to assume that everyone is going to be armed this evening, and it's not just social death for anyone who doesn't meet the dress code. It's not that he really expects there to be shooting. The Holiday Inn bar in Bexleyheath is hardly the OK Corral, but he is nervous. Meeting Omen always makes his skin crawl, the spooky dead eyed rapist. It wasn't just the postcode thing, although the fact that he was 100% Lewisham and Damien Anderson was a Peckham boy didn't make things easier.

The Car does a right onto the A2 at the Sun in the Sands Roundabout. The spray is heavy, and the window wipers can only just cope. Passing a lorry is like being dropped into water. It would be frightening if there weren't so much more to be scared of.

"So why are we meeting some fucking Peckham boy and his Paki mate in fucking Bexleyheath?"

It's a good question.

"This is between us?"

"Yes."

"He's not a Paki, he's a Turk, the main man. He was celled up with Omen when he was in Belmarsh last. Some rich student boy doing a lump of bird for killing a kid in a car crash and he didn't have a friend in the jail. Omen says he sort of took him under his wing. Looked out for him and shit."

There is a snort from the driver's seat.

"No lies. Man is the nastiest cunt in London, but that's what I heard from people who were in there with them. Turkish boy stuck to Omen like a shadow. Turns out that although he's a good little student, his uncles are big into heroin. So when Omen gets out, he's straight on to Mustafa about how he owes him. Which he sort of does, although half of those bad black boys he's been protected from are Omen's mates and Peckham Boy scum anyway, so you can take a guess about how much real protecting's going on. Omen calls me and asks me if I can get my hands on some serious money and here we are."

"Why you?"

"Omen's a greedy cunt. He doesn't want to share with all of
Peckham. Me, I'm family. He needs someone to get half the
money together, and it's a blood thing. He's my cousin. He
knows I can do it, and he knows I ain't going to be chatting his
business all over and getting him into trouble with his old
friends. Simple."

Bexleyheath. Sugs makes the turn off just before the road rises
up onto Dartford Heath. MacHeath slides the gun out of the glove
box. He keeps it low, under the level of the dashboard. The rain
is so heavy that any CCTV is going to be useless, but it pays to
keep good habits. He pushes the gun into the back of his
waistband and pulls his coat around him as he jogs to the hotel
reception.

There's not much talk with the hotel staff. Mr Smith and Mr
White are escorted through to a meeting room, and if the
receptionist's curiosity extends beyond the weather or their
journey, he keeps it well hidden. Four men are already sitting
around the table, drinking water and eating the boiled sweets
that have been set out next to the pads of paper. Sitting at the
head of the table is an older, swarthy man. He is wearing a white,
collarless shirt and a black suit. His pepper and salt moustache
would be a credit to a World War One general. Next to him is a
man who cannot be older than his mid twenties. His upper lip
barely supports the sparse imitation of his neighbour's. He's in
head to toe Calvin Klein and looks uncomfortable. There is a
taller, broader man standing behind them. A bodyguard. Damien
Anderson sits on the right. His dark skin is grey under the
striplights, and his face undergoes the painful process of
changing into what he obviously thinks is a welcoming smile. He
is sprawled in his seat, and doesn't get up as they come in,
disguising his height. His legs stretch out underneath the table
and his tracksuit has ridden up to show thin ankles. MacHeath
wonders how easily they would snap as he leans over to shake
his hand. The heating is cranked up to suit the Turks'
sensibilities. The windows are frosted with condensation. It is
almost tropical, but Damien Anderson's hand is cold and dry.

"Cuz."

"Germaine. Meet Mr Suleiman."

MacHeath nods to the older man. Shakes hands.

"And Mustafa. He's my old pad-mate I told you about."

More greetings. Handshakes. To business. Mustafa speaks to the older man in Turkish. Interprets.

"The proposition is that you pay £500 000 and in return we will provide you with good heroin. 99% pure. You pay us in seven days. We provide the product two days later. That's it. You will speak to Musti when you have the money."

Damien Anderson ghetto smiles, gold and white.

"OK Mr Suleiman. I'll be in touch. I'll bring the money. Germaine and me will sort it out between us."

More muttering.

"My uncle fears that the connection between us is documented by the authorities and this puts everyone at risk. He says that all contact should be between Mr MacHeath and me."

There's no gold on show now. Germaine MacHeath looks from one to the other. Surely Omen isn't crazy enough to lose it with these people? Damien Anderson gets himself under control and smiles. He's aiming for obliging and friendly, but misses and gets predatory pedophile passing a crèche.

"Sure, Mr S. Germaine will be in touch with Musti."

More handshakes. Back on the road. Germaine MacHeath sits in silence. It seems to have gone well. He has a mobile number of a new and promising drugs connection in his pocket. There is the small obstacle of raising £250 000 in a week, but he has already got plans to sort out the cash flow. Stepping up. At the moment, he and Omen need each other. True, cousin Damien had always been a sneaky, vicious lowlife, but they're family, or the closest thing to it. Even rats don't bite their own. But then again, they may have known each other since they were kids, but they are certainly not friends, and the "known" thing is probably an exaggeration. What do you do on those Sunday afternoons when you are all little kids and your mother and her friend think that because they are besties, their kids must enjoy a good chat and a cup of tea as well? You watch a bit of TV, play bloody board games and watch the boy your Mum has told you to call "Cousin Damien", tease, pinch, twist, punch, dead arm and dead leg your little brother. You watch because you are so shocked that someone could be this bad you can't react. You can't quite believe how nasty it is at first, and by the time that you are sure that he's not having a laugh it's gone on for too long. The adults have probably heard you laughing too, and you'll be in trouble for not saying anything sooner even if you say something now. Sunday is a day for families. Round it comes again, and it leaves you a little bit more complicit every time Auntie Country and Cousin Damien say their "see you next week" and she gives out cider and fags tasting kisses. He shakes your hand, stares you down and thanks you politely for having him and letting you play with the toys he's borrowed. All until you get to eleven years old, when you put the main lesson that school has taught you into practice and beat the shit out of him. Sitting on his chest and banging his head on the floor until he's begging for mercy, your Mum is pulling you off him by your hair, slapping your thighs and sending you to spend the rest of Sunday in your room alone. You have shaken hands and there has never been any trouble. He grows up into Omen, and you grow up into Shanks. Big men. You make deals, sell drugs and don't fuck each other over, but it's still there. Standing behind you both. History. Even with the gun in the glove box, plans in his head and serious money in the very near future, Germaine MacHeath can't get rid of the thought.

But family is family and business is business. Germaine MacHeath shakes his head and stares out of the window. Tail lights turn the rain into drops and smears of blood.

Chapter 4

The sun has been up a couple of hours. The street cleaning vans have been and gone, giving the homeless their wake up call and incidentally washing the pavements and gutters clear of last night's takeaways and fag ends. The traffic is just beginning to build up, but is still moving with gelatinous freedom.

The elderly man running up his security shutters and watering his hanging baskets is a creature of habit. His father opened the shop at 7am when it was on the Mile End Road, and he was not going to change. In the old days, people would come to pawn their jewelry before work. His customers didn't surface until much later these days, swooping down from Knightsbridge and Mayfair for a hard day's shopping. He still opened early. It is tradition. The shop's security is a regrettable necessity, but it is claustrophobic. It is nice to be outside on a bright morning when the world's washed clean and new.

The blue BMW glides to a halt. The driver is wearing sunglasses. Not about to attract attention in a city where the slightest increase in temperature increases the shorts wearing population by thousands. His Raiders baseball cap is pulled low, with the brim touching the top of the frames. His head is slightly bowed over the wheel, obscuring his face from the pole mounted CCTV cameras. Three men get out of the car. Their walk to the jewelers is measured, unhurried. A slight miscalculation by one of the three means his red hair is caught on camera for a second from behind as he pulls his balaclava over his head. The three men break into a run. Before the jeweler can react they bundle him into the shop. One draws a handgun and holds it on him. He is forced to lie on the floor. The two robbers not involved in crowd control smash the glass display cabinets. Jewelry and watches are transferred into sports bags. The men leave the store at a run, sliding into the BMW and Sunday driving away from the curb with the urgency of a mini cab paid by the hour.

The CCTV inside the shop is high quality. The best that money can buy in an establishment dedicated to the concept that money is no object. Every fold in the robbers' clothing, every tear on the shopkeeper's face, every tremble, twitch and gesture is reproduced. The raid takes less than a minute and a half. The footage is silent, and the contrast with the frenetic aggression gives it an unreal quality. It will be several days before the police can be provided with a full inventory. The witness is treated for shock, but suffers no lasting ill effects. Nothing of evidential significance can be gathered. No identification of the perpetrators can be made, despite it being widely circulated to all Metropolitan Police employees. "Average height or slightly above, average build, although hard to tell through bulky clothing and wearing generic sportswear" does not provide even the most eagle eyed officer with much to go on. There are no forensics. A thoroughly professional job.

***

Germaine MacHeath checks his phone and smiles. It is just after midday and he is waiting for his new car. The crowd outside New Cross railway station is thinning, and he can see the silver VW Golf stop-starting through the traffic towards him. He has a hotel reservation booked, and a restaurant before that. He is reasonably sure that this is what a girl like her would expect.

The blue BMW should be burning somewhere in the back of beyond. He suggested Dartford Heath, but anywhere would do. He is not bothered about the specifics. A manager has to trust his team. Same goes for moving the goods. He's sent Sugar off to see a man about it. They all have something to gain, and too much to lose by double crossing each other. There was more than he thought. Watches, diamonds. Might even have done the lot in one job. Possibilities play in surround sound as he takes the car keys from the kid who's driving and slips him £100 for his trouble. Possibilities for the afternoon. Possibilities for the future. Time will tell about that. Plans may well be changing. The car is kitted out to his specifications. There's some weed in the glove box. He thinks about rolling a joint, but he wants to be sharp. On his game. He lights a cigarette as he drives over the brow of the hill onto Blackheath.

She's waiting for him by the tea hut. A bit of South London working class culture with all the taxi drivers and Millwall boys for authenticity before showing his more sensitive side with dinner at the Oxo Tower. Everything is in place. She stands out a mile. She practically shines, her hair loose about her face and the light behind her. She's wearing high heels, but even if she was in sackcloth and ashes, she'd tower over the others around her. Germaine MacHeath gets out of the car and greets her with a kiss. He's a man on his way.

Chapter 5

Day two. An enquiry on hold until the answers come back from the first wave of questions. The sound of people looking busy.

It's a relatively long walk from the SOCD office to the lepers' corner of the car park. When he returns, the phone is ringing and he has to break into a run to catch it. He listens, his head on one side. The voice is urgent. He is putting on his coat while the other man is still speaking and is out of the door before the receiver is cold.

"With me, please, Sergeant Stevens. Peckham Police Station."

He briefs her as she drives.

"Peckham have just called in that they have arrested one of their frequent fliers trying to use a credit card in Jane Canavan's name in Footlocker. She was being booked in when they got the message to notify us."

Stevens' face shows her disappointment. The prisoner is female. No early baths and champagne for the SCD, but a promising development.

"The strategy is simple. I don't want to interview her about some two bob credit card fraud. We'll leave that for the locals. This woman is not going to want to be a witness, and she'll be very reluctant to be an informant as well."

"What are we going to do?"

"An informal chat. See if I can't get her to see that withholding evidence in a serious enquiry would be an error of judgment."

Stevens looks incredulous.

"I'm going to put the fucking fear of god into her, Sergeant. See if she's up for a bit of enlightened self interest. Off the record, naturally."

The car inches along the bumper to bumper gridlock of the New Cross Road. The traffic irritates him. He wants to be flying in on a helicopter with Ride of the Valkyries blaring. More fitting to the arrival of an avenging angel. He smiles. You catch yourself thinking things like that, and you realise you're one step away from saying it out loud. Another step along that road and you'll be applying for a firearms ticket or signing up for riot training.

A quick flash of the official ID and they are through to the Custody Suite. McGuiness leans against the desk reading the Detention Log while Stevens makes small talk with the locals. Chantelle Joseph. Born in the seventies, making her in her forties now. Lengthy record. Possession, prostitution and thieving. The junkie's CV. The station has been refurbished recently, and the Custody Sergeants sit on a plinth in the centre of the room, masters of all they survey. The cell block is opposite the interview rooms, meaning that any prisoner has to be walked past the officers the law say are responsible for their welfare on their way to and from interrogation. A safeguard he has absolutely no intention of following. He catches Stevens' eye and nods to her. Cell 12. Let's go. He politely declines the assistance of a privatised rent a cop acting as your minimum wage jailer of the afternoon. He puts his hand out for the keys, which are handed over with just enough hesitation to point out that orders are being obeyed against better judgment. Murder Squad told me to do it, Sir, and who am I to argue? Childish Nuremberg.

They walk down the corridor together, footfalls echoing off plaster and concrete.
The cell door opens disappointingly smoothly. Chantelle Joseph is stretched out on the bed. She is tall, over six feet. She'd stare him in the eye easily if she wasn't ostentatiously registering her contempt and lack of interest by lying with her back to the door.

"Knock knock, Chantelle. You don't mind if we call you Chantelle, do you?"

Years of heroin have made her more gray than black. Her eyes are yellow, pupils like black marbles. Skin stretched over her face so tightly it looks as if it could rip. A skeleton in a nylon tracksuit. She doesn't react.

"Chantelle, I'm DCI McGuiness from the Serious Crime Directorate. That's murder squad to you."

Her shoulders tense. It is almost imperceptible, and suppressed in a fraction of a second.

"I'm arresting you for the murder of Jane Canavan on Peckham Rye yesterday. You do not have to say anything, but it may harm your defence if you fail to mention anything now that you later rely on in court. Anything you say will be used in evidence against you."

She sits bolt upright. Her eyes are wide and her mouth opens. McGuiness carries on before she can say anything.

"Those cards you were using, Chantelle. They belonged to a woman who was raped and stabbed to death. Her body was found on the Rye yesterday. It's been on the telly and in all the papers. Maybe you've seen it."

She whips her head from side to side. Emphatic disagreement.

"You wouldn't have needed to though, would you? You were there. There's no way one person could have done that to her on their own. "

Her voice is distorted and raw with cigarettes and methadone.

"Fuck off. I want my solicitor."

"I'd want a solicitor, too, if I was looking at the business end of a life sentence with thirty five years behind a door before you get a sniff of parole. Thing is, Chantelle, it's not a solicitor you need. It's a fucking magician."

"I'm not saying a word."

McGuiness sits next to her. They are almost touching and he can feel the thin cell mattress shift as she flinches away from him.

"I don't expect you to talk, Chantelle. I know you're a solid junkie thief and talking to us is something you don't do. So listen to this. We have got you working a credit card that belonged to a murdered woman within 24 hours of her murder. That's called recent possession. You say nothing now, and the jury will take enough time to have a fag and a cup of tea before coming back with a guilty. I'm happy with that. Job done."

He turns to Stevens.

"Better rustle up some legal representation for Miss Joseph. You using duty these days, Chantelle, or do you have someone in mind?"

The disrespect is calculated. The duty solicitor scheme supplies unrepresented suspects with a lawyer. It is for the inexperienced; the first timers and those so far gone with drink and drugs that they don't show any interest.

"Julia Villiers"

"Bloody hell, Chantelle. Do you think you're a celebrity or something? Showbiz Julie isn't going to leave the ivory tower for the likes of you."

Stevens coughs.

"I'll call her now, guv. Maybe she'll be interested in the profile. I mean; there can't be many female whole lifers. "

"True, Kath. Chantelle here is going to be the most notorious woman in the country until the next one comes along and everyone forgets about her. The press will have a field day. Holding someone down, cutting them open. It shouldn't affect the Judge, but it will. Have you noticed that they always seem to go harder on the girls?"

Stevens considers for a second.

"Reckon you're right about that. Shock of the unexpected, I suppose. I mean, you expect a murderous rapist to be a man, don't you?"

McGuiness gets to his feet.

"Well, Chantelle. Enjoy the view. It's as good as it's going to get for a long time. We'll come and get you when your brief gets here."

He makes it as far as the cell door before she breaks.

"Wait."

He stops for a second. The words pour before he can turn to face her.

"I got them off of Omen. He gave them to me to work. I have to give him back the stuff I buy and he'll weigh me in for some brown. I didn't murder nobody, Mr McGuiness. You check my record. I never do violence."

"Omen?"

"His real name is Damien. I don't know the rest. He's a Peckham Boys older. Used to run a crack house on the Yellow Brick Estate. I don't even know him that well. I just happened to be there."

"When was this?"

"A couple of hours ago. That's all. You've got to believe me."

McGuiness doesn't bother talking to the prisoner directly. There's no point. He's got what he wants and she doesn't merit a second look. Story of her life, and while he can't say he feels good about it, there are more important things on his mind. As he leaves the Custody Area, his phone rings. Sarah. He considers answering for a second, before rejecting the call.

Chapter 6

It has yet to rain today. The sun is bright enough to give the industrial units and flats a fresh coat of paint. The church is not empty, and father Anthony Mitchell congratulates himself about the reasonably good turnout for a morning service. The church has cleared, and while he sits in the confessional, he reflects that the absence of repentant souls seeking forgiveness for their sins is as likely to be down to Monday afternoon commitments as the moral strength of his new parishioners.

The church is a cave. What little sunlight that manages to infiltrate the dirty windows keeps the interior in a state of constant twilight. There is an all-pervasive smell of incense and damp, which crawls inside his nose and throat, making him feel suffocated. He is unsure whether the smell has permeated his vestments, or whether he can feel it sinking into the cloth. The odour of sanctity in a secular age. The bench is reasonably comfortable, and if he sits perfectly still he can avoid the resurrection of the clouds of dust that choked him when he sat down for the first time. Father Anthony rubs his face and pinches the bridge of his nose hard. He can feel pressure building inside his sinuses and worries that he will not be able to make it to the parochial house in time to take his medication before the migraine takes hold. He begins to feel uncomfortable. Hot, and as damp as the church itself. The gloom slows direct light's agonising assault for the moment, but the pain is growing inside him. He checks his watch. Ten more minutes.

He doesn't hear the door open. He is slumped with his head against the sill. The cool of the polished wood is soothing. He is only aware that someone is sitting the other side of the screen when he takes his seat. There is a strong smell of stale tobacco and degeneration. It is a different decay, stronger and more pungent than the genteel scent of mildew rising from the cassocks. It reminds him of hard lives and bad sanitation; a walk past the damp and neglected places where the destitute and homeless gather. Father Anthony Mitchell sits upright and listens to the labored breathing from the other side of the screen. He allows the other man to compose himself before muttering a blessing. His head is pounding now, and the stench is overwhelming in the confined space.

The other man coughs deep in his chest. It is as insistent as a barking dog, and it echoes inside the confessional, booming and repeating as if it was inside the priest's skull. Father Anthony winces, shutting his eyes tightly and opening them slowly. His vision is beginning to clear when the man starts to speak.

"Forgive me Father, for I have sinned. It has been…"

There is a pause, followed by a liquescent chuckle.

"..a good few years since my last confession."

Father Anthony is aware that he is muttering something reassuring before he falls silent.

"It was a Saturday night and I'd been out. Can't even remember what I'd been up to now, and it's not important anyway. I could see the lights in the living room so I took a quick look through the window. Just to see if she was still up. Not that I was frightened of her, mind. I was far too old to be scared of her. I was nineteen and a man, and everyone knew it. I just wanted to see what I was coming home to, Father. You can understand that, can't you?"

Father Anthony recognises a rhetorical question. He cannot place the accent. It is truncated, with whole syllables being swallowed. Not quite Irish, but pushing it. Almost American at times. He shakes his head. It's probably not important.

"I was hoping that she'd be in bed. If she was up she'd either be pissed up, wasted or angry because she wasn't. There were no kids in the house then. Me and my brother were too old when the Social started taking the kids off her so we got to stay. I thought he'd be out as well. Neither of us were exactly home loving, Father, and if she was right when she shouted at us for treating the place like a hotel then all I can say is that it wasn't a hotel either of us would have wanted to stay at, and that's the God's honest truth.

The curtains were open and I could see my younger brother sitting on the floor. It wasn't the main light I'd seen. There was nothing on but the TV. He was siting there in his boxers and a t-shirt watching the TV. It was a cold house. She never had any money for the gas, and wouldn't have an electric fire in the house, so I knew she was pissed off with him. It was one of the things she'd do, see? If you got on her nerves she'd get her own back. Take your clothes off you or lock you out. She had a nasty temper on her, and it didn't matter whether you'd done anything or not. Just being there when she was raging was good enough. Anyway, I was looking through the window and I could see my brother had his legs pulled up to his chest and he was sort of hugging himself. I couldn't see her, and I couldn't hear her neither. I nipped round the back.

I was planning on coming in through the garden door and creeping past the kitchen just in case she was lying in wait. First think that came into my mind is that she'd been cooking. The house smelled of it. Not in a good way, either. Burned milk and bacon. There was no noise from the kitchen. I didn't look in. Best to let sleeping dogs lie, I thought, and I went up the passage and into the living room. I stopped at the door. I could see him side on from there, and he looked like he'd been taking drugs. Not weed or coke or suchlike. Tranquilisers. I could see him and I was sure that he could see me right back, but he sat there, eyes on the telly, hugging his legs like a bloody statue. I whispered to him from the door, "All right brother?" He turned to look at me and I almost puked. His face was red all down the left side. His skin was bubbled up like burned plastic. The mark was a funny shape, and at first it made me think of a ship with portholes sailing up from his chin to his ear. Then the penny dropped."

More coughing and more echoes. Silence. Father Anthony scarcely dares to exhale. The coughing continues long enough for him to make an enquiry

"Are you all right, my son?"

"Sorry Father. I've a bad chest. Shan't happen again. Anyway, I tried to get him to stand up and come with me. He needed a doctor. Any fool could see that. He was having none of it. He didn't say a word. He just shook his head. I carried on at him, with him saying nothing until he mouthed the word "kitchen" at me. I didn't understand, so I asked him what he thinks he's talking about and told him to put his shoes on so I could get him to hospital. He said it again, and I think that's where she's got his clothes. "Fine," I said, "I'll get them for you" and off I march down the passage. I was hoping she was passed out. I was angry, but I wasn't stupid. Just trying to make myself feel big so I'd have the bottle to go in if she was there.

I saw her as soon as I put my head round the door. She was lying on the floor by the cooker. The air is full of smoke, but it's not so bad that I can't see the kitchen knife. It's sticking out of the middle of her chest. There's this hissing in the background, and it takes me a few seconds to work out that its coming from two places. There's a pan on the hob and whatever was in it has boiled dry long since. I went to take it off, and just as I leaned down to grab a tea towel so I don't burn my hand I saw the iron. It was still plugged in and resting on her leg. Burned milk and bacon, Father. Two mysteries solved and the only one left was what I was going to do about it.

I went back to the other room. I looked at him and raised my hands. Like, "what happened?" He's like he's in some kind of trance. I thought I knew, though, and for all I knew he needed to be in hospital I knew I couldn't take him. Not with her dead on the kitchen floor. As soon as any of her kids went to any hospital between Bodmin and Swindon their computers lit up like a Christmas tree, even back then. She'd had six kids taken away. Every colour of the rainbow, they were. None of them lasted more than a few months with her. They must be all over the country now. I never saw any of them again, and it's not such a big place. Just his bad luck to be too old for the Social Workers. Mine too, I suppose. The Social would come to the house to ask her what happened as soon as they put two and two together.

I lit a fag for my nerves and tried to think of what to do. He was rocking backwards and forwards while I'm doing this, and a little bit of spit was coming down his chin. I went over to him and wiped it away with my sleeve. I watched the spit sink in and it looked like nothing. Like it's never been there at all and I knew what had to be done. He was going to be no help, so I got the rug from the living room. Ugly looking thing it was. I found it in the street when they were doing up a curry house, so no great loss. I wrapped her in it. I didn't think to take the knife out until I'm half ways done, so I had to start again. Fingerprints, see? I wasn't a bad kid, and I wasn't a fool. Once she was wrapped up, I tried to pick her up to take her to the car, but I couldn't. She was far too heavy for me, the fat cow, and I had to drag her to the back door, grunting and heaving like a tug of war. I put her in a wheelbarrow, dumped her in the boot and drove to where she used to go on the batter. I dumped her out of the carpet in a car park at the back of the station. There was nobody about. It was in the papers for a few days, and then everyone forgot about it. Just another dead fat prossie. I spent a few months looking over my shoulder. Every time the doorbell rang I had to stop myself going over the garden wall. Then I forgot about it too. Truth is, the police and the Social were glad to see the back of her. Out of sight, out of mind. There were only two people to care that she was gone and neither of us did."

The confessional creeks and rocks like a tree in high wind. Father Anthony puts his hand to his forehead. He is on fire. He grinds his eyes shut as lightning bolts of pain shoot down the right side of his head and sprays of colour dance on the back of his eyelids. It takes him at least quarter of an hour to recover. He walks to the church door, following the ghost of the man's smell out into an empty street.

Chapter 7

Ken McGuiness checks his watch. It is 5:30. He is conscious of the missed call on his phone and is putting off calling her back until he is finished at work. She would have called again if it was business, and pleasure is a reward for work not an end in itself. So the cigarettes stay in the drawer and the phone in the jacket pocket. It may not be much in the way of morality, but it sounds good until you say it out loud.

It's not a bad piece of work either. A background check on the victim, and her Oyster Card movements, tracking her journey through London's transport system on the night before she died. Jane Canavan moved from South Wales to London ten years ago, to take up a job with a housing charity working with young people. On the face of it nice to have a victim whose lifestyle hadn't put them in harm's way. The organisation's personnel file is revealing. A difficult character. Unpopular with junior staff. Someone who could get carried away with her authority and throw her weight around. Complaints about her usually followed by periods of sickness. Depression and anxiety. Sick notes signed by a doctor in Bridgend. McGuiness notes the name. No long term diagnosis. Back to work within the year before the sick pay ran out every time. She may get down, but she was never out. A bit of a cycle, and on her past form she was reaching a peak. She'd had a complaint made by one of her staff partially upheld. No real sanction, but not something that had sat well with her. Due to have some more time off back in Wales? Worth checking.

She had gone into work on Saturday. The charity's offices were off Old Compton Street in Soho, and she had taken a train from Croydon to Charring Cross. It was only about a quarter of an hour's walk from the station. Too early for a night out and no movement for a couple of hours. The trail picks up at 9:30, when she took another bus South. She must have got off at Waterloo, because the card showed her going through the barrier into the station before leaving ten minutes later. This was at 10:23. Seventeen minutes later, a credit card payment for two bottles of wine in a riverside pub. Had she been alone? This was the last post. Then nothing until the cards turned up in Chantelle Joseph's pocket along with Jane Canavan's work identification.

McGuiness considers the options. She must have met someone, or decided that there was something that she needed to do around the station. She hadn't forgotten anything, as she wouldn't walk back along a route she thought was long enough to justify the cramp and discomfort of a London bus in the first place. What was there? A stroll down the South Bank? A cultural evening in the National Theatre? A meal? Alone? He busies himself sending the usual "seize all available CCTV" email. Making work and winding down the clock until the day is done.

7:30. Ken McGuiness walks out of Lewisham Police Station. The working day is done. He has an unlit cigarette in his lips and his mobile phone to his ear. Sarah. He fumbles for a lighter as the phone rings out to voicemail again. He considers leaving it, going home to his pregnant wife and a night spent watching property porn. Considers it, rejects it and walks to his car. She's probably at home. He leans against the car and finishes his cigarette. Waits for the phone for a second, thinks and gets into the driver's seat.

He is almost surprised to find himself driving West. Past the Rye, the scene of the crime filled with dog walkers and joggers. Horror fades as quickly as nightclub ink, and in South London life goes on as streamers of crime scene tape flap lazily in the early evening breeze. East Dulwich. The traffic is solid down Lordship Lane, moving so slowly he is able to window shop in the delicatessens, bookshops and restaurants. This area was rough once, when he first joined the Met. People got robbed at knifepoint at the NatWest. Now you can pay £7 for a sandwich. Times and crimes change. Progress of sorts. A right turn takes him towards Brixton. More gentrification. Someone told him that there is a champagne bar in Brixton Market now. Oysters and Moet for the new locals as they toast the demise of a working class culture that they found edgy and exciting enough to price out of existence.

Parking is a bitch. That much is unchanged. It's quite a walk from the one untenanted meter on Acre Lane to Sarah's flat. He passes her little red car on the way, and finds his heart beating slightly faster. Nerves or anticipation? He won't, can't think it might be guilt because what has he got to feel guilty about? Everyone is doing it. It's in all the papers. On the news.

Politicians. Footballers. Every ordinary Joe and Josephine is playing away. Why should he be any different? It's just a bit of harmless fun, and it's not as if anyone is going to get hurt. He's not going to leave Maxine.

The door to the block has been wedged open. Some local traditions die harder than others. He makes his way up the stairs. The flats are part private and part council, and the stairwell lights are dim. There is some graffiti, and it smells mildly of piss and bins. She is on the third floor, and as he climbs the stairs he feels a sense of foreboding. He can't explain it. He's a police officer. He deals in facts. He has always despised the Psychic Sallies. If you can't touch it, pick it up and put it in an evidence bag it doesn't bloody exist. Footfall follows footfall into concrete echoes. It's all a bit haunted house, and he can feel the hairs rise on his forearms. Nonsense. Stop acting like a kid.

Third floor. He can hear music through her front door and smiles. She's in. The doorbell interrupts Elvis Costello's heartfelt plea about not wanting to go to Chelsea with its electric rasp, but Elvis doesn't seem bothered. He waits, listening for movement. Nothing. He waits, and then rings again. Nothing. The song reaches its end and restarts. He pushes open the letterbox. He can see the corner of a sofa. Her red coat is draped over it. If he cranes his neck he can see one high heeled shoe in the middle of the hall floor. The song restarts for a third time. Something cold in his stomach wakes and goes south. He puts a hand through the letterbox and finds the key on a string he had warned her about in his most stentorian policeman's voice. He is glad that she ignored him now.

The air is moist, steamy, and he can hear the faint splash of water from behind a closed door. McGuiness smiles. She's in the bath. He stands still, indecisive. She will go absolutely mental at him for letting himself in, and no protestations about unspecified fears for her safety will sound like anything other than the standard police excuses for an illegal invasion of her privacy. Fuck it. Can't very well turn round and walk out. Besides, she has probably heard the door and is lying in the bath worrying that it's Billy the rapist waiting like Norman Bates for her to come out of the steam, sharpening his kitchen knife on her worktop.

"Sarah?"

He tries to make his voice seductive, but he sounds like he's inviting her to surrender peacefully, and he knows it. He emphasises each footfall. Not sneaking up on her. Nothing sneaky about a married man in his girlfriend's flat at all. His hand hesitates on the handle before he pushes the door open.

"Sarah?"

Her name catches in his mouth. She is lying in the bath. The hot tap is running, the water gurgling inadequately through the overflow and splashing onto the floor. Her hair has spread out like weeds around a face that three inches of water turns into a blur. There is a bottle of wine on the metal bin, covered in a thin coating of condensation and half empty. An ashtray on the corner of the bath contains a half smoked spliff, and the dog ends of two others. He takes a step and sends a half filled glass sloshing and chiming across the tiles. He doesn't pause to roll up his sleeves, and plunges his hands into the water. It is uncomfortably hot, and he wonders how she can stand it. His hands support her head and upper body as he tries to raise her. This takes more strength than he anticipated. His back complains as he realises that her neck is stiff. Rigor mortis. Her body is still as supple as he remembers it from the Travelodge. Same triangle of dark hair. Same legs. Lips beginning to go blue, and eyes grey on bloodshot red.

He feels his eyes water, and narrows them as his tears turn bathroom lights into blades. He wants to fall on the floor, to kneel next to the bath. To cradle her and bring her back, but it wouldn't help. Between two and six hours. Eyes, jaw and neck. A hundred post mortems, maybe more. Time of death is an inexact science. You couldn't set your watch by it, but she's long gone. A classic accident for the recreational drug user living alone. He's seen a lot of dead people. He's not quite eating a McDonalds in the autopsy level of case hardened, but if that's the end of the road, he can see it from where he's standing. It doesn't prepare you. He doesn't think anything could. It's always bad news when your work comes home.

He hasn't cried for over thirty years. Mum's funeral. He's not about to start now, aged forty two. Looking at Sarah's body in the bath he realises that she has become as cold as a painting. Preserved on her boat filled with flowers, suspended in water. The Lady of Shalott drifting down the Effra, out of Brixton, out of life and away from him forever. He has to hold it together. Fucking up won't bring her back, and he tells himself that there are true innocents to be considered. He can't leave her to be found in three months time, bloated and purple, covered in flies and turned to an organic soup a council cleaning team in gasmasks will scoop into bags and take away. He owes her that. The last act of a severed connection, a single act of kindness as a ring tone cuts off in the dark.

Practical man. Blunt hands and clear eyes focused on the details so as not to see the picture they make. Wiping the door handles and the sides of the bath. Down the stairs and through the door as quickly and quietly as prey. Hunted by windows that stare empty eyed from every side. Forcing himself into a leisurely stroll back to the car and gone. Mirror, signal maneuver into the traffic, cigarette regulating his breathing like cancer in a paper bag. Back to his life. Dry eyed and ready to kiss his wife on the cheek. Trauma's shadow explained by the job. A man who sees bad things for a living can always hide another ghost in the crowd, and nobody asks questions because nobody really wants to hear about it. Not when there's cash in the attic and homes under the fucking hammer.

He drives out of his way. A very long route home, avoiding main roads and cameras. He stops at what must be the last payphone in England, miraculously working and while drinkers smoke and smokers beg for change outside a pub on Brockley Road, he calls in Sarah's death. It's not much of an act of remembrance. It's a less than adequate tribute to their...what? Time together sounds anemic, and he cannot bring himself to say the word affair. Whatever it was. Policemen and adulterers are spread thin. There's not much to go around and he's given all he can spare.

Chapter 8

Ken McGuiness wakes up early. It's not exactly sitting up and screaming, but the sheets are damp. He lies awake watching the orange glow behind the bedroom curtains raise to a morning milky gray, waiting for his heart rate to slow down and fall into step with his wife's rhythmic snores. He would like to read, but doesn't want to wake her. Eventually a full bladder and a need to be distracted from his thoughts drives him out of bed and downstairs, where he sits at the kitchen table, drinks a cup of coffee and lets the news whip him into a healthy anger. After an hour and a half, he makes his wife tea and gets ready for work. He picks up the post on his way out. Three items. A gas bill is dumped on the hall radiator cover for future reference, an invitation to change his home broadband supplier doesn't make it further than the recycling box in the front garden. He puts the brown padded bag into his jacket pocket. The handwriting looks familiar, but he can't place it.

He opens the package at work. It contains a datastick. No covering letter. The handwriting looks like Sarah's, but she has crossed his mind a lot and he's not sure. She had a habit of sending him pictures of herself. Some were definitely not suitable for work's IT, so it is probably a good idea to wait and use his laptop. It crosses his mind that this might be some form of suicide note, and he spends a few minutes in frantic worry about who else she has sent it to, before turning on his office computer and beginning the day.

The email blinks onto the screen as he is reviewing the reports into the CCTV surrounding Peckham Rye, and watching the name "Doctor Sarah Reed" fade out leaves him shuddering and wondering whether last night had been some kind of hallucination. He clutches at the reassurance that it had been sent to another scientist for validation yesterday afternoon and forwarded, opens it and reads.

The report is in the form of a witness statement. He finds the truth declaration and dire warnings about the consequences of telling lies in court reassuring. The first page is taken up with her qualifications and experience, setting out why the Court should listen to the opinion of Dr Sarah Reed. It is an impressive pedigree. Degree in biology, postgraduate study at Imperial College in London then straight into the Forensic Science Service. Driven. Professional. Measured. McGuiness shakes the word obituary away, rubs his forehead and concentrates on the content.

DNA testing. The greatest investigative tool since fingerprints. Better, even, as you can find DNA in places where fingerprints won't stick. It's presented as a spiraling away into the infinite heart of humanity, but so far as forensic science is concerned, identifying someone depends on ten points on the helix. Ten stations on a line. Two markers at each station, like passengers getting off a train on either side of the carriage, one inherited from the mother and the other from the father. And Bob's your suspect with odds of a billion to one unless he's lucky enough to have an identical twin without an alibi. That's the theory, and mostly that's also the case. Not here, though. She continues,

"Here we were able to extract a mixed, partial profile from the samples taken from the high vaginal and vulval swabs. We were able to separate these into two partial profiles. One is female and consistent with the deceased. The other is male.

A search was conducted against the national DNA database, and a match was found with Damien Noel Anderson, date of birth 24th December 1986. The chance of someone else sharing this partial profile who is not related to Mr Anderson is 250 000 to one."

Ken McGuiness likes those odds. It's not the magic bullet, but it's something to go on. He checks the police national computer against the name and date of birth, half fearing that Damien Noel Anderson would be a severely disabled drink driver living on the Shetland Islands. The results flash onto the screen like New Year fireworks, and he has to restrain himself from punching the air. Damien Noel Anderson. Street name "Omen". Last known address on the now demolished North Peckham Estate. Previous convictions for rape and a GBH that involved the use of a knife on a witness in another gang related trial. Member of the Peckham Boys street gang from his early teens. Drug dealer, enforcer and rising star. Supplier of credit cards to junkie shoplifters. A thoroughly viable, local suspect. Forensic evidence and intelligence. He closes the file, collects his thoughts and emails the notification of a team meeting in two hours time. The datastick lies forgotten in his pocket.

***

Germaine MacHeath walks up the stairs and out of Oxford Circus Underground. He usually avoids public transport, but today is special and even a man of his soon to be status has to make some sacrifices.

There is enough threat about him to make wading through the Oxford Street tourists possible, and he manages a decent slow walk as far as a Café on Wells Street. It's next to the Family Court, and deserted apart from two men in suits deep in conversation over a bundle of papers that towers over the plastic tomato ketchup dispenser and sugar shaker. He eases himself into a booth and orders a black coffee.

Two sips and Polly is in the doorway. The sunlight behind her turns her skirt transparent, and even the lawyers look up from their discussion to check her out. She slides across the leather bench opposite him and leans across to kiss him on both cheeks. His lips brush the air next to her and he smells her perfume. Two years ago and fresh out of Belmarsh prison, Shanks would have thought it was fake, but Germaine; he's moving up and this is how the upwardly mobile behave. And it's not without its perks.

"So Germaine, why are we in Oxford Street?"

She smiles. He takes his time before replying, grave as a Godfather.

"We are going to look at something. I have had a good month and I thought it would be nice to get you something to celebrate a new thing. Got to share good luck to keep it coming."

He finishes his coffee and they leave. As they walk towards Regent Street and the shops she links her arm with his and leans her head against his shoulder. Her blonde hair swings and her hips nudge his thigh with every step. Her body heat radiates, and he can feel his skin tingle. He notices a man stare at her as they walk past and restrains himself from staring back. The sort of man who has a woman like this on his arm doesn't need to intimidate people. Not on Oxford Street anyway.

It's a short walk to the shop he has picked out. A traditional jewelers. The name of the proprietors is lettered in gold across the display window. The doorway is wood paneled with a tiled floor. The Victorian look doesn't extend to the security, which is very 21st century. The door is locked, and a camera swivels to check them out before a buzzer springs the door open and they go inside.

There are display cases around the walls and a counter at the far end. The entire shop seems to be made up of dark wood and glass. Light reflects from mirrors and polished cases creating tiny sparks on the dark surface of the walls. It smells of beeswax. Polly's heels rap on the marble floor, beating out a march as she and Germaine drift from case to case. She is smiling, and her eyes sparkle back at the diamonds that have animated them so prettily. A middle aged man stands discretely behind them. They seem like a nice couple. Reassuringly expensively dressed, particularly the gentleman. His Prada shoes and Givenchy leather jacket are noted and filed under the heading of potentially serious customer. One mustn't make assumptions about people's status based on their skin colour any more. Besides, it's far more effective to look at their clothes. The girl is transfixed. The man less so, and his gaze does wander about the shop from time to time. So typical of a man to get distracted, and if his occasional glances around seem a little calculating and linger upon the alarms and cameras, it's probably nothing. He can overhear the girl's conversation and her voice is absolutely of the right kind to be shopping there, even if her companion seems a little taciturn.

They spend a long time looking at diamond rings, before MacHeath asks her which one she would like. She points to a simple platinum band with a large diamond. The price tag reads £3 000, and her smile is part joke and part challenge. Her knight will have to be able to kill the poverty dragon to win her favour. He doesn't hesitate. He doesn't even double take. He nods, and beckons the attendant over.

The ring is too large. A danger, the attendant explains. It's a lovely piece and it would be such a pity if it were to fall from her finger because she was too eager to be seen with it, however understandable that might be. A measuring. Germaine

MacHeath hands over a bundle of cash that the jeweler meticulously counts, first into ten bundles, then three and finally one that is placed in a cash drawer that glides out from beneath the counter as silent as a stealth bomber. A receipt is produced, and he leans over the counter, palm down upon its smooth surface to sign. Polly takes his arm, and with a promise of seeing them in a week, they walk to the door. There is a glow of colour in her cheeks, and as they pause for the security system to release them, he turns to her and they kiss. Not long, but her passion is stoked by the cash pheromones in the air. He smiles, and looks up into the camera's fish eye. Another smile and they are gone. The camera returns to its impassive surveillance of the doorway.

Chapter 9

Lewisham Police Station stands at the top of a street market. Fried chicken boxes roll like tumble weed in and out of the herd around the cashpoints and the gateway to the shopping centre. Queues slither along dirty pavements. Busses wheeze and groan under the weight of commuters and the sound of falling scaffold poles rings the end of another trading day. High on the seventh floor Ken McGuiness holds on while the hubbub subsides. He imagines himself trembling like a greyhound waiting for the trap to open. He can see the hare, and he can name it.

There are thirty officers in the incident room. McGuiness stands in front of a white board. There is one photo pinned to it. A black man stares into the camera with impassive eyes, head and shoulders above a date and time indicator and the name "Damian Noel Anderson". The team has arranged themselves in a semi circle of plastic chairs. There is an ecological disaster of paper coffee cups and some shouted banter about Chelsea's forthcoming game against local FA Cup no hopers Millwall. Crown trouble is expected, and after the Millwall fans fought a pitched battle with the police outside the ground a few years ago, the general consensus is that the Met want and will win any rematch. Scores are suggested for injuries on each side. Met one, Millwall twenty is a popular bet. The blue team has the horses and the riot gear against the Burberry team's home advantage. A double humiliation. Beaten on the pitch and on the streets. McGuiness claps his hands once. Silence falls.

"Ladies and gentleman, the rather charming portrait you can see on the board is Damien Noel Anderson, street name Omen. I am happy to be able to tell you that he has been forensically linked to the death of Jane Canavan. Even better, his name has come up in connection with the use of Miss Canavan's credit card in Peckham, so he is a person of significant interest to us.

The photo was taken after Mr Anderson was charged with GBH in 2008. He stabbed a rival drug dealer 11 times in the stomach, and it is only because the ambulance service managed to land a helicopter on a nearby football pitch that this wasn't a murder. You can all appreciate the similarities with the fatal injuries Jane Canavan sustained.

Mr Anderson was acquitted of the assault because all the witnesses got seriously cold feet. The best we could manage was his being recalled to serve the remainder of his twelve year sentence for rape. He had been released on license six months before the stabbing.

The rape is a depressingly typical gang initiation attack upon a fourteen year old girl who didn't realise quite how bad her new friends could be. He was one of seven defendants, all of whom got long sentences despite the fact that they were all aged between fourteen and seventeen. Anderson was described as the ringleader. He was the one who posed as the victim's boyfriend, so we can say that he can be plausible and has a history of persuading women into dangerous situations. This isn't evidence enough to convict him even if the CPS can persuade the judge to let the jury hear about it, but taken along side everything else, this man is a very good suspect.

Anderson was an up and coming member of the Peckham Boys at the time of his rape arrest. Recent information suggests that he has reached the status of gang older, so it is no exaggeration to say that this is a very dangerous man indeed. His previous convictions suggest he is willing to use extreme violence. His gang affiliations mean he has access to firearms and an extensive network of members and sympathisers. We have no current address for him, and the only recent information about his whereabouts is that he has been an occasional visitor to the crack house on Pentridge Street in Peckham.

Our strategy is to raid and round up as many known gang members as we can. Nick them for anything, and then give them the very distinct impression that this problem could be made to go away as soon as Damien Anderson is in custody. It should be made very clear to all people arrested that the reason that we want him has to do with his personal predilection for sexually motivated homicide and nothing to do with what these people would regard as decent honest criminality. They'll be more willing to give up Ted Bundy than Ronnie Kray. We'll have the meatheads in their meat wagons on side. Full TSG support. The operation starts at six tomorrow morning. I want five interview teams of three, two officers to conduct interviews and one supervisor to collate information and liaise with me and DI

Walsh, who will be providing roving support and dealing with leads as they come in. I'll even step in and do a few interviews myself."

He pauses for ironic applause.

"We'll be using Peckham and Walworth Road primarily. Overspills will go to Bromley and Windmill Road.

Sergeants Wilson and Stevens will organise you into the teams. Get a good night's sleep. Tomorrow is going to be a very busy day."

Ken McGuiness gathers his belongings for a silent walk through the activity of the incident room. He is relieved to make the stairs without challenge. He is a conscientious leader, and does not like lying to the men and women under his command. If he was asked where he was going, nothing on earth could persuade him to tell the truth. The Metropolitan Police is no longer the organisation it was in the 1970's. Women are not sexually harassed, or at least not as much. Racism is a clandestine practice that no longer enjoys official approval. It is still a police force, a body of strong, hardened men and women, fighting crime and protecting the community they serve. A leader has to command respect; a respect that would not be earned by the revelation that he was on his way to a meeting of the Natural Childbirth Trust.

He has arranged to meet Maxine there, and it is a relatively short drive from Lewisham. Could have taken the fifteen minutes he gave it, only of course it doesn't. Sitting in the traffic as it grinds up Loampit Vale, Ken McGuiness checks his watch and thinks about the possibility of smoking a cigarette in the car. Will Maxine notice? She's developed a nose like a bloodhound since she fell pregnant. He's already late, so things can't get much worse. Perhaps if he opened the window? By the time he pulls up outside a double fronted house in Dulwich, he's three cigarettes down and there is a blue haze in the car that no amount of pointing the air vents at the windows and putting the blower full on can clear.

Maxine is wearing a gray pinafore dress that stretches tight across her stomach. She is sitting with her legs beneath her in an enormous chair, an antique more suited to a Victorian gentleman's club than a suburban living room. She looks fragile, childlike, a misleading impression that is reinforced by her pale skin. No make up for the NCT, who obviously favour the natural look. She is staring intently, concentrating. Across the room is the object of her attention, a middle aged woman holding a doll in one hand and a plastic model of a human pelvis in the other. Ken McGuiness sits to her left, keeping one eye on her and the other on the scene being played out opposite them. He is torn between his irritation at being there at all and his knowledge that Maxine's attentiveness is built on a foundation of being so pissed off with him that she doesn't even want to acknowledge his presence on the same planet, let alone at the antenatal class. He notices that despite the fact that every face in the room is resolutely Caucasian, the doll is black. Keeping his sneer internal takes an effort of will.

When Maxine gets angry she acts as if he's barely part of the same species. It should wind him up. He is the authority figure, the policeman, the senior investigator, man of the house and breadwinner. It does not. He feels what she wants him to feel. Unworthy.

The woman is talking now, reeling off statistics. McGuiness has always loved facts and figures. He cannot help but listen. Breastfeeding. It increases the baby's IQ. It makes them stronger, faster and fitter. It's the elixir of life, apparently. Percentages are given. They sound implausible, although he is not sure whether this is because of the statistics themselves or the cut glass accent in which they are delivered. He shifts uncomfortably. He is squatting by her side, preferring the position of supplicant to the offer of a seat on the sofa next to a man with whom he is sure his only connection is forthcoming fatherhood. He's wearing a goatee and pink corduroys. Probably sandals as well. He is sure he saw a cycle helmet in the hall. The pelvis and the doll are put away. He makes a plea for an armistice. He touches Maxine's arm and whispers, "should give me a go on them once you start, love. I could do with the edge."

She doesn't even twitch. He stares at her for a moment, searching for any trace of a smile. Not a chance. Her mouth is squeezed so tightly into a line her lips are practically white. She gives off disapproval like a faulty gas fire gives off fumes.

The subject of the second part of the lecture is the process of birth. The contrast between the explicit words and their 1950's BBC delivery is ridiculous. It's like having phone sex with Joyce Grenfell. He struggles to contain himself, but the phrase "vaginal dilation" is too much. He snorts, turning his laughter into a cough, which in turn becomes a spasm. Heads turn in unison. The entire room meerkats and stares at him in silence as he chokes. He reddens. The only person who doesn't look at him is his wife, who is still unaware that he exists, apparently. Muttering excuses, he blunders to the stripped pine door and out into the street. He will sit in the car and wait for her.

He turns on the radio and lights a cigarette. A play. Not a chance. He is not in the mood for BBC radio middle class. Might as well go back inside. He searches the dial and finds some music that doesn't sound like people shouting over a drum machine. The windows are closed, misting up with condensation and smoke. No point in hiding it. Maxine had probably smelled it on him as soon as he had walked in, dismissing any possible excuses and waiting to publicly out him as a man whose selfish addiction puts the health of his unborn child in danger as soon as he left.

A gust of wind shakes the car on its suspension. There is more than one storm coming. Ken McGuiness lights another cigarette, thinking about sheep and lambs. He checks his watch. In another fifteen minutes school will be out. The plastic pelvises and dolls will be packed away. Maxine will descend upon him through curtains of rain. Her anger has always had something of the elemental about it. His father used a similar image to describe his mother. "Might as well argue with the weather, son," he would say as man and boy left the house seeking sanctuary out of doors. "Might as well argue with the weather."

It had been a day like any other and he wasn't looking for an argument. His concerns were far more mundane. He'd been sergeant McGuiness back then and hadn't joined the police to become a social worker. His secondment to the Home Beat Team involved too much tea and sympathy to make a young man reared on Jack Reagan and George Carter comfortable. A means to an end he had been told, and he focused on the future as he encountered the inhabitants of the Pickwick Mews Estate in his capacity as the human face of the Metropolitan Police Service. This involved meetings. Not the useful incarnation of the word, in which faces were noted, intelligence gathered and that could be passed off as serving some greater purpose, but a limbo of Formica topped tables, Maxpax coffee, smoke free zones, doodles and minutes. The Area Anti Social Behaviour Panel. A grey, low rise, Local Authority office block at the edge of the estate. He didn't come prepared for trouble. As he was buzzed through the security doors into a concrete womb of pink pastel paint and safety flooring, all he anticipated was a slight cramp in his cheek from maintaining his attentive face.

Sometimes you only find something when you stop looking for it. There she was. Maxine Imogen Slade. Invisible to the eyes of the state. Untraceable. The end of cold trails. Undeniably there, sitting on a plastic chair and looking at him with a lack of recognition that he could not help but find a little hurtful.

She sat with her back to a large window. He gathered that she was some kind of community activist by osmosis, as he was preoccupied by the detail of her. Her hair was chestnut coloured now. He remembered her as a bottle blonde. She was still slim, and wore a denim skirt that rose above her knee as she leaned forward to emphasise her point. She still favoured shapeless sweaters, and if gravity had claimed her she hid it well. Her chest looked exactly the same as it did in its eighties peak. Her cosmetics were so subtle that she looked clean, scrubbed; and he was concerned that she was so pale.

His scrutiny was so forensic that he missed his cue. They were discussing youth crime. It was a subject upon which he held no particular opinion other than scepticism about the usefulness of youth clubs. Why would anyone want to swap the buzz of crime for a plastic cup of orange squash and a game of pool on a tilting table? He managed to drag himself away from his contemplation of the delicacy and determination of her jaw line to realise that the rest of the panelists were looking at him. He coughed, feeling the top of his ears redden. A reedy voice. Male. The deputy under director of youth services, or something. "So, Sergeant, will the police commit to the Cratchitt Street Project? The Local

Authority is prepared to match any other funding stream." Then she spoke. To him. And he replied. He had no idea what he said, but it was obviously the right thing, because she smiled. At him. He noticed how white her teeth were, and how her smile was wider on the right side of her mouth. He noticed the sun on the rooftops and how even municipal slate could shine like precious metal. Maxine Slade had smiled at him. He was on top of the world.

Dogs bark, birds sing and doubts nag. It's what they do. They get inside your head, under your guard and bring you down to their level. They take away your wings and force you to crawl. If you let them. No doubts nagged Ken McGuiness on the drive back to the police station. Nothing could touch his mood, however much it muttered or agitated. Doubts had other things to do, other business to take care of so they decided to wait for him instead. There was a general sense of foreboding as he walked in. The station officer's, "Hello Sarge. Good meeting?" started it. The meeting had been good, yes, but other than his meeting Maxine again, why was this? Hard to specify, and best put out of his mind. He sat at his desk, switched the computer on and read the unopened mail. All routine. The icon blinked, "incoming message." Why was the deputy under director of youth services emailing him? These people! He'd only left the man half an hour ago. He shook his head, waiting for the message to open and confidently expecting it to contain nothing more than the minutes of the meeting. Reassuringly bureaucratic, if you thought about it. He scanned the content reflexively. Fuck. He bowed his head, rubbing his eyes with the palms of his hands and taking calming, deep breaths. It was still there. The subject was funding. It read:

"Dear Sergeant McGuiness. May I thank you and the Metropolitan Police Service for your participation in the Cratchitt Road Project Funding Partnership. As you know, this is an important enterprise developed by the private sector together with the Local Authority and now the Police. Its mission statement is to work with young people at risk from crime and antisocial behaviour providing a community based solution to the family, personal, employment and training needs through purposeful activities. Only last year we were able to help a number of young persons achieve positive outcomes. We look forward to receiving the Metropolitan Police ' s allocation of

£8000 and look forward to working in partnership with you in future."

Shit. Fuck. He checked it again. No change. A short message indicated that it had been sent to Superintendent Mulholland and to the Borough Commander. Shit. He imagined himself directing traffic in Deptford for the rest of his soon to be sorry career. Scratch that. He'd be collecting trolleys in Safeway's car park. The phone on his desk rang. He flinched. He thought about going straight to the occupational health and faking post traumatic stress before picking up the receiver.

Politics and luck. You can't predict them. A short walk and a trip in a lift. McGuiness had imagined five separate permutations of his demotion and dismissal by the time he reached the corridor outside Superintendent Mulholland's office. Voices. A discussion. He knocked, louder than he intended. Three of them. Lots of scrambled egg on the uniforms and the Superintendent treating them with deference. Explanations not so much demanded as suggested. Adjectives advanced. "Astute", "political" and "modern." McGuiness bewildered, but not so confused that he was going to argue with them. Played it modest and gave credit where it was most likely to do him some good. Thanked the Superintendent for his support in this innovative community engagement. Handshakes. "Smoke if you want to, Sergeant." A glass of Scotch. A promise to personally assist by volunteering. On his own time, naturally, not the job's. More handshakes. Back into the corridor, a bright future in front of him. A reputation as a policeman who understood the changing world. Happy accidents. An excuse to see more of Maxine Slade.

A dogged pursuit. McGuiness the thief taker chasing Maxine the community activist. Not without baggage, as she finally confided in him. Bipolar. A new word. Understanding through research and conversation. Medication, marriage and finally pregnancy. It hadn't been an easy decision. She had to stop taking her tablets to conceive. Fetal development and medication don't mix. She needed support, and he needed to work to take care of the tedious necessity of keeping things afloat. He tried, but he was spread as thinly as jam on a pensioner's breakfast. There are only so many hours in the day, and sometimes he fell through the gaps. He couldn't blame Max for getting angry. She was taking all the risks, making all the sacrifices. She has a right to demand a few from him, and Max knows her rights. She tells him so, and he tries his best or so he thinks. It's a trigger, though. Pavlov's cop. He can't hear the word without a tremor of resentment, can't help but look at her like a suspect although he would have to admit that he's the one with the guilty conscience not her. He lights a cigarette. His third. The car is thick with smoke. It penetrates the upholstery and hangs in the air, filling the space from foot well to ceiling. She will be furious. It will be his fault. Something concrete. A peg to hang his guilt upon. He cracks the window, allowing the rain and cold in. The discomfort is reassuring.

The door opens. Maxine slides into the passenger seat. He studies her profile. She is as cold and expressionless as a carved angel. She sniffs. McGuiness braces himself, knowing that no answer he can give will be adequate. There will be no happy accidents. He will take his punishment like a man and long for the order and reassurance of work. He cannot wait for the pregnancy to end. For things to be normal. For something to take his mind off water, death and the lies that he can't help thinking caused them. For them to be Ken and Max again.

Chapter 10

Hundreds of people ring the police every day. Some call to give information about crimes. Most of them have seen a crime in progress. Those who are not watching the incident unfolding in front of them have their details taken and passed to the investigating officers. Others give up names. Some of these are settling scores, making trouble for rivals, enemies and people who have got in their way. Others are genuinely trying to help bring criminals to justice. There's a big overlap, and a lot of work has to go in to sorting out the irate ex girlfriend denouncing her straying partner as the nightstalker from the irate ex girlfriend who has decided that if her boyfriend is going to sleep with her best mate then she's not going to keep where he hides his gun a secret any more.

The telephone call hits the switchboard at 3pm. "Shanks' crew did that jewelers up west on Monday. Shanks." It's short. To the point and not on the line long enough to trace where it was made from. Further enquiries reveal that it was made from an unregistered pre paid mobile. Both give it credibility enough to have its contents investigated. Intelligence confirms that the nickname "Shanks" is quite common, and that one of the 27 known gang affiliates to share it is a Germaine MacHeath. Based in the Borough of Lewisham in South East London. Previous arrests for commercial premises robbery, drugs and assault. No recent arrest record, but he's 29 years old now. He could have burned out, got out or got better at it. Risen through the ranks to the point where the usual ways of coming to attention no longer apply. No gang older is going to get arrested shotting £20 wraps to junkies. Chain of command, just like the police. You never see a superintendent on a foot patrol. The verdict is that this is worth checking out. A colour printer whirs and clicks a high definition photograph into existence. Not exactly recent, but only five years old.

The civilian admin worker places the file in a tray. It's marked "for attention", but it is already mid afternoon. It will be looked at in due course. Another piece of grist in the enquiry's mill. It's not urgent. How could it be? A high value robbery isn't exactly an opportunist crime. There's a lot of planning involved, and if it's successful the prize is worth the risk. People don't like to change a winning formula, so the best way to catch a robber is by watching him and catching him when he does the next one. After he's caught, the phone he has on him will probably link him to the scene of his other crimes. Everyone loves mobiles. They help us keep in touch, and the quick, romantic text to the girlfriend just before you do the job. The one you sent for good luck, and to show that you are doing what you do for family and a better life. That's the one that will put you at the scene when the scientists triangulate the masts the call bounced off. Paved with good intentions. That's the road to Belmarsh prison. It will take organisation, and that's another day's work.

***

The object of all this unwelcome attention and the woman he is now beginning to think of as his girlfriend spent the afternoon at a hotel in Folgate Street in the city. It wasn't luxurious, but the bed was comfortable and neither of them was going to spend the whole night there. It's 8pm and it's time to leave and head south. Polly lies on the bed. She's still naked, but all good things have to end. He has showered, and is starting to get dressed, when she asks him:

"Do you fancy coming round to mine for dinner?"

He's unsure how to react. She won't be the first girl to cook for him, but he remembers her saying that she still lived with her parents.

"Are you asking me for dinner, or asking me to meet your family?"

"Both, I suppose. Is that a problem?"

He thinks about it. He's never met any of his previous girlfriends' parents, but then again, he's never been asked. A new way of doing things for a new life. It sounds good to him, at least it does in his head and he isn't about to try it out loud. This is how people like Polly carry on. People like him. He puts on his best smile.

"I'd love to."

Chapter 11

It hasn't been the easiest of drives home. McGuiness was almost surprised to see Maxine. He'd half expected her to take a taxi home, leaving him to sit in the car marking off each radio news bulletin and cigarette until his fear of being seen to abandon his pregnant wife at the Natural Childbirth Trust faded into a suspicion that she had left him waiting in the street like a prank-called mini cab. She is silent as he drives, his hands at the perfect 10 to 2 position, checking his mirrors, indicating and maneuvering with exaggerated care. Precious cargo, and all that. Something to focus on that stopped his attention drifting to his left and the glacial avoidance of eye contact that waited there.

Home. Smooth to the curb and out of the driver's door at speed. Brisk walk to the passenger side and McGuiness opens Maxine's door. She doesn't speak, but she doesn't refuse to look at him either. It's progress of a sort. The house is dark. Maxine hasn't drawn the curtains in the front room and the glass reflects the streetlights like a tarnished mirror. As he turns, he sees a movement. Small, but definitely there. Inside. "Police, Max. Call 999" and he is off, taking the couple of steps that it takes to cross their modest front garden at a sprint.

It's instinct. Protector. Policeman. Pregnant wife outside and intruders inside the gates. McGuiness turns the latch key and hits the door with his shoulder, mentally thanking Maxine's total inability to use a dead lock. He can hear his voice bellow, "Police. Stay where you are!" and is shocked by how strong his Liverpool accent sounds. Echoing in the dark. All the ironing out re-creased by seconds of angry outrage. A figure exits the living room. Male. Tall, and either well built or in bulky clothes. McGuiness lets his momentum carry him forward and hits him side on, shooting out his left fist and aiming for the jaw hinge. He can feel the give and knows he's hit flesh not bone, his knuckles twisting into the material covering what he assumes is the man's cheek. Shit. More movement. A second man exits the back room and runs towards the kitchen, heavy footfalls. He feels a blow to the temple. Not hard. Finding range and purpose. Fingers snake across his face to his eye. He drops his chin to his chest, and bends his legs. The fingers slide across his face and scrabble for purchase in his hairline, grabbing and pulling. McGuiness doesn't resist. He straightens both legs and arches forward. He can feel the impact down through his neck and shoulders as his forehead strikes the man in what he hopes is the bridge of his nose. For a moment it's November 5th as red and white flashes in front of his eyes, then the dark is back. The man begins to slump, but keeps his grip on the handful of hair as he goes, pulling them both down. McGuiness grabs clothing and uses his last purchase to spin him round, landing on top of him with his full 14 stone and aiming a punch that connects, satisfyingly. The yelp almost masks the sound of footfalls and he has barely enough time to turn his head to the side before the kick hits him and knocks him sideways, rolling into the front room and away from this new threat, his feet slipping on the rug as he tries to stand. He's half way up when he hears sirens. There is movement in the corridor and he chases. Out through the kitchen and into the garden. The fence is high, but not impossible. Seven feet at most. The first one makes it over with ease, hurling his upper body over and swinging his legs to follow, as efficiently as if he was on an assault course. The second has taken a few blows to the head. He makes it half way before McGuiness grabs his leg and pulls with all his strength. The man resists and then falls back into the garden. McGuiness is on him with a roar. Hurling himself into a hissing cloud that leaves him coughing and clawing his eyes, rolling blinded and helpless on the grass as the uniforms arrive.

***

John Peach can hear conversation in the dining room. He is on the stairs as he catches the lower pitch of a male voice, and he assumes that this must belong to a friend of his daughter's. It will probably be some teenage student radical, hyped on a cocktail of slogans and self righteousness who will hold him personally responsible for every death in police custody since 1975. He tells himself not to rise to it. She'll grow out of her dinner table rebellion, and so far as the boy was concerned- there'll be another one along in a minute.

He pauses at the door then opens it like the man of the house. He looks around. There, sitting at the side of the table opposite his daughter, is a tall, black man. Peach thinks he looks a little old for a student, but then again some people mess up education the first time round, and fair play to the lad for not giving up. There's something about the face that looks familiar, but he is too wise to let himself jump to the obvious conclusion. His wife smiles up at him.

"Hello, John. I've made you a gin. Dinner's in about ten minutes."

The man stands as he comes in. Very respectful. Peach goes to the head of the table. He doesn't sit. He picks up the tall glass, drinks then says:

"Who's your friend, Pol?"

She looks up at him, a sly smile on her face. He knows that expression. He's seen it before, and it pisses him off each and every time. She thinks that she's winding him up by bringing home a black man. John Peach is not a fool. He knows that being obviously racist is career suicide in the Met. Stephen Lawrence's shadow is a long one, and he's nothing if not ambitious. But everyone is a product and a prisoner. He came up in the job when political correctness was voting for the government who gave out the pay rises. It's not so much that she's trying to piss him off. She's succeeding. He forces a smile on to a face that is as tight as a surgical glove.

"This is Germaine, Daddy."

He holds out his hand and they shake. The man's grip is firm. His hands are smooth. Well maintained. They do look after themselves. Probably why they seem to age so much better.

"John Peach"

"Please to meet you Mr Peach."

He does not correct him. John would be too informal. They sit, and Polly starts a lengthy story about some university friends that he thinks he should probably recognise but doesn't. He nods and smiles along. It is a relief when his wife appears with plates of lasagna and a salad bowl.

John Peach finishes his meal and pushes his plate to one side. He leans back in his chair and yawns, a full stomach warming him and accentuating the day's fatigue. His wife pauses behind him, one hand filled with empty dishes and the other on his shoulder.

"Poor John. Are they working you too hard?"

He smiles.

"We're like the KGB, love. We never sleep. It can get a bit tiring."

She laughs, picks up his plate and bustles out into the kitchen. He can see her through the hatch, sipping her wine as she busies herself loading the dish washer. Peach yawns again. Polly is chattering about some fashion internship she wants to do. It's in Milan, apparently, and while it will cost him his monthly overtime to keep her there, it will, as she says, be worth it in the long run. He's heard it, or something like it, so many times he doesn't need to listen. He reaches behind him and takes a bottle of brandy down from the sideboard.

"Get me a glass, love, and one for Germaine if he wants some."

The bottle is a good one. Remy Martin champagne cognac. It catches the light and glows deep amber as he puts the bottle onto the table. Polly brings 3 glasses. He is on the verge of telling her that this is a man's drink, but catches himself just in time. He fills the three glasses, raises the largest and takes a very satisfying pull. The amniotic gurgle of the dishwasher starts up in the background, and all is right in the world.

"So, Germaine. What are you studying?"

There is a pause. Short enough to be ignored, but it's there nonetheless. The warming lethargy slips off John Peach like discarded bedding. Germaine MacHeath smiles his most disarming smile. His teeth are very white, and reassuringly free from the slightest hint of gold. He spreads his hands out, salesman's palms upturned.

"It's my younger brother who got the brains in my family, Mr Peach. He's the student. I'm just a humble worker."

"Really? What line of work are you in?"

It's conversational. Nothing to take offence at, but it takes Peach some effort to suppress what his wife calls his helping with enquiries voice.

"Oh I'm an entrepreneur. I do some music production, run a club night. Promotions. That sort of thing."

It's only as evasive as you chose to make it. John Peach choses a peaceful evening.

"So how did you two meet, if you're not at university?"

"Germaine came to pick Danny up from the football match on the Rye. You remember, Dad, the one I told you about. The game that got stopped by the police because they found a body in the bushes. Danny's in the same year as me. He's Germaine's brother."

Peach vaguely remembers something about a body on the Rye. He hasn't paid it a lot of attention. Different priorities and enough work of his own to be getting along with.

"What do you do for a living, Mr Peach?"

"Well, Germaine, let's just say I keep London safe for hard working people."

He hates telling some people he's a police officer. He's not ashamed, just weary and wary. Life's too short for a discussion about stop and search or civil rights with his daughter, let alone some friend of hers he's probably never going to meet again. It's not exactly a lie, either, and it has a suitable air of mystery. Could be a spy, a fireman or even a road sweeper.

"Gosh. That sounds exciting."

Peach checks every inflection for a note of sarcasm. Polly chatters on about her friends, her plans and the parties she will be attending. Every item comes with its own request for parental funding, and Peach deftly deflects them until her friend decides to leave. He shakes hands and goes back to his brandy.

Chapter 12

At least Max and he are friends again. Being CS gassed by a burglar seems a small price to pay for the thaw, and although she has gone to bed and he could get away with it, he resists the temptation to have a sly cigarette. It's only respectful. His eyes don't hurt all the time now. It comes in waves, and he struggles to his feet to wash his face. Cold water. Just like the training, only the training doesn't do it justice.

He's visited a lot of victims. There's no script that tells you how you should react. He has already been through angry. That was after he had taken the uniforms round the house and found that although they had switched on the bloody computer and checked all his pirated DVDs nothing was missing. They had been upstairs. The wardrobe was open and draws had been pulled out. Maxine's jewelry box was untouched. They hadn't bothered to unplug the telly, which he could understand, as it was a huge, early '90's, fat tubed monstrosity. His stereo and speakers were a bit of a prized possession, making their failure to even contemplate stealing it feel a little insulting.

McGuiness slides into the armchair. There's some rubbish on TV, a politician being interviewed about crime statistics. Usually, he watches this sort of thing and gets some catharsis from shouting the truth at the shiny, sanctimonious gobshite, but tonight it just not the night for it. He considers going to bed, but his fingers are still trembling with a combination of adrenaline and pepper spray. Restless. He switches between channels until the late night talk soothes into an analgesic susurration. He stands, walks through to the kitchen and pours himself a whisky. On the way back through he sees his jacket on the bannister post. He rifles through the pockets, looking for cigarettes, telling himself that it's just the one to calm him down a bit, then he'll go up to bed. He pulls out the packet, slightly crumpled and ripped, another casualty of home protection. He ferrets around for a lighter until his fingers hit upon a lozenge shaped plastic object. He pulls it out. It is a memory stick. Sarah. For a moment he sees black hair floating in water, green against enamel, before shaking his head, sitting down at the computer and plugging it in. The box clicks and whines itself awake, and he is momentarily concerned enough about the contents to mute it. He didn't want

Maxine being woken up by the sound of Sarah's voice, whatever the contents. Forensically aware is the police term. It translates to "don't screw up and make yourself look guilty by leaving obvious clues." The screen fades into life, with the forensic science company's logo. All very official and he wonders why she couldn't have sent this electronically with the main report. He lights a cigarette and begins to read.

There are three sub-files, neatly headed "Introduction and DNA Discussion" and "Original Case Papers" and "Appeal". The first is a quick read. Sarah had decided to go off the reservation and compare the scene samples for Peckham Rye with profiles obtained through the work the newly privatised forensic science service had taken on. Some for private investigators, some even for the defence. McGuiness does not approve. He doesn't like it that this data exists at all. Everyone should know where they stand, and that includes knowing who pays the piper. He doesn't like that Sarah has accessed it. This went beyond the forensic brief, and probably strayed into illegality. A black mark. Unprofessional even, but you don't want to speak ill of the dead so McGuiness glosses over this breach of protocol and reads on.

There wasn't a full profile at Peckham, and what there was is a partial match not only for the much-hunted Damien Anderson, but also for the blood and semen recovered from the scene of four murders committed in Bristol in the 1980's. The Avon and Somerset Police linked these to three others, also committed at the same time and in roughly the same area. Seven women, ranging in age from 15 to 43, all tortured, all presumed to have been raped and all dumped on open ground around Bristol. McGuiness yawns and wonders why she has bothered to send him all of this. It's not as if Damien Anderson could be on offer for the Bristol case. He was born in '86, and at least two of the Bristol murders predated this. The forensics are a reasonable match, though, the loci and alleles present in both the Peckham and the four Bristol samples. No full profiles, and no one to one billion clean hits in either case. It's frustrating, like one of those photographs where everything is blacked out except a few central details and you only have a sense of the whole picture.

He thinks that he gets her point. It was one of her favourite rants; how police officers and the ignorant public at large think forensic science is like magic. You only have to point it at the guilty and they confess. A sort of Agatha Christie drawing room reveal with white coats and test tubes. He thinks about closing the computer down and going to bed. It has been a long day, and tomorrow the Met will show their trademark insensitivity to the victim's wishes and expect him to go to work. Closing it down and ignoring her last message to him feels wrong, though. Disrespectful. You should never ignore someone's last words even when you are pretty sure that you have heard them before. He clicks on the case file and begins to read.

July 21st 1982. Teenage glue sniffers found Laura Sumner's body on disused land behind what looked like a depressing, concrete children's play area complete with broken swings and a witches' hat in the inner city Montpelier area. She had been stabbed in the throat. Post mortem examination revealed lesions on her wrists and ankles that were consistent with being tied with a non-fibrous ligature, such as a clothesline. Her breasts, stomach and genitalia were covered in a lattice of hook shaped burns and she had been beaten with a blunt instrument, breaking her left forearm and a number of ribs. She had sexual intercourse shortly before her death. The sheer number of injuries made concluding that intercourse had been non consensual medically impossible.

McGuiness winces. He recognises the hook shaped burns from his stint in child protection. A heated coat hanger. A brief flashback to an interview room, a man in a white paper jumpsuit that exaggerated his druggy pallor, sweating under the strip lights and making eye contact with his own reflection in a Styrofoam cup of institutional tea. A bundle of photographs: bruised and burned flesh interspersed with pictures of cots and baby bouncers. A heated coat hanger is hard to hold and lacks heft. It's not a murder weapon. The victim needs to be pretty well powerless or the attacker is as likely to hurt himself. Tied up, tortured then beaten to a bad and lonely death. Serious among murders.

More statements set out the victim's background. McGuiness skims these, reading enough to establish that whatever early promise Laura might have had drowned in the heroin habit she was working as a prostitute to support. A vulnerable victim, but not one that would ever have the tabloids headlining with Justice for Laura.

The investigation stalled. No witnesses, forensics or suspects; and all that the police had left was to cross their fingers and hope that Laura Sumner had been a one off. August 23rd 1983. Stephanie Harrison went for a night out with friends. She had argued with her boyfriend and stormed off, saying that she was going to walk home up the Gloucester Road. Her parents contacted the police the next afternoon, and were told that she would probably come home under her own steam. The disappearance of another young woman didn't ring any alarm bells. Stephanie was an admin assistant at an estate agent. There was no history of drugs or prostitution. No reason to link her absence with Laura Sumner's murder until her body was found. A park called Ashton Court, the sort of name that means either stately home or council estate. Her body was partially submerged in a small pond by the side of a track used by the odd intrepid mountain biker or kid putting his stolen moped through its paces. Invisible from the neighbouring golf course and tea hut. Abandoned in a public place, not hidden so much as put somewhere that it would take a bit of persistence or luck to come across, like a clue in a treasure hunt. Found by a park ranger, alternately vomiting and resolutely denying that he had been patrolling this isolated spot to find a place for a break from golfers' complaints. The same marks on her wrists and ankles. More torture, not burning this time but four fingernails had been removed from her left hand and her upper front teeth were missing. Sexual activity. Semen recovered from clothing and from internal swabs. Beaten and stabbed, the gastric artery severed. The absence of massive bloodstaining at the discovery site suggested that she had been killed elsewhere. No leads. No witnesses. No hope.

19th September 1984. Christina Kelly. Another prostitute. Questioned as a potential witness in the Laura Sumner investigation. Looks like what he would have described as a "crusty" in her photograph. A white girl with dyed red dreadlocks. Some flurry of activity around anyone who had been both women's client that got nowhere. No mobile phone records to trawl through. No CCTV. No social media. None of the get lucky fast aspects of a modern investigation back then. McGuiness senses the frustration and impotence. The enquiry knowing that there'll be another one along in a year. More interviews with sex offenders and more dead ends. Saturation policing for St Pauls and Montpelier that gave up nothing more constructive than a few arrests for possession of cannabis and curb crawling. Hope sliding into the desperate desire to be seen to be doing something.

McGuiness is skeptical about the idea that murderers read their own press cuttings. It's too American. Natural Born Killers is a good film, but still a film, and prisoners can't earn money writing books about their crimes in the UK. The fourth murder makes him question this. Louise Griffiths. Pregnant mother. Unemployed. She was a big girl, tall and strong with a resolute set to her jaw that still projected confidence despite him knowing how it had ended. Last seen leaving a pub called the Cadbury Vaults to take the short walk home. Found behind some metal commercial bins in an alley leading to the back of a Jamaican restaurant. If the other murders had been horrific, Louise' was a showstopper. Strangled, eviscerated and posed holding the fetus like a Madonna and child. Thirty years doesn't diminish the nauseous jolt the scene photographs give him. Nothing could.

Silver linings. Louise Griffiths was seen carrying a large vinyl handbag. This was recovered from a skip. It was the Holy Grail, the lucky piece of evidence that pulled everything else back on track. The contents had been removed, and fingerprints had been left on the strap and the fastening. Good quality, and identifiable as belonging to a knife-carrying shoplifter called Richard Hartington. Better still, he had been caught peeping through windows and exposing himself to women walking through Eastville Park as a 14 year old. Cautioned and allowed to go about his business when it emerged that he had a low IQ, and social services agreed to place him in a therapeutic children's home. He was arrested and interviewed. He made a full confession.

McGuiness vaguely remembers the case. The confession was disputed at trial. The interviewing officers were accused of violence and torture. There was a photo of Richard Hartington looking like he had been given a pretty serious kicking that did the rounds. The official response was that he had to be physically restrained during his arrest. Public horror at the crimes and the relentless press coverage meant that people either didn't believe him, or didn't care. A mob banged on the prison van windows as Richard Hartington was whisked away to begin a life sentence that the trial judge said should be at least thirty years but the home secretary increases to a full "life means life".

There was an appeal. There always is. It failed. They often do. Murderous sex offenders don't seem to attract the same support as footballers and armed robbers, and Richard Hartington looked like he was going to slip into the system, a nameless pallid face in a burgundy toweling prison tracksuit. You could hardly blame him for committing suicide in 1993. The only surprise was that he made it that long with spit and shit in every meal and violence waiting on every landing. His mother went to cancer two years later. She had started a campaign to free her son, but that had died with him. Nobody cared, and the world moved on to other crimes, other villains and other victims. Nothing remained of Richard Hartington but a black and white photo on documentaries with low production values and lower factual accuracy. He didn't even merit a serial killer nickname.

McGuiness lights another cigarette and pours himself a drink. He is tired, but cannot shake the belief that he would be letting Sarah down if he stopped reading now. Mixing her memory with any thoughts about loyalty makes him uncomfortable, and it is easier to read on, take a pull of his cigarette, a swallow of whisky and not think about it. He blinks the smoke out of his eye and opens the appeal folder. Another report. Short, and to the point. The DNA from the Bristol scenes could not have been Richard Hartington. No grey areas. No possibilities or probabilities. He scratches his head. Could the real Bristol killer be some kind of relative? Even if this was true, so what? It didn't get him any further towards finding out who he was, and what was the point of sending him a file that exposes a 30 year old miscarriage of justice when anyone who gave a shit has been dead for at least 20 years anyway? He sighs. A quick skim back through the statements to see if he's missed anything, then bed. He owes her that much, he tells himself. One of the interviewing officer's names is familiar. Martin Bright. DS Bright. The Deputy Commissioner responsible for anti terrorism had the same name. It's not exactly unusual, so it could be a coincidence. A quick check in Google should do it. Started out with Avon and Somerset, apparently. CID in Bristol before transferring to the Met in 1992.

Everything looks very far away. He can see his hands on the keyboard and he wishes to god they were someone else's. What the fuck had Sarah been thinking sending this to him? It is like handing him a rattlesnake or a ticking bomb. Clear evidence that the second most powerful police officer in London had kicked a confession out of a spastic back in the day. Not just career ruining. Sent home in disgrace stuff, but public enquiry and charged with perverting the course of justice 24 carat poison. Fuck. Had he done something to upset her? Why him? A flash of her lying on a bed naked and him spouting some shit from a film like a proper Hollywood hero cop, making himself feel better and her look at him like he wasn't just some middle aged wanker cheating on his wife. Connections. Burglars who didn't steal anything and a clever, beautiful woman drowned in the sort of accident that took idiots and junkies but not people like her. He squashes the idea that he put her at risk, that he was somehow responsible. It's easy enough. Realising that you might be in danger focuses the mind rather well. Another cigarette inhaled furiously. If this is true, if the burglary and Sarah's accident were connected, then the only thing keeping him safe is that they didn't find it. As soon as they recover it, then he's fucked. He can't throw it away, though. Sarah might have died for this, and he needed time to think before he decides to ignore that. Ken McGuiness rifles Maxine's desk, mentally reproaching himself for every lecture he has ever given her about never throwing anything away. He finds what he's looking for. He hastily writes his own address on the padded envelope and puts what he thinks is about the right amount of stamps on it. There are no occupied cars in the street, and he has known the neighbours for a while. None of them are on holiday. He's pretty sure he's not being watched. Maybe the burglary put them off. He opens the door and creeps out into the night. The post box is three streets away. It only takes five minutes, and he goes to bed as soon as he gets home. Maxine's shape under the blanket looks like St Paul's cathedral and he shivers in besides her, searching for sleep.

Chapter 13

Kath Stevens' hands are in the driving position her instructor taught her nearly twenty years ago, and she is not distracted by the morning news. She's tired, though. It's nine o'clock. She's been driving since five, and god knows her sidekick for this jaunt to South Wales hasn't been exactly exemplary in keeping her awake. He's been asleep since Swindon. She's got a lot on her mind, and it's a good chance to work through it provided she doesn't space off and start talking to herself. Some things aren't for saying out loud.

She takes a pull of coffee. It's cold, but she likes it black and bitter, so it's not too disgusting. Evaluation is what her situation needs. She's thirty six and single. She's been married but Dave took off long ago leaving her literally holding the baby and paying the mortgage. Holding it all together, and she'd done her best. It wasn't her fault that the schools where she lived in Catford were pretty well all feeder schools for Feltham Young Offenders. It wasn't her fault that she thought that her daughter was special, far too special to tip into the sink school and flush away with the rest of the bathwater babies. That meant going private, and even with a sergeant's salary, it is hard. Beth winning a scholarship made it impossible to say no, and she found out that scholarship meant something different to the definition she had always used quickly. Tuition wasn't free, just cheaper. £5 000 was a lot to find every year, and no amount of patronising advice about going without expensive foreign holidays, designer clothes or changing the car every year made it any different. As if she's been spending thousands on Vivienne Westwood originals and fortnights in Dubai? Cutting down on camping holidays in Dorset and replacing her two grand second hand car every five years bought Beth about three weeks of St Dunstan's precious time. You had to do your best. She'd given up smoking, and become a supermarket wine shelf drinker. It helped a bit, but every time the fees were due, and the inevitable painful interview with the headmaster was called, she couldn't help resenting the smug upper class wankers who talked about the sacrifices they made to pay school fees. Couldn't take that skiing holiday in winter and had to make do with a fortnight in Monaco? Bleeding hearts, tiny violins and rivers of tears. She had been ordering tap water and a starter when she found out that she was going Dutch, saying she couldn't go out because of "childcare issues" and watching her "date" mentally deleting her number for years. What is there to show for this at the end? Another meeting with the headmaster, another letter setting out the arrears and muted suggestion that perhaps Beth might be happier in a school where she didn't feel out of place. All that scrimping and saving to make sure her daughter felt she belonged there was apparently a waste of time. Message received. Loud and clear. She had wanted to grab the headmaster by his throat and ram her fist into his face. It had shut him up when she'd handed over an envelope of cash the following week. They were all very respectful then. Perhaps Beth was Saint Dunstan material after all.

That was the problem. She'd paid in cash. They'd given her a receipt. It was there for anyone to find, and she is sure that sooner or later someone will come looking. She regrets it, of course, but she knows that regrets won't save her. She thought about putting the money back, almost as soon as she had taken it. It's too late. She knows that the miraculous appearance of £5 000 will be even more suspicious. She is going to follow the DCI's advice and try to pass it off as a clerical error. There's a good chance that nobody will bother to look into it any further than an insinuation by the Defence in court, and who listens to those? She's not corrupt. This is family. She loves her daughter and wants the best for her. It was a spur of the moment thing. The solution to her problems presenting itself when she was angry enough to go for it. The milk has been spilt and it's too late for tears now. Nothing to do but hope for the best and try to stop waking at four every morning worrying that the noises she can hear are the start of a dawn raid.

Detective Sergeant Kathleen Stevens sighs, reaches over and punches the sleeping DC Simon Welbourne in the shoulder. A signpost for Bridgend, Junction thirty five flashes past. Time to be a police sergeant. She should savour it. There might not be many more.

"Wakey wakey. Nearly there."

Her colleague yawns.

"Are we going to be long here? It's a total shit hole. They probably started building the wicker man when we phoned to say we were coming."

"Enough of that. We're here to see Jane Canavan's grieving mother not to start a bloody diplomatic incident. If you can't deal with exercising a bit of sensitivity for a couple of hours, then you'd probably be happier in the TSG."

"All right skip. Keep your hair on. I'll be the soul of charm until she drugs us and we wake up to Peter Cushing bolloxing on about the harvest."

She tells herself that he's not a bad officer, and that he'll be fine once they are face to face with the grieving relatives. The Satnav guides her through unfamiliar streets to a bungalow. A deep breath and she puts her professional face on. She's trying for sympathetic in a no nonsense way, but she is aware that she can look hard faced. A proper Bermondsey girl, all dip dye and heavy make up underneath her sensible suit. She waits for Welbourne to get out of the car and they walk to the door together. She walks carefully, making sure her heels don't get caught between the bricks on the herringbone drive.

The doorbell plays "Men of Harlech." Frenzied barking starts immediately. It's high pitched. Not too frightening, although the prospect of removing a Jack Russell's teeth from her extremities makes her take step back. Welbourne mouths, "bet it's a fucking corgi" to her as the door opens. It isn't. An elderly lady in a pink, acrylic housecoat holds a nondescript ball of furious black fur by its collar.

"Are you the police from London?"

"I'm Sergeant Stevens, this is DC Welbourne, my colleague. Is your dog safe, Mrs Canavan?"

"He's perfectly harmless unless somebody provokes him. Come in"

She leads the way into a room dominated by a three-piece suite and television. Pictures of Jane Canavan stand on every surface. From cradle to graduation, taking in first days at school and work, a visit to a theme park and all points in between. Stevens notices that she is either on her own or with her mother in every photograph. It is oppressively hot. The radiators are on full, and a three bar electric fire glows in the grate. She prays that her underarm deodorant lives up to its advertising.

"Mrs Canavan. We just need to ask you a few questions about Jane, to get an idea of who she was and what she was up to when she was murdered. She worked for a housing charity, didn't she?"

The older woman roosts on one of the armchairs, and seems to puff herself up when she thinks about her daughter.

"She was headhunted, you know. She had ever such a good job with the council here. Worked for the homeless. They treated her terribly though. Always putting more work onto her, the lazy so and so's. Practically running the place on her own, she was. Doctor Pritchard had to sign her off with the stress."

Stevens recognises the name from the medical certificates on her London employer's file.

"Was Jane prone to stress. She'd had a bit of time off sick up in London, too."

Motherly anger.

"Not until the council started trying to get rid of her she wasn't. It was all so unfair. They were jealous of her. She gave her job everything, and all she expected was that the idle sods she worked with would do the same. Bullying, they accused her of. Outrageous. As if Jane could have bullied anyone. She was so fragile."

"So why did she leave? London's a long way to go for a job."

"She wasn't sacked! And as for all that disgusting nonsense. The lies these people told. Jane was lucky to get out when she did. Nobody could have worked with people who said that about her."

Stevens looks at Welbourne. He looks as lost as she feels.

"I'm sorry Mrs Canavan, but can you repeat that?"

She takes out a notebook and balances it on her knee. The other woman is cautious, suddenly realising that she has taken the conversation down a road that might not be entirely friendly to her daughter's memory. Stevens keeps eye contact for a moment, willing her to carry on. Mrs Canavan coughs, stands and bustles out of the room.

"Where are my manners? I expect you'll both want a cup of tea after your drive"

"That would be lovely." Stevens gets up and follows her. "Let me give you a hand."

The kitchen is small, almost a galley. There is a dog bowl and water dish by the back door. The work surface is spotless. The kettle begins to boil.

"Mrs Canavan, I don't want to upset you or go over any painful memories, but we need to catch the man that killed your daughter. Anything you can tell us about her might help us do this. Please."

Three mugs are slammed onto a tray. Stevens lowers her voice.

"Please?"

"You'll have to ask them. I let no corrupt utterance proceed from my mouth, as the good book says."

She crosses her arms across her breasts. Interview over. Stevens considers, her hand on her chin as Mrs Canavan hurls tea bags into pot, her housecoat fading to pastel behind wreathes of steam.

"Can you tell us her boss' name?"

Mrs Canavan shoulders tense as she forces the name out of a mouth that is drawn as tight as a robber's hood.

"Drinkwater. Moira Drinkwater. The tenants loved Jane, and that Moira was always a jealous liar."

Custard creams and jammy dodgers. Tea from the best china. A muted discussion about the court process, and why Jane Canavan's body couldn't make the final journey down the M4 until the person charged with her murder had the chance of his own post mortem. More sympathy. The system was wrong, cruel even, but what could they do? Surely it was better that the monster who did this to her daughter faced justice and didn't escape on a technicality. Everyone lapped that one up. They knew that the legal system was set up to acquit the guilty in the face of overwhelming evidence. Every judge was a mild mannered liberal stooge who couldn't wait to set free a paedophile before knocking back the tax payer funded claret over the Guardian crossword. The British press, making it easier for every police officer trying to explain the unpalatable to the angry and bereaved. It is so much better when there is someone else to blame. More tea and then back on the road, bladders sloshing like water balloons.

The civic centre is concrete and glass. It is next to a river and the dull green water's reflection in its windows makes it look camouflaged. Stevens parks the car. She and Welbourne walk under a concrete, cigarette-seeded awning and into a reception area. A receptionist inspects their warrant cards with barely suppressed excitement before breathlessly calling the Housing Department and announcing a lady and a gentleman from the Murder Squad in London. They are ushered into the presence of Moira Drinkwater, the Deputy Director of Housing Services.

The reality doesn't really live up to the title. Moira Drinkwater is short. She can't be much taller than five foot. Her head is small, and slopes upward from a broad jawline to a narrow forehead that is accentuated by the sort of severe ponytail that would be called a Croydon facelift if she had been twenty years younger and two hundred miles further east. She stands and holds out a hand. Stevens notices that her hips have to be twice as broad as her shoulders. The whole effect is of a pyramid draped in man made fibre. There is a sharp static shock as they shake hands.

"Sergeant Stevens. Constable Welbourne. I'm Moira Drinkwater. What can I do for you?"

She's curious about why they are there, but Stevens can't detect any signs of nervousness.

"We're here to ask you about one of your former colleagues. Jane Canavan. Do you remember her?"

Moira Drinkwater exhales as she sits.

"I can't say that I'm surprised, although I'm sorry to hear she's got herself in trouble, naturally. What has Jane done now?"

"She hasn't done anything that we are aware of, Moira."

Stevens catches Welbourne's eye then leans in. Confidences are about to be passed.

"She's been murdered."

The Deputy Director of Housing Services gives a shriek, and settles back into her swivel chair, breathing as heavily as if she has just dived into freezing water.

"Murdered."

It's a gasp, barely audible.

"By who?"

"That's what we're trying to find out, Moira. My colleague and I couldn't help noticing that your first thought was that Ms Canavan would be the perpetrator not the victim."

"Jane was always a difficult person to have on the team. She was very hard working and enthusiastic at first, but she worked here for ten years, and I'm afraid that her performance became more and more erratic. I don't want to give you the wrong impression. She was never arrested or anything, so it's all allegations, but a lot of staff complained about her manner. There was one incident when some poor girl who was working as an admin assistant committed suicide. Jane was her manager. Her family made some very serious allegations about her during the inquest. They said that she had bullied her until she couldn't take it any more and killed herself. The girl had problems, of course. She had a dreadful childhood and she had been taking drugs and drinking a lot. They so often do, don't they? She'd even tried to hurt herself before. Highly vulnerable. The coroner said that this couldn't be proved, so no more was said about it. There were complaints from other staff, as well, but none of them were prepared to make it official, so what could I do?"

She pauses for breath, and Stevens takes the chance to nod sympathetically. It can be hard when the rules protect the guilty. Welbourne has his head down, his hand moving furiously across the Evidence and Action book in his lap.

"It all came out when she was managing our Homeless Persons Unit. That's where people come in off the street if they were looking for somewhere to stay. The police were looking for a young man, and traced him to Jane's house. He was in her bed. Naked. She was in the shower. She denied sleeping with him, of course. Told the police that she felt sorry for him, and they had to let her go, but it turned out he wasn't the first. None of the others were what you could call credible. They had drug and alcohol problems or had been in trouble with the police, so it was decided that it would be best if Jane moved on. "

The M4 is reasonably clear. They have made good time to Bristol before either of them speaks.

"Fucking Hell. That is some dark shit."

"That's more than true, Sarge. I mean, I'm a single man and I spend most of my time trying to make myself look good for the ladies. I go to the gym. I even moisturise if I'm going out, although for Christ's sake don't tell my Dad. Maybe I've got it wrong, and that's why I'm still single. I should put on a coat that smells of rat piss and get myself down the council. Guaranteed a shag."

"I think you'll probably find that our Jane was a special girl, Simon. Mind you. Rat piss has to be an improvement on Old Spice, so why don't you give it a go. Do you think there's a name for it?"

"What?"

"Tramp shagging. I mean, I've got to write this up and I can't call it that, can I? I mean, kiddy fiddlers are paedophiles, naughty undertakers are necrophiles, so tramp shaggers are what?"

DC Welbourne considers.

"Vagophiles, I think, Sarge."

"Bloody hell. How do you come up with that?"

"Vagos is Greek for tramp. You have to use the Greek to match up with the "phile" bit"

"You are truly a man of hidden talents, Constable. If there was a medal for naming perversions I would recommend you."

"Benefits of a classical education, Sarge."

"Spell it for me"

It is getting dark. A sign reads, "London 124 miles". Stevens looks in the rear view mirror and sees a string of lights behind her.

Chapter 14

Lunch is over, and the elderly retreat from the community hall, the rag and tag of mobility scooters and mini busses a geriatric Dunkirk. Father Anthony Mitchell breathes in vegetables, washing up liquid and air freshener, then turns his back on the exodus. He nods to the volunteer who is busily stacking dishes, a pretty red haired girl whose name he searches for but has mislaid.

"Just get off when you're finished. I'll lock up."

He has the Daily Mirror folded under his arm and a packet of ten Benson and Hedges in his pocket. He is self conscious that the young woman can see the bulge that the cigarettes make in his trousers, and maneuvers the paper down to his side to disguise it. The sunlight is strong enough to cut columns of light into the interior gloom. The morning's work is done. The next call upon his time is not until six o'clock and later this evening Manchester United will take on Bayern Munich in the Champion's League. Half an hour, a couple of cigarettes, the sports pages and the tranquility of solitude in the Community Hall's lavatories is a blessing. Time to clear his head.

The plastic seat is cold against his thighs. He lights a cigarette and exhales, his eyes already on team selection and an informative discussion about the relative lack of success of English teams. A light tube buzzes like a trapped fly. He folds the paper neatly as he reads, one hand to his temple and the other held in front of him to compensate for his short sightedness. He has a slight headache that will need monitoring.

He becomes aware of the smell as he reads. It overwhelms the urinal cakes as subtly and slowly as mustard gas. It is a lifetime of cigarettes, refuse and alcohol filtered through open pores and dirty clothes. It makes him gasp, and the pulse above his right eyes starts a familiar arrhythmic drumbeat. There is a rasp of match and sandpaper and an exhalation from the next cubicle.

"Afternoon, Father."

He recognises the voice, the breath rattling behind each word and the accent that could come from a number of places or nowhere.

"The council didn't take the house off us after they found her. After the social workers left us alone and the neighbours stopped feeling sorry for us we never really spoke. We didn't ignore each other, or live in silence. We just never sat down and had a chat. We just weren't that kind of family, and although I had thought that killing her might have brought us closer we rubbed along just the same as we did before, but without the worry that she'd be home, pissed and angry. He turned into a secretive little sod as he grew up. He left school and took to hanging around god knows where. He must have had some mates, as he was always smoking weed, but they never came round the house. I'd ask him, and he'd pretend I hadn't spoken. I couldn't get anything out of him. We were basically both grown men by then, and that was the reason that the social left us to it. There were times when I thought that he wanted to say something. He would stare at me with his mouth open as I was making tea or watching the telly.   He looked like a bloody goldfish. I would wait, even try to encourage him a bit, but he'd shut his and go about whatever it was that he did.

I was working on the mini cabs. I had an old Ford Granada like the one on the Sweeny, with the big back lights and the square bonnet. I worked nights, and it was all right if you didn't mind the drunks. Money was better, too.

It was a terrible night. Rain like something out of the Bible, drops the size of golf balls bouncing off the road and hammering on the roof of the car. I was driving back to the centre along the ring road when the wipers went. You couldn't see a bloody thing. I tried driving with my head out of the window but it was hopeless, the rain punching me in the face and bursting against my eyes. I needed somewhere off road with a roof on it so that I could fix the car and get back to earning. I drove along at walking pace trying to think of somewhere, half blind and the rain smothering the headlights so all I could see was water and a couple of feet of white line.   I was going to settle for a petrol station forecourt when I remembered the old garage. I hadn't been there since I was a kid. She'd rented it off the council when she'd been dry for a bit and was looking for somewhere to keep a load of chairs and tables that would get her a few Jesus points with her church. It was about half a mile away from the house, down the back of the blocks at the edge of the estate.

The double doors were chained and padlocked, so I went round the side. I reached round for the lights, flicked the switch. Nothing. I shut my eyes and opened them again, hoping that they would get used to the dark. I stood there, not wanting to move in case I barked my shins or tripped over, and wondered what to do. There was a smell of damp and frying bacon. I could hear the rain dripping off my clothes and onto the floor, and my breathing in and out. I pulled out a lighter. I couldn't get the bloody thing to work at first, and when I did the flame cast hardly any light at all. I turned in a circle trying to get a sense of what was in there. When I got to half way round he was just standing there, pale and staring in the dark like a bloody ghoul. I nearly jumped out of my skin and burned my thumb. The lighter skittered away across the floor. "Hello" he said, like we just met outside the Co-op.

It took my eyes a while to adjust, even though the light was dim and it came up slowly. Candles and a hurricane lamp. Big shadows painting the walls. I could see he'd made it his place. There were empties on the floor, a bit of old carpet and a couple of chairs that looked like he'd had them out of a car. A pub trestle table, god knows how he'd got that up here on his own. A gas bottle connected to a ring and grill. Sliced Mothers Pride in a bag and a plastic tub of margarine. Tea bags and a pint of milk. A metal Fosters Lager ashtray filled with so many dog ends it looked like a sandcastle. Home from home, really. He sat in one of the seats and gestured to the other. "Sit down", he said. "I'll make us a cup of tea," and he gets busy with the cooker. I did as I was told, my wet trousers sticking to the vinyl. There was no radio or TV. Nobody shouting or talking. Just the drumming of the rain on the corrugated iron roof, the hiss of the kettle and the burner and the sound of breathing echoing off the concrete walls. It could have been thousands of years ago and we were cavemen.

He handed me a cup of tea then sat down. I could feel my hands beginning to thaw out against the sides of the cup and I took a sip, looking over at him through the steam. He rolled up a spliff. He only took a little draw himself, then passed it. I took a hit, pulling the smoke deep into my lungs. I didn't want to get stoned really. It was the tobacco I wanted. I finished the spliff and he pulled another one out of a tin. We sat there smoking in the half-light, spliff after spliff. I started to hear voices and rhythms in the noise of the rain, the creaking seats and our breathing. Before I knew it, my foot began to move to it, twitching in the smoke like a dreaming dog. I caught him looking at me and tried to stop. He was perfectly still, sitting in the chair staring at me with his eyes wide and white and a smile on him. I could sense that every bit of him was alive, roiling and crawling under his skin, and if I took my eyes off him for a moment he would change.

It was so quiet that it was almost lost in the background. An inhalation, caught in the throat somewhere between a whimper and a sob. His eyes slid off to the side and mine followed. It was hard to tell what it was at first. She was tied to an old table, like one that you'd have in the dinner hall at school. It was lying on its back, its legs standing upright in each corner. She was in the middle, her back to the floor and her wrists and ankles tied. She had some clothes on still, a leather skirt and a t-shirt. There was masking tape around her mouth and eyes, which made her head look huge, like an insect. I could tell she had been crying because a line of mascara had leaked under the tape and down across her cheek. There were raw lines on her skin that had dust and dirt from the floor sticking to them. I realised where the bacon smell had come from and it made me feel sick. My head went down, between my knees. When I looked up, I realised that I could see up her skirt. She didn't have any knickers on. He caught my eye and shrugged at me, like it was the most natural thing in the world to have a girl tied up in the garage, all naked and burned. Like it wasn't a problem. Like I had been out of order coming in and disturbing him and I owed him an apology that he was happy to let go because I was family, and we looked out for each other. I tried to stare him down. I was the oldest. I had always been the one in charge. But my eyes kept being pulled back to her. Up her skirt. She had black hair down there. I could see she trimmed herself. Kept it neat and ready for action. I felt myself go hard. The burning smell made my throat fill with bile. I swear that I didn't want to. The smoke made me horny. I could feel my trousers bow outwards like a tent. He smiled at me. He looked at my crotch and back to her and said, "It'll be my treat. You can have a go if you want because we're brothers and brothers share everything."

I expected to say no. I was waiting for the words to come out of my mouth and nobody was more surprised than me when they didn't. I felt a trickle down between my shoulder blades. The garage smelled of bodies and breath and something strong and sharp behind it. I noticed that I was panting, my chest rising and falling in time with the pulsing of the blood between my legs. I couldn't have torn my eyes away from her even if I wanted to. And I didn't. It was never about what I wanted. I wanted what anyone else would have in the damp, dark heat. He knew that. Knew me better than I knew myself. He was staring at me as intensely as I was staring at her. His breath and my breath were in time, echoing off the walls so it sounded like the whole building was breathing in and out as it stood over her wondering what would happen next. I looked at her, listening to her whimper, and I expected there to be an angel on my shoulder arguing with me. Laying down the law. But this was real, not a cartoon. There was no voice in my head telling me that it was wrong. No good advice for me to ignore. All I could think of was what would happen if I did? Would I get away with it? Who knew about her? How had he got her? I looked at him, and he smiled at me. It was wide, "everything's going to be alright" smile that made me think of being at the seaside or Christmas morning. I looked at him and he shrugged, like someone at a door who tells you to go first, a sort of "be my guest" shake of the shoulders. So I did. I helped myself. The table legs weren't that far apart, and she struggled at first. I could hear him snickering at my white arse and I felt myself hotting up. I slapped her once, and she made a whiney noise like she was trying to beg me to stop through the tape. It made me feel like my cock was going to explode, so I slapped her again, and again, until she lay back down shaking her head from side to side and making cat noises. Then I did her.

I pulled up my trousers, and gave the thumbs up. His turn. That was the point of it all, wasn't it? She went very still. I could tell that she could hear his footsteps and she was trying to work out whether she was about to get a second helping. I smiled to myself and thought of a phrase I remembered from some magazine I had read. I don't know where. At the doctors or something. "Female intuition". She had a lot of that, or so I thought. Knew what was coming to her. I saw him raise his foot and stamp on her, hard. She screamed, but it was through the tape and you could hardly hear her. He crouched over her and to begin with I thought he was just giving her a beating because he was leaning forward and his fists were going in and out so quickly they were blurring and blending into lines. Then I saw the red and the yellow glimmer of the candle reflecting on what he had in his hand. I smelled nosebleeds and butchers shops. I wanted to stop him, but it was like I was stuck. And I couldn't say anything. I was afraid that she would recognise my voice. Stupid when you look back on it. Me and him were talking before I even knew she was there. And there was no way she was going to pick me out. Not after what he had done to her. Then he turned round. We were breathing in time again, the only sound apart from the rain on the roof and the dripping of her blood off the edge of the table."

The flush is deafening. The door bangs against the cubicle and Father Anthony sits, shocked, his trousers around his ankles, a still smoking filter in his hand. He stares blankly at the football pages, unable to move and frightened that any noise would bring some terrible fate upon him. He stares at the newspaper, unable to make sense of pictures before his eyes. It is fifteen minutes before he is able to stand. The keys jangle in his hand like wind chimes as he locks up and walks off into the afternoon on shaking legs.

Chapter 15

The Central Criminal Court is busy at 1:45pm. Lunch is nearly over and there is a large queue of barristers, witnesses and police. Nobody coming through is a tourist. Although you can see justice being done at the Old Bailey if that's what floats your boat, the general public is strictly segregated. You have to be in the system, or at the very least touched by it to use the main door. Security is tight. London's most famous criminal court is a target, and risk has to be managed. Ken McGuiness joins the line, steps into a Perspex tube that reminds him of Star Trek, before allowing himself to be searched.

He is at Court to shepherd a case through one of the numerous pre trial hearings. He is here to be the visible police presence and reassure any of the grieving relatives and their supporters that things are being taken very seriously indeed. Privately, he thinks it is a waste of time. It's a domestic murder. A husband who stabbed his wife during an argument then called the police. His tearful confession to the 999 operator seems to McGuiness to be pretty good evidence and it's hardly a whodunit, but nobody pleads guilty to murder. What's the point? There's only one sentence, and he can see why even the guiltiest murderer isn't rushing towards life in prison with open arms. He decides to wait for the prosecuting QC outside Court Three. It's in the old building, and he likes the marble floors, memorabilia displays and statues. It makes him feel like he has made it. He's not just a cog in the Met machine, arresting drunks and petty drug dealers. He's a Murder Squad officer and here is where he does his day-to-day.

The hearing takes ten minutes. It is followed by a short discussion with the prosecuting barrister, who has taken some very expensive lessons in being patronising, and whose advice could be summed up as, "do the absolutely obvious things that I am sure you have never thought of because you didn't go to a decent school". Finished by 3:30. He's due back at Walworth for 5, to start interviewing and reviewing the gang members that his team, the TSG and local CID have spent the day rounding up, and he is not anxious to rush back to what he is sure will be hours of grunted "no comments", the smell of trainers and Maxpax coffee. Rush hour crush and the press of work weary bodies on the train aren't too appealing either. He remembers that Kath Stevens has her day in Court as exhibits officer and decides to cadge a lift from her. He walks down to the notice board on the first floor, checks the case name and walks to court Eleven.

This is in the new building. Less marble and dark wood, more stripped pine and uncomfortable seating. He takes a look through the glass window in the court door. The trial is still sitting. There is a uniformed police officer in the witness box. McGuiness doesn't recognise him. The prosecution's team is in the front two rows. A QC, female, short and red faced. McGuiness knows her by reputation. She is living proof that people start to look like their dogs. Her junior is tall, young and eager looking with long hair in a flicked fringe and a fashionable beard. A Crown Prosecution Service Case worker hides behind them, safe inside a rampart of case files. The third bench is empty. He takes a quick look around the Court. She's not there.

The public canteen is on the second floor, and as the public is not allowed in the building, the only patrons are police officers, witnesses and the odd advocate who isn't confident enough to sit with the great and good in the area where the barristers' eat their cucumber sandwiches. He sees her as he's walking past up the stairs to the police room. The peroxide hair and thin shoulders are unmistakable. He is just about to go in when he notices that she involved in an intense conversation with a man in his thirties. He has short hair, not exactly a skinhead. A non descript haircut and a high end off the peg suit that signals "job" at court as obviously as hi-viz and a utility belt. Square jaw and good looking in an "Action Man" sort of way. His hand is stretched across the table towards her. They aren't touching but the gesture is possessive. She is leaning forward. He gets the impression that they don't want to be overheard, and leaves. He'll wait for her outside.

Two cigarettes later, and there she is, pushing the door open with her head down.

"Kath"

She turns, and he can see her face is red under the pancake. Some kind of lovers' quarrel? It's not his problem. He scrounges his lift.

Walworth Road Police Station. Operation Disrupt is off to a flying start with the morning's six o'clock knocks. Thirty-six arrests: twenty-six already in the cells with the rest stacked up in vans waiting to be processed. The count so far is twelve for drugs, eight for money laundering, two for firearms, nine for assaulting the arresting officers and five wanted for not showing up at court.

There are two to each cell and rising, and the custody area smells of inhumanity and microwave curry. McGuiness can hear cell doors being kicked and snatches of shouted conversations as he swipes his way through the door. Every gang member under seventeen needs an appropriate adult, a responsible person to sit with them while they are being questioned to make sure they understand what is going on and aren't tempted or bullied into admitting things they haven't done. Every single detainee has the right to legal representation, and as gang members usually know the system as well as the police, every single person processed so far has asked to speak to their lawyer. The phone is ringing off the hook as four harassed custody sergeants ignore it and try to get on with the never-ending task of sorting out the paperwork that transfers prisoners into the cells. This has been going on for about nine hours straight, and is not showing much sign of letting up. Two civilian jailers duck and weave through the throng of people at the sergeants' desk delivering microwave meals and cups of tea to prisoners. At least if they are eating they aren't kicking off or shouting. In a concrete and metal environment, every banging door and shout echoes and repeats itself, all blending into a blizzard of inarticulate protest.

One prisoner is ready. His mother and solicitor are sitting on an uncomfortable slatted wooden bench. McGuiness spots DC Welbourne standing at the desk accompanying yet another prisoner.

"Simon, book whoever these two are here for out, and let's crack on."

The prisoner is 15 years old. His trousers hang at mid buttock and he's pimp rolling down the corridor with a swagger that writes a cheque that his eyes can't cash. McGuiness ushers him and his entourage into the interview room. It's small and windowless, airless too. An arthritic air conditioner weakly circulates a smell of damp. McGuiness unwraps two tapes, puts them into the machine and after an electronic whine, the interview starts.

It's over pretty quickly. The kid has only been arrested for possession of a bag of cannabis, and the gang links seem fairly minimal. He "no comments" all the questions like he's used to the game, and even manages a yawn, but McGuiness can tell that he doesn't recognise Damien Anderson's photo when it's put in front of him. That's the problem with trawling. You catch all the little fish if the net is too wide, and you have to throw them back. He brings the interview to an end, seals a tape and returns his prisoner to the human zoo. One down.

It takes three hours to work their way round to a fish worth keeping. Delroy Simpson. The Intel file says his street name is X-ray, and looking at him either he's put on a lot of weight or it's evidence of a sense of humour. He is eighteen stone at least, and the debris in his cell shows a dedication to eating that even takes in the local institutional catering. He walks the walk, and his shoulders almost brush the sides of the corridor. He's in his mid twenties. Not exactly a contemporary of Damien Anderson's but old enough to have known him. There's proper leverage too, a handgun in a ziplock bag in a cistern. Serious time. Five years minimum even for a clean skin who pleads guilty. Delroy Simpson has a lot of skin and none of it is clean. He's decided to be questioned without a lawyer, too.

McGuiness is a low key interviewer. He can't see the point in shouting and he doesn't have that edge of outrage that many of his colleagues seem to find it hard to hide. He leans forward across the desk, elbows on the table. It's just a chat.

"A Baikal pistol, two magazines and a silencer, Delroy. That's 5 years and rising."

The big man grunts and shrugs.

"It's not mine, mate. I've never seen it before you lot pulled it out of the bog and waved it about. How do I know you didn't put it there yourselves?"

"Now, I can see that there might be some difficulties for us. You live in a house full of bedsits for a start, but you're not helping yourself by accusing my officers of planting evidence. It sounds a bit desperate for a start, and that sort of nonsense never flies with a jury. Not for a man with your previous."

He lets the idea of a way out register before moving on.

"Do you know this man?"

A photo. Custody image. Left, right and centre. A nod.

"That's Omen."

If you were to help us with finding Omen, I could be persuaded that we needed more enquiries into the gun. Who knows, the forensics might not match. Anything could happen."

Delroy Simpson knows where this is heading. He doesn't look convinced.

"I'm not a snitch."

"I'm not asking you for information, Delroy. I don't need you to make a statement. I've got all the evidence I'm going to need."

McGuiness fans the Peckham crime scene photos out on the table like a casino dealer opening a new pack of cards. Jane Canavan's wounds smile up under the strip lights, red against blue white. The big man flinches.

"I need to talk to Omen about this. You can't tell me whether he did this or not; at least I don't think you can. Were you there, Delroy?"

"Fucking hell. Of course I wasn't. I'm not a fucking psycho."

"I've got nothing that says that you were. This isn't some drug deal gone wrong or some dead gangbanger who at least chose to live like that. This lady worked for a charity. She was raped and stabbed to death then left inside a bush on Peckham Rye for a ten year old kid to find. I don't need a witness statement. I don't need you to tell me that Damien Anderson killed that woman. I know all I need to know about that. What I do need is to find him. If he's an innocent man, I need to clear him and get on with the job of finding the person who really did this. If not, he needs to be off the street. If he's done this once…well, you've seen all the films Delroy. Do you really think that this will be the only one?"

He's shrewd. McGuiness can see the cogs turning. One nudge should do it.

"I have to think about whether we've got enough to charge you with the gun. I might need to bail you for the forensics, and to check on who else had access to the toilet."

He pushes a card with his mobile number across the table. Delroy Simpson looks at it, puts his hand over it then scoops it into his pocket. It looks like a drug deal.

"Fine. I'm looking at two weeks. It's a serious offence, so there should be no problem in getting the forensics on the hurry up. Simon, take Mr Simpson to the custody desk and get his bail date organised."

He dead eyes into the other man's face for a second.

"I expect to hear from you, Delroy. I'll be very disappointed if I don't."

Delroy Simpson nods, stands and walks into the grey world of the not quite informant. McGuiness sighs and stretches. It must be gone ten by now, and time for a cup of coffee before the next round. He walks through the Custody Suite and notices a priest sitting on the bench opposite the sergeant. The man is in full dog collar, black suit and overcoat, but still manages to look as fragile as a child playing religious dress up. He nods as he passes. He hasn't been to mass for years. Old habits, though.

Chapter 16

The jeweler off Regents street has had a busy day. The pavements outside are full, and traffic snorts slowly past as the day draws to its close. The owner is tired. It's not demanding work, but his assistant called in sick and there has been a steady flow of customers. He's usually careful with the security system. One has to be these days, but it's nearly time to shut the shop, and he is thinking about his commute. The bell goes once. A short buzz and he has pressed the release before he thinks to check the external CCTV.

Three men are inside before he has the chance to react. The cabinets are smashed efficiently. Watches and jewelry are stuffed into bags. One man jumps the counter and reaches behind for the takings. The owner cannot help himself. It's a territorial thing. Primeval. As the man reaches towards the draw where the altered purchases are kept he grabs him. It is madness. He's sixty-three, and hasn't been physically fit for thirty years. The robber is young. Tall and broad shouldered. And he has a gun. He can see it as he tries to pull the other man's hand away from the drawer. It is black. Not new. The finish is worn to silver along the squared edges of the barrel. He cannot see a cylinder, and he has seen enough films to know that it is an automatic. For a moment he comforts himself with the thought that these things are usually replicas. The gun crashes down against the side of his head. His knees buckle and he grabs his attacker around the waist. He looks up and sees the barrel pointing down at him. The noise is huge, freezing everyone in the shop. Once, twice, three times. Overkill or panic. Passers by look though the windows and scatter. Motorcycle engines cough and grind, base notes under the screaming. The sound of trainers on pavement and they are off. Weaving through the traffic like predatory fish.

***

It has just gone eleven o'clock and Detective Inspector John Peach is still at work. There are still police showing the public a reassuring presence in the West End, but the forensic and tech teams have done their jobs. It's time to sift, to evaluate and to work out a strategy to catch the people who shoot shopkeepers in broad daylight before they do it again. He clicks on a Scenes of Crime Officer's report and begins to read.

There are numerous fingerprints. It's a shop with a lot of glass surfaces and people in and out all day. The real trick is checking what has been found against the database. It's all computerised. All that it needs is for someone to take the time to put the scene prints onto a computer and search, and for a crime this serious it is high priority. Twenty matches. Peach scrolls through, discounting the obvious dead ends. Women seem out of the picture. So do the elderly. You can't stereotype. Some women can be muscular and some older people can be pretty sprightly, but he has seen the CCTV. The way they move and dress looks typical. Some crimes are equal opportunity. Anyone can be an Internet pervert or a fraudster. Robbery is a young man's game and John Peach reckons this crew are in their thirties at most.

That narrows it down to four. Two are unlikely. A hedge fund manager with a recent previous conviction for drink driving and someone who got arrested for breaking a window at the age of fifteen. They aren't off the radar, just relegated until the other two can be arrested or eliminated.

The first of these looks promising. 32 years old, with a previous conviction for street robbery. It's quite old, committed when he was 17. Nothing since. Could mean that he learned how not to do it. Not every armed robber has been in and out of court for some time. Peach flags him up for further investigation. Stand up, Paul Murphy, your life is about to be picked over. The second looks even better. Germaine MacHeath. Twenty-nine years old, his last previous conviction for cash in transit robbery six years ago. A five year sentence and early release a couple of years later. Since then, nothing concrete. A fine for possession of cannabis.

The next step is to check whether there has been any intelligence on either Murphy or MacHeath. It's a stroke of a computer key away, with the Metropolitan Police having the resources that Big Brother could only dream about. There is very little on Murphy, other than a couple of call outs to some no crime detected domestic arguments. Not pleasant, but not in the same league as robbery and murder. He types in Germaine MacHeath and it's payday at Las Vegas. The robbery he did time for was well planned. The security van was boxed in and raided as it delivered to the NatWest bank in Catford. It ended badly because a security guard put up a fight, and one of the robbers was detained at the scene. MacHeath came to light after investigations into people who had been in contact with the arrested man's mobile phone. No guns. It was violent as hell, though, with one guard having his arms broken and the other fighting on with a fractured skull. Hardcore. Juvenile convictions for robbery, drugs and assault as well.

Peach checks for anything recent and finds the report from a few days before. Unattributed to this suspect, admittedly. Shanks is not exactly a rare nickname, but it is too close to be a coincidence and well worth a deeper look. He pulls up a photograph. Germaine MacHeath gives a custody suite camera his best thousand-yard stare, full face and both profiles. Its old, taken five years ago. There is something slightly familiar about him. John Peach cannot put his finger on it. He has seen so many people throughout the years that it is sometimes hard to recognise them out of context.

He thinks about leaving and going home to his family. There is some CCTV he wants to watch before calling it a day. He's already seen the robbery, and there isn't much point in going over it again until there is a suspect in custody. He already knows what went on. It's always worth checking out the days around any robbery, particularly one that has been so well planned. Working that one out didn't happen over night, and robbers on reconnaissance are a lot less careful with hoods, masks and gloves than they are when the job is on. Worth checking out whether Paul Murphy or Germaine MacHeath have been doing any window shopping. He sets the range to two days either side. Paul Murphy and Germaine MacHeath stare out at him from a window on the screen. He can watch it on fast forward. If either of these two charmers show up, then it will be easy enough to slow it down. The traffic has died down outside and London settles into a weekday night. Nobody is going to be awake by the time he gets home anyway.

He doesn't recognise the man at first. It's not that he is disguised or anything obvious like that, but he seems to have a knack of making sure that the camera only catches his face from slightly behind. The woman that is with him is instantly recognisable.

Blonde, and wearing the Prada leather jacket that she had pestered him about so tenaciously before Christmas. He slows the film down to real time and watches it again. She turns, smiles up into the camera as the man leans over the counter, deep in conversation with the assistant. He looks round. His head is bowed. More hair and forehead than face is on screen with a slight glare making identification harder. He beckons her over and she tries on a ring. It's obviously not a good fit, as there is some more conversation with the assistant before he hands over money that he peels from a bundle of notes that looks at thick as a banker's smile. They turn and walk out. John Peach fiddles with the computer and changes the camera to the one covering the door. There, in profile, they kiss. The footage is so detailed that he can see his daughter's cheeks suck slightly in as their mouths lock. He can see the side of the man's face and he recognises him. Not just as Germaine MacHeath, armed robber, gangster and suspected murderer, but as Germaine the entrepreneur, his daughter's dinner date. The man he had shared a meal with and who had been surprisingly polite and respectful.

He shuts the computer down and sits, staring at the screen as the afterglow fades. He knows how this will play out. The CCTV will be disclosed to the Defence, and the Defence will use his daughter as Germaine MacHeath's alibi. He thinks about getting rid of it but it's not an option. It will only make things worse. John Peach sits with his head in his hands. The ghost of an idea begins to form as the world reels around him. He stands, ejects the disc and slips it into his desk drawer. It's not as if he'd be fitting up an innocent. Germaine MacHeath is a violent armed robber. He's shot a man dead for no other reason than to take his property. He's not the Guilford Four or the Birmingham Six. He's not even the Lewisham One. It's not really fitting someone up in the conventional sense of the word. He's done the crime, and he has to be put in a position where the CCTV and the fingerprints won't matter. John Peach tells himself that it's not about crime stats and clear ups. It's certainly not about money. It's not even about family, although Polly not having to deal with the consequences of her own stupidity and him not having to hear the conversation stop as he walks into the office every day would certainly be a bonus. John Peach tells himself it's about getting justice for the victim, and gets to work.

People own a lot of stuff these days, and criminals usually own the same sort of stuff as everyone else. There's no point in knowing that the i-phone with the text about serving up white and brown is the same one you confiscated from the drug dealer when you arrested him. You have to prove that the phone you took from the scene of the crime is the same as the phone that went to the lab and had the texts downloaded. If you can't, it's red faces all round at the prosecution team and a good post match drink up for the defence. Continuity of evidence: every case has it and because it's everywhere it's all been reduced to templates. It is easy enough to change the scene statement seizing the shell casings. A couple of clicks of the keys and two were picked up not three. It's as simple to change the number on the exhibits bag to one he happened to have with him. He folds the hard copy statement and puts it into his pocket. He's going to burn that, but not here. Sod's law is that it will set off the sprinkler system. He prints the new copy and sends a terse email to the DC who made it, pointing out that it hasn't been signed and urging him to get his shit together. It's the sort of attention to detail that makes him the best sort of senior investigating officer.

The next bit is more difficult. The exhibits are in storage. It's on the premises, but guarded by CCTV. It's not lost on him that it would be ironic if the source of his problems actively brought the chickens home to roost. He opens the desk drawer and takes out the CCTV. It's an exhibit, too, and a less diligent officer might be prepared to take the line of least resistance and not log it back in. It's only a working copy after all. John Peach is not the sort of officer to bend the rules. He seals the disc, and takes the lift to the storeroom. He meticulously writes the date and time in the exhibits book, locates the bag of shells, removes one, replaces and reseals it and leaves. His hands are shaking slightly as he collects his jacket, but he smiles once he is sure that he is off camera and on his way to the railway station. He hates to admit it, but it's a buzz. There is a conversation he is rather looking forward to. His daughter has always run rings around him. It will be refreshing to have the upper hand. It will probably cost him, but one way or another she is going to help him bring Germaine MacHeath to justice.

Chapter 17

Ken McGuiness is awake at six. It is a new habit of his. He has to be up before the post, jiffy bag in hand and his ear cocked like a dog for noises outside the door. He's tried to think through what he would do if the Professional Standards did kick the door in. Try to swallow the stick, he supposes, although he hasn't quite got his head round the mechanics of it. It's quite large and he has problems with anything larger than a bloody Haliborange at the best of times. The post is rarely there before eight anyway, and he has joined the latecomers and stragglers. It's a worry, but he can't think of anything else to do. The problem with dangerous secrets is that once you are in on them nobody will believe that you have forgotten. It has occurred to him that being able to return the datastick on demand might be a valuable last line of defence at some stage, and he needs all the defence he can get. Maxine sleeps on, snoring gently as he tries to move silently around the room, barking his shins and tripping over his shoes. He is swearing under his breath on the way to the shower. The prefect beginning to the day. He leaves Maxine a cup of tea by her bedside. It's a symbolic gesture as she can sleep for England at the moment. He kisses her on the forehead. She rolls over and mutters something about calling him later. He tries to close the door behind him softly as he leaves.

He sees a car in the street he doesn't recognise. He can't be sure whether it is empty or not, and doesn't dare look at it directly. It occurs to him that posting the package from the same post box near his house every day is asking for trouble, and opts to drive to work. He stops outside the sorting office in Brockley Road and makes a run for the post box.

Back in the car and he takes a call. Western Way in Plumstead. Another body. It is beginning to rain as he starts the journey. Thin rain and the intermittent pulse of window wipers. Over Blackheath. Stockbrokers' wives, boutiques and restaurants. Fine wines and a good time had by some. On through Charlton's terraces, drawn up in dilapidated ranks like a third world army on parade. To Woolwich. Past the barracks and Lee Rigby's shrine.   McGuiness smokes and keeps silent, staring out of the window and wondering if there is a shop he recognises on any High Street East of Lewisham that doesn't sell fried chicken.   Half built flats with windows like empty eyes stare balefully at the dilapidated covered market and promise a glass and chrome tomorrow.

The traffic is heavy, banking up and crawling. Walking pace. McGuiness checks his phone. "Call me." He dials Maxine's number. Ringing and silence. Voicemail. Impersonal and well modulated. Reassuring. If there was a problem she would have answered. "Returning your call, Max. Thinking of you. Hope things are all right. Won't be able to get to the phone for at least an hour. Speak soon." The end in sight. Barriers and uniforms directing disgruntled motorists. He stops the car and indicates right. A young woman approaches. Her peaked hat is pulled low over her eyes, paramilitary style. Her expression is hostile, unwilling to recite the same tired explanation to yet another indignant commuter. "You can't drive down here. Sir." There is heartbeat between the order and the honorific. Reminding the public who's the servant. McGuiness flips open his warrant card. "DCI McGuiness, love." It never hurts to pull rank. Lets the foot soldiers know who is in charge. Her face changes from default hostile to a welcome that makes him shudder. He parks the car on the other side of the barriers and walks.

Western Way. Four lanes. Patches of straggling grass scab a bare central reservation. The Thamesmead Estate sits on the left, opposite a council recycling centre. Further down, Thameside prison. Box fresh and new as trainers. Privatised. Plastic prison officers on minimum wage unwilling to take on the inmates for seven quid an hour, and who can blame them? A gangster's Butlins, by all account, with a phone and TV in every cell. Next, brittle white in cladding and breezeblocks, stands Woolwich Crown Court. Behind that, squat behind its grey perimeter, Belmarsh high security prison. Finally, Isis Young Offenders' Institution, barbed wire and a name like a 1980's gay disco. The whole place is a municipal joke, a town planner's wry smile at his desk. This is where unwanted things are dumped. The stations of the crushed.

A wind is channeled down the line of least resistance. It batters him as he walks, whipping his coat around his legs and rattling overgrown bushes. Cold sinks between his shoulder blades. He feels his pocket vibrate. His phone. He shakes his head, annoyed and ashamed by his annoyance. Maxine. It's probably nothing and he will ring her back later. He's got important work to do, and it's not the time for idle chat.

The body is on the other side of the carriageway, under hastily erected arc lights and a white tent. Five marked police cars and an ambulance blink silently. Requiem in blue. McGuiness shows his warrant card and is through the outer cordon. He recognises a DS from his team.

"What's the situation, Steve?"

The man hands him a forensic pack. A plastic boiler suit, mask and hat in a vacuum sealed bag. McGuiness dresses himself, handing his coat to Welbourne and pulling the unwieldy costume over his suit.

"Female Caucasian. Estimated age is early to mid twenties, but not that easy to tell in the circumstances, Sir. Doctor's been and pronounced life extinct a few minutes ago. Formality, though. You only needed to look at the poor cow."

The man's upper face is visible between his white facemask and hat. He has dark eyes and prominent eyebrows. McGuiness nods as he listens. They walk towards the inner cordon. The tent straddles the footpath, bridging the undergrowth on both sides and hanging between two lampposts. McGuiness feels his lungs constrict. The anticipation of challenge as an investigator or the prospect of slaughterhouse visuals? It is a question he doesn't want to answer. He ducks through the flap and sees her. She lies in the middle of the path, her head pointing towards the carriageway. Spread eagled and naked. She has red hair; vivid against skin that would have been pale even had it not been bloodless. It has been arranged in a halo around her head, the colour sharply contrasting with the washed out grass. Her remaining eye is green. The other is subsumed in a weal of blue, black and red. A blunt injury that has collapsed her cheekbone and left an empty socket. Six wounds gape across her abdomen. There are no blood trails across the white flesh that surrounds them. No blood on the grass or the fragmented concrete. No sign of the missing eye, either, although the forensics boys could have removed this. He notices a technician looking at him as he angles his head to see if there are any injuries to her genitals, and feels momentarily ashamed. He holds back an impulse to explain himself. Anyone with the right excuse can look as much as they need, and the more violent the demise, the greater the numbers whose profession makes them voyeurs. The dead have no privacy. No rights. McGuiness makes a mental note that she does not appear to be wearing cosmetics. Choice or cleaned up? She would have been striking enough with that colouring. He does not want to make any assumptions, but is willing to bet that forensics and pathology will show that she was killed elsewhere and abandoned. He inhales; filling his lungs and feeling the craving rise inside him. He turns on his heel and marches back to the car. He has an investigation to run, tasks to allocate and a cigarette to smoke. There is nothing he can accomplish here.

Chapter 18

Polly Peach's phone rings at 11:43. The caller identification is "G" and the ring tone blares out Meridian Dan's "German Whip", making John Peach cringe inside as he gestures to his daughter to answer.

"Hello, Germaine."

MacHeath's voice is low and husky. It's part affectation and part late night. Weed and cigarettes combined with genuine affection.

"How you doing, sweetheart? Are you busy this afternoon or have you got time to meet up?"

Polly's mouth is full of saliva. She has always been a confident girl socially, but performing gives her stage fright. Her mind goes blank and she can't remember her lines.

"I'd love to. I've got lectures until four, but I'm free after that."

Her voice sounds rushed and artificial, as natural as a call center script. She wonders whether he can tell that she's nervous, and pushes her fringe off her forehead. She wonders if her father can see that she is sweating. He's looking at her with that "I am so disappointed with you" face. Part hangdog and part inquisitor. Polly Peach can't put the kettle on, didn't make the netball team and has let the whole school down again. She stifles an impulse to blurt out that the police are after Germaine and to tell him to run. She's not like that girl in the film who warned her husband that the police were waiting for him even though she could have ended up going to prison herself.

Her father had been at his patronising worse last night, calling her silly and naïve, and implying that she didn't know exactly what sort of man Germaine was. He acted like she was some kind of child, 12 years old and just out of pink and One Direction, not a nineteen year old woman who had been born and brought up in Beckenham. True, she had gone to Sydenham High, but that was her parent's choice. She told people she met at University that she was from South London, and she enjoyed the frisson this brought. Besides, her dad was a detective. He was on the Flying Squad, for Christ's sake! How much grittier could you get? He didn't exactly look the part. He had no scars and wouldn't even wear a sheepskin coat ironically, but being the daughter of one of the Sweeney was almost like being a gangster princess. Yes, it had been a bit scary. Conspiracy to rob, and possibly even murder were serious. She couldn't deny that. The idea that she would be arrested and charged with either just because she had been to a shop with Germaine and he had brought her a ring was ridiculous. The bottom line was that she hadn't known anything about any robbery, even if Germaine had done it, and she wasn't even convinced about that. Polly Peach thinks reassuring thoughts and tells herself that all she has to do is do as she is told and everything will be all right. There are places she wants to go and things she wants to do and good behavior is always rewarded.

Germaine MacHeath smiles into his phone.

"I'll meet you at five at the Elephant. South American café by the station inside. See you then."

"See you Germaine"

He thinks about adding something else, something suave and affectionate that isn't too slushy but lets her know that she's more than just someone he sleeps with, but can't think of anything in time.

As soon as the call ends, the next begins. It's a busy world.

"Shanks, you alright?"

"Omen"

"We need to link. Have you got everything you need?"

"Don't worry about me."

"Can you be at the Clockhouse on the Rye at four?"

"I'm meeting some girl up Elephant at five. I'll be by there at seven thirty."

"Sweet."

The day is arranged. Germaine MacHeath lies down on the bed he slept in as a child, lights a cigarette and looks out of the window. Trees move to the sound of trains and a cloudless sky makes Brockley Barcelona for the day. Money, a girl and a very short meeting with that cunt Omen in the sort of public place even he is not going to kick off in. All is well with the world.

There's no point in driving to Elephant. The traffic's a bitch and there's nowhere to park when you get there. Germaine MacHeath is pushed for time. See the girl, get back South and do the deal. There are only so many hours in the day, and he's too much of a big man to be walking, so he drives to the train station. It's a simple plan. Park up, get the train and no delays when time will really count, but the streets around the station are filled with commuter traffic. He waits, drumming the steering wheel and trying to keep his temper as a woman in a four-by-four makes a complicated twenty-six point turn out of a parking space. The train is pulling out of the station as he acknowledges the grateful flash of her hazards. It's hardly worth swearing, but he does it anyway as he climbs out of the car and walks to the station entrance. Another half hour before the next train. A cigarette and a cup of coffee. He thinks about calling her but decides that she'll wait.

It is one of the ugliest buildings in the universe; a vast, concrete shopping complex that has fallen harder than the times around it. There is no Marks and Spencers or French Connection. Stalls selling phone cards and e cigarettes compete with Polish and Latin American cafes. There is a bowling alley and an amusement arcade, a street market where you can have a stolen mobile phone unblocked while you shop for a snide Gucci handbag and a thriving culture of street drinkers congregating around quid a throw massage chairs. In the centre of the first floor is an open plan café selling Columbian coffee and cakes. This is the meeting place, and it is rammed. A steady flow of people breaks around the group of tables and chairs, heading towards the railway station and the exit onto the Walworth Road.

Polly Peach sits at a table and runs her fingers around the rim of an espresso cup. She's had two already, and her skin feels like it is vibrating in sympathy with the reverberation of traffic and trains. She looks about her, taking in the crowds and trying to avoid thinking which ones might be policemen. Her eyes feel gritty and sore. It's a bad day, but it will pass.

DI Peach has the area covered. He's in the car outside, parked on some double yellows outside a railway arch and blending in with the mini cabs. Four officers inside. Enough to take down someone in a public and crowded place with the minimum of fuss. There's one man in the Café, one by the station entrance, hiding in hi viz among the chuggers, one by the stairwell on the way out to the tube station and one by the steps leading to the street market. He checks his watch as the Blackfriars train comes in. Any time now.

DC Calvert cranes his neck to take in all the passengers coming up the stairs. The flow decreases to a trickle then stops. No MacHeath. A few young black men, but none of them match the briefing photo, and none of them stop by the café to talk to the blonde girl. He sighs, and leans back against the wall. There are two girls laughing and messing about in the photo booth. They are fourteen or fifteen, and should be in school. It's not much of a distraction from his bladder and he begins to regret the cup of coffee he drank before setting out. He's not a stranger to surveillance, but you can hardly piss into a Lucozade bottle standing in front of a load of teenagers in a shopping centre. He wanders into the station and checks the arrivals board. Nothing for another ten minutes, and he is beginning to lose faith in the suspect showing up at all. He tenses his stomach but it's a losing battle. There's plenty of time and there's no more sure way of blowing your cover than soiling yourself in public. Calvert crosses the concourse to the public lavatories. He's light on his feet, bouncing against the desire to let go. The turnstile needs twenty pence to pass, and the act of searching for change is almost unbearable. He pushes through and runs into the tiled sanctuary.

The 4:15 from Crofton Park to Blackfriars is running three minutes early. Germaine MacHeath disembarks and walks down the stairs from the platform to the exit. He's in no hurry, and he allows a couple of school kids to push in front. He even swipes his Oyster card. The day is too important to fuck up by getting nicked.

DI Peach is on the radio. The first train was a no-show. Polly is sitting in the café reading the Metro. She checked her phone a few minutes ago. He authorises DC O'Riordan to make contact. A discrete word through an earpiece and a young white man stands up and walks to Polly's table. He bends at the waist and rests his hands on the table. He smiles, just making conversation with a pretty girl. His jacket rides up and shows a glimpse of rigid handcuffs attached to his belt.

Germaine MacHeath's first thought is to revert to type when he sees the man chatting up Polly. He's just out and onto the concourse, and he almost breaks into a run. Then he sees the cuffs. Fucking Feds. It doesn't feel right, and he knows that trusting your gut is what keeps you free. He turns and walks back into the station. He is on his way out of the back entrance at a slow walk when Calvert comes out of the toilets. The policeman looks around him, nervous that this little dereliction of duty might come back to haunt him, but the slow trickle of humanity leaving the station doesn't include any black men of the right age and build. He resumes his position by the photo booth.

DI Peach is on the radio. He is entirely focused on the conversation. The text had been from another student. Yes, O'Riordan had seen it. No, it wasn't disguised. A picture of an Asian girl and the name Sunita came up on the screen. Nothing to report.

Germaine MacHeath stops for a second. It's been a while since he's taken a bus, but as far as he can remember the one to Peckham leaves from Walworth Road. There's a cab station outside, but his need to get away is greater than his desire to travel in comfort. Taking a cab makes a witness who can identify you. Better to take the bus and chuck the Oyster when he's done.

The operation is stood down at 6:30. DI Peach drives his daughter home. He suspects her of tipping off her boyfriend, and she worries that she has given herself away to a man who might even be as dangerous as her father says. The silence in the car is opaque, and they are both relieved to be back in Beckenham and to go their separate ways.

Germaine MacHeath sits on the 176 and thinks. One person knew he was going to Elephant, and that was Omen. Cousin Damien who was pissed that the Turkish mafia didn't want to deal with him direct. Cousin Damien who hated him almost as much as Germaine hated him right back ever since he gave him that beating all those years ago. Cousin Damien, the fucking rapist. Cousin Damien, the snitch. His hands are clenched on the back of the seat in front and his knuckles are white. He forces himself to be calm, to think. There's a way out of this that takes him to where he needs to go and leaves Damien Anderson where he deserves to be. Germaine MacHeath smiles, and makes a call. The Audi is waiting for him as the bus pulls up at Queens Road Station.

Chapter 19

Three flat sharers in a student house in New Cross reported that the fourth hadn't come home from a night out this morning. They had taken the trouble to walk to Lewisham Police Station, and they were concerned because it was out of character. Heather Buchan wasn't the sort of girl for a casual hook up. She was dedicated, a politics student with genuine ambition. She was also religious, and went to church even though her parents were in Edinburgh, far enough away not to see any falling. She did voluntary work at a soup kitchen. The photo that her flatmates had been sent back to New Cross to collect lay on McGuiness' desk and he was pretty sure that he had found Miss Western Way. It wasn't easy to tell. He hadn't exactly seen her at her best, but the height age and colouring was the same. He is grateful that the death knock belongs to someone else. He rings DS Stevens. Time to spread good news and cheer. He realises that he has forgotten to turn his phone back on after the post mortem, and reaches into his jacket. The phone springs to life, and 7 missed calls flag up. Maxine. Every one. He rings her back and goes to voicemail. He can feel the panic beginning to clutch his throat and breaths. In and out. Calm and oxygen. He looks at his messages.

"Ken. It's happening. Going to Kings. Max. x."

"Nightingale ward. Come quickly."

He is up and running. The drive is a patchwork of voicemail and unease. He cant help worry pulling on his stomach slightly, as he dials Maxine and hangs up without leaving a message again. It's a few weeks early, just eight, and that's nothing to be worried about. She's probably in the delivery room now, and can't get to her phone. He imagines her in stirrups surrounded by starched and reassuring 1950's nurses as he parks, roots for coins for the meter and pays for four hours. He can't see how it won't be over by then.

Kings College is modern. A Victorian shell enhanced with glass and concrete. He follows a pastel colored sign and takes the lift to the sixth floor, eyes down and no conversation with the woman with the drip stand and packet of Bensons. There's a code for the door, and an itching wait to be let in. McGuiness cranes, trying to catch sight of Maxine through the glass panels. A stammered request and an ushering into a side room that is no less disturbing for its politeness. Information is given neutrally. He is told what will happen to him, to his wife and, although it seems a little abstract at the moment without evidence of his or her existence, to his child. He takes in phrases like "fetal distress" and "surgical intervention" piecemeal, recognising them as negative but unable to register the greater meaning of what is being said. The same questions surface and sink, churning through unspoken anxiety. "Will she be alright?" "Will the baby be alright?"

He is escorted down a corridor towards a double swing door labeled "theatre". There is no sense of time or effort in this movement. He is dragged by a tide of bustle and purpose that surrounds him. As he passes a window he catches sight of himself. His face is blank, unemotional while his eyes track from right to left, constantly searching for a way out that doesn't exist. A prisoner lead through the yard. He is helped into a set of blue surgical scrubs. A mask is tied across his lower face with practiced efficiency. There is no panic. Every movement is conserved and efficient. Finally, he is escorted through another set of doors to Maxine.

She is lying on her back. He is shepherded to a chair by her head. He expects her to be asleep, but she turns at his entrance and murmurs his name. She reaches out a hand and he takes it. Her grip is warm and strong. Her hair is plastered to her forehead but her hand isn't clammy. She is paler than ever, and her lips are dry and cracked. He feels his chest clench and the theatre lights split and refract into shards until he manages to compose himself.

"You're doing well, Max. I'm here now."

She smiles.

"Ken"

She squeezes his hand. He notices that she is screened from the waist down. There are muttered discussions and the sound of rustling from behind it. His eyes wander upwards to the chrome light fitting and he sees a reflection of his eviscerated wife, purple, white and red in miniaturised mirror image. He drags his attention back and captures a strand of her hair, pulling it back behind her ear and off her face. She is utterly still now, her hand dead in his. Her eyes imprison his with the intensity of a plea he can do nothing to answer. It's out of his hands. Whatever it is, he can't make it all right.

More movement behind the screen followed by the sound of a baby crying, angry and insistent. Wheels squeal on flooring. Maxine raises her head.

"What's going on? Where's the baby?"

"You've had a baby girl, Maxine. She's only two and a half kilos, and she's quite jaundiced so we're taking her to the Special Care Unit. You'll be able to see her once we've sorted you out."

Maxine looks bereft.

"Ken. Follow her."

McGuiness hesitates. He wants to stay with his wife. Maxine raises herself onto one elbow. It costs her, and the effort pulls her face tight at the eyes and the corners of the mouth like bad cosmetic surgery.

"Kenneth McGuiness. Follow that fucking baby."

He is an institutional man at heart, and while he may resent authority, his instinct is to obey. He nods, registers the name of the ward she is to be taken to and sets off at a run.

The Special Care Unit is a fortress. Doors open, admitting McGuiness to a sterile area where he must wash his hands with a sanitizer before he can be permitted to go inside. A nurse writes down his name and takes a photograph. The area is covered by pictures of children of various ages, all in healthy poses. Bicycles and horses feature, as do swimming pools and sports kit. The nurse nods at them.

"Our graduation photos. Almost all of the kids we look after go on to have normal and happy lives, Mr McGuiness. Come and see your daughter."

He follows her into a large room. There are glass boxes around the edges, and he thinks for a moment that they are fish tanks, set out to calm fractured nerves like a dentist's waiting room. It is hushed, the silence broken only by the sound of machinery and muted footfalls. The particular box of interest is in the far corner, by a large window overlooking the main road. He sits and listens as the procedures are explained. He cannot hold his daughter yet. That will come in time. He can watch her and, provided his cleans his hands properly, he can put his finger through the hole in the side and stroke her head. It's not much, but it's a start. The nurse leaves him to it.

McGuiness stares. She is tiny, about the length of one of his hands. The heart monitor pads look like soup plates in comparison with her chest and there is a tube up her nose that leads to a feeding bottle. She has dark hair, thin and slick against her scalp. Green, red and yellow graphs flow across a monitor, reassuring in their regularity. Tentatively, he puts his finger into the box and touches her forehead. Her eyes spring open. They are cobalt blue, wide and serene and she looks at him gravely for a moment before her face crumples into a howl that brings a health care assistant across to change her nappy. Order restored, father and daughter resume their contemplation. Eventually she falls asleep sucking the dummy he can't help disapproving of despite the explanation that it helps her to maintain her reflexes so she will be able to drink normally in time. He stays with her, taking in every crease and fold and hoping she will open her eyes again as night falls outside. There is a rhythm to the room, a steady wheeze and bleep. A harmony between his daughter's cot and the others in the ward. He finds himself rocking to it. He can feel his eyes moisten, salt tracking down his face and stinging the open pores on the side of his nose. He rubs his daughter's cheek, feeling the ridges and whorls of his finger rasp against the delicateness of her skin. The weight of his world rests upon him as reality sinks in like ointment. Eventually he is encouraged to leave. He does not protest. Worry has made Ken McGuiness fragile as glass, and he walks to the double doors with exaggerated care.

He has seen Maxine settled with Lucozade, fruit and magazines.

It is cold outside. Moisture hangs in the air. The yellow glow of streetlamps lights up petrochemical rainbows in the gutters. He can hear an idling engine as he enters the car park. High pitched and insistent. A two-stroke whine. He walks briskly to the far corner where he has left his car with his head down against the elements. The motorbike is parked next to his car. His first thought is that it is youngsters, messing about in the car park. Probably stolen. He wonders whether he should intervene and decides against it. He is off duty and he wants to go home. He notices a figure standing by his car. The red jacket identifies him as a parking attendant. Shit! He jogs the last twenty yards to see the man pull out an electronic device from his coat pocket.

"Hold on a minute, mate, will you?"

The man turns to face him and smiles. His face is narrow. Sallow skin and whiskers around thin lips. McGuiness notices that his teeth are white and even.

"Is this your car, Sir?"

"Yes. Look mate, I've been in the hospital. My daughter and my wife are in intensive care and I lost track."

The attendant leans over the windscreen. His movements are exaggeratedly slow. He breathes heavily, as if the effort of checking the ticket is almost too much for him.

"Says 8:56."

McGuiness feels heat rising to his cheeks and hopes that it is the contrasting air temperature that is to blame. He checks his watch. 9:04.

"I'm less than ten minutes over. Can't you just let it go?"

"That's not my problem is it, Sir. You've got a watch, and you've just shown that you can tell the time so it's really down to you to make sure that you come back to your car before your ticket expires."

The smile hasn't wavered. One more appeal to a better nature that is as redundant as an appendix.

"Look, my daughter's really ill. She's only a day old and she's in intensive care with wires all over her. I'm sorry I lost track of the time and I'm a few minutes late, but I'm sure you can understand how that happened. Now can't you give me a break here? It's only a few minutes."

The man must have been born to a Cheshire cat. His smile is literally from ear to ear. McGuiness finds himself clenching and unclenching his fists. He wills himself to stay calm. The attendant's head is on one side and his palm cups his chin. He deliberates, ostentatiously.

"I'm very sorry, but every person who overstays their ticket has a sick kiddie or a dying grandmother. I'm not saying that I don't believe you, but you must admit that it is a bit of a coincidence, isn't it."

The voice is nasal. It would have been irritating at the best of times, and McGuiness can't shake the suspicion that it is put on to wind him up. He had a temper as a younger man. He was told to watch out for it. Martial arts, sport and self control. That was the ticket. Never lose it. He is almost surprised at how it feels. He expects a snap, something physical. The smell of ozone and the sound of breaking glass. Not even close. The sensation is gentle, a broken rope giving way under constant pressure. One minute he is standing in a car park being called a liar by a man in a nylon tabard making maximum abuse of power for minimum status. The next, the impact jars up his forearm. He can feel the movement in the jaw as the head snaps back too slowly to absorb the force of a punch thrown too quickly for sober reflection. The motorcycle helmet echoes as it hits the ground. The attendant slumps against the car and lies among the potholes and puddles.

Ken McGuiness is cold. Eyes down. Head down. Don't look up to give them a good view of your face. Don't turn on the lights until you are out of the car park. Hope against hope that the cameras don't catch your number plate. Christ all fucking mighty, how could he have been so stupid. Father of a sick kid and husband of a sick wife. He'll be lucky not to add unemployed and ex convict. All he needs is alcoholic to collect the whole dysfunctional set.   He shakes his head violently. Once he is clear of the hospital he lights a cigarette and is careful to open the window.

Chapter 20

Germaine MacHeath wakes early with a plan. It hasn't been a good night's sleep. You don't snitch. That's as far as it goes. Even if you do, you certainly don't snitch on family. He looks through the contacts on his phone. Mustafa's number is still there. Saved under TFC, a Turkish supermarket in Catford. He's the contact. The last job brought enough money for both sides of the deal. He selects a few numbers and writes them down. He'll go to Lewisham and buy a burner. Some conversations need to stay untraceable. He'll be having those about Cousin Damien. They'll be later, but now it's time to talk to the devil before he appears.

"Cuz?"

"How's it going, D?"

"We need to meet. I've got something for you. What happened yesterday?"

"Shit. As in "shit happens" Cuz. Sorry to leave you hanging. You done what you have to?"

"No problem."

Can you meet me on Elfrida Crescent in Catford? It's off Southend Lane near the Lidl. Six o'clock. "

"See you there."

He ends the call. He should be free by seven. Seven thirty at the latest. Time to arrange the evening before the day takes over. She answers at the third ring.

"Germaine?"

He hears a catch in her voice and thinks she has been missing him.

"You all right, Polly?"

"Yes. You stood me up yesterday."

He hesitates. There are some things that girls can't be told.

"Sorry, love. Something came up. Can we meet this evening? Maybe have some food?"

"That would be lovely. Where do you want to go?"

"There's an Indian in Brockley. Supposed to be one of the best in London. It's opposite the Criterion pub. See you there at seven thirty?"

"Of course. I'll be there."

He hangs up, smiling. It doesn't last long. There's work to be done, and Germaine MacHeath knows that the finer things in life have to be earned.

***

Although it has been raining heavily, and he was shivering in the lift to the third floor of King's College Hospital, Plover ward is heated to a temperature that reminds him of Kinshasa. Harsh artificial lighting overwhelms the grey gloom that struggles and expires upon the windowsill. Father Anthony Mitchell sits by a bedside. The figure in the bed does not respond to his presence, or that of the woman who hovers at his shoulder. Mr Flaherty is imprisoned in life. Machines guard a perimeter around his bed. They drip and click, marking out cycles. John Flaherty is frozen on the way to death, and with no last rights to be said, Father Anthony finds himself at a loss. He clasps his hands more out of habit than in an appeal to the Almighty, and politely refuses Mrs Flaherty's third offer to fetch him a cup of tea. He cannot find words of comfort for her, and he speculates that his role is redundant when the time of the soul's departure is so obviously in the hands of man. The thought depletes him, and in his weakness he accepts a cup of vending machine coffee. They agree that there is little to recommend it, before a second cup is offered and declined. Steam begins to rise from his legs and shoulders, misting his glasses and forming a layer of condensation upon the metal housing of the ventilator. He is relieved when the nurses begin to distribute medication and he is released. It is lunchtime. As he leaves the ward he enquires about a canteen. The staff nurse gives him directions, and a slip of paper.

The cafeteria smells of chip oil and custard. Ahead of him, two young men in scrubs talk animatedly about football, pausing only to bark their orders at the middle aged woman behind the counter. The portions they receive are gargantuan. Mountains of chips loom over a sea of baked beans in which a Cornish pasty's back surfaces like a whale. It is his turn. He hands over the slip and, after allowing a polite interval to permit its authenticity to be established, diffidently requests his meal. The woman does not meet his eye. Ladles clash like colliding cars and a plate of food is placed on the counter. Father Anthony surveys it carefully. There are eight chips. He can count them easily. The expanse of plate between them and the thimbleful of baked beans leaves little margin for confusion.

"Is it nouvelle cuisine today, then?"

The woman crosses her arms. She does not look at him. They stand in silence. Eventually, she gestures to the man behind him, inviting his order. Father Anthony wills himself into tranquility, wishing that he could repeat whatever it was he had done to placate the mob now.

"Excuse me. There are only eight chips on my plate. I have paid for a portion. Eight chips is not a portion."

Her eyes take an inventory, noting in his dog collar and raincoat.

"You aren't a doctor."

There is no inflection.

"The two young men before me got far more, and I can see that the tray is almost full."

It seems prudent to fight fact with fact. Her chin rises with hydraulic slowness.

"They were doctors. You're not. This is a hospital canteen."

"I know that. It doesn't mean that eight chips is a portion even if I am not a doctor, madam."

She smiles, and he realises that this is a confrontation that she has enjoyed many times. It has been leading to this moment.

"That's it. You're causing trouble now. I'm going to call the police and have you removed."

Father Anthony does not approve of profanity. It's part of the job, like a lifeguard not being keen on drowning. He accepts that for some people swearing is more a matter of punctuation than something intended to cause offence. It is not something he cares to tackle head on, but given the choice, he would rather not listen to it. It is a failure of vocabulary. He tells his confirmation students that as God has blessed them with a rich variety of language, it is lazy to resort to it. Idleness and blasphemy are mortal sins. He is shocked to find himself wanting to applaud as his neighbour leans across the counter, waves what he assumes is a warrant card in the woman's face and snarls:

"For fuck's sake. We're already here. Give the man his chips before I nick you for fraud, you stupid cow."

He takes his time selecting a drink and various sauces in plastic sachets, hoping that the policeman will have found somewhere to sit so he can join him. He wonders what brings the man to the hospital and discounts the professional. He doesn't look like the sort of policemen whose job takes him to hospital canteens. He looks across the refectory and sees the man slouched over his tray as he relentlessly shovels chips into his mouth. His face is a study in emptiness. Food as fuel. Father Anthony knows the anatomy of distress. It marks the soul as distinctly as illness, and cannot be hidden beneath self control. He can see it on the policeman. He walks to his table and points to the seat opposite.

"Do you mind if I sit here?"

The other man looks up. Father Anthony notices the broken nose and scar on the lower lip. There are lines around green eyes that squint up in professional suspicion. It is not a handsome face, but not ugly enough to stick in the mind.

"Help yourself."

The tone is not unfriendly.

"Thank you for that."

"All part of the service. I'd give you one of those "I've met the Met" badges, Father, but I must have left my last one in the car."

"You're not here improving community relations, now, are you?"

The face is closed. Not hostile. Shutters down and nothing to declare.

"Well, if you need to talk, I am a trained counselor among my other talents. Here's my contact number. If you want to get in touch I'll be happy to hear from you. Church service is optional, although many of my patients do find it beneficial."

He hands over a card. The policeman takes it and puts it into his jacket pocket without examining it. They finish their meals in silence. Father Anthony picks up his tray and walks to the exit without looking back. He knows that he will be hearing from the policeman again in the same way that he knows that a terrible fate awaits the damned. It is a matter of unshakable certainty.

Ken McGuiness watches the priest and wonders whether he has started to look like a charity case. He checks his reflection as he leaves, head down and a cigarette ready in one hand. He is not reassured.

***

It's just getting dark. Streetlights are stuttering into pale yellow light and the ghosts of television sets flicker through undrawn curtains. The traffic is stacking on Southend Lane, ambling slowly past the supermarket and through the estate to Catford, Bromley and beyond. London is coming home, listening to the radio and thinking about life outside work. The low-rise buildings on either side catch the engine noise and channel fumes downhill in waves.

A young black man loiters at the window of a third floor flat in a four story block that stands at the top of the road like a sentry. He checks the mobile phone he holds in his hand occasionally, his eyes sliding forward and back, slippery and swift. He's looking out along the rows of parked cars, checking from side to side as every new set of headlights slides past. He knows cars. They're a bit of an obsession with him. He's looking out for wide spaced headlights that slant towards the grill. A Mercedes. Silver grey and sleek as a shark.

It's not cold in the flat, but he shivers anyway. It's easy not to be scared when you've had a line of coke and you are being asked to help out the big man. It's different when you are alone. The walls of your baby mother's living room close around you like a cell and the streetlights throw bars across the window. Still, it's not as if you are doing anything. Just making a call when you see a car. That's all, and where's the crime in that? He takes a long pull of a joint and carries on staring. The Mercedes might not even show up. Maybe nothing will happen, and he can bank a bit of credit without any risk.

Three seconds later, and break lights burn in front of the block. The spotter takes a closer look and punches a number into his phone. The Call connects. He says, "it's on", and hangs up, walking away from the window towards the TV.

Damien Anderson pulls up to the curb. He leaves the engine on. He sits and waits, window down and cigarette in his right hand resting on the sill. He's acting relaxed, but his knee bounces up and down in double time to the music he's playing. He's got an empty suitcase. He'll hand that to his "cousin", make a call and let the police take him as he drives away. Simple. He's got to make the money up somehow. It'll be a lot of work, but he's a grafter. He's confident that he can bring it together. Shanks isn't the only one who can jack a jewelers. He looks around, wall eyed, his best intimidator's glare. He's not scared and he isn't expecting trouble. Not really checking for threats. Habit, more than anything. The street's empty, and he ducks down to roll a joint. He's early and there's time to kill.

A black Prius pulls into a parking space outside the supermarket. It has a Transport for London cab license in its back window. It's the Uber driver's car of choice and as anonymous as a corner shop carrier bag. The driver doesn't look round as the passenger gets out and crosses the road to the estate. He checks his mobile phone. Looking for the next job.

Germaine MacHeath jogs across a green area towards Elfrida Crescent. The gun is restrained against his waist by his belt and the jacket that is fastened over his hooded top. He can feel it move slightly, and worries that the trigger might catch against his clothing, but it seems to settle. He puts his hands in his jacket pockets and checks, subtly. No danger of accidentally shooting his dick off and waking up handcuffed to a hospital bed. He jogs on, barely above the speed of a fast walk. His hood is up, and his peripheral vision is filled with black toweling. It's a cold evening, and intermittent raindrops spatter down like stray bullets. He looks around, his head moving slightly from side to side. Low key. Nothing sudden, and as much a part of the street furniture as the blue council bins.

Damien Anderson finishes the joint. The weed has mellowed the bump of coke he took before coming out, and he feels relaxed and alert. No rough edges. The streetlamps are vivid; their orange glow mixes with the black tint of his windows and makes him think of bonfires. He remembers a line from his childhood. Treason and plot. He giggles and checks his phone for texts. This will soon be over and he has other things to do. He's looking forward to it.

Germaine MacHeath reaches the edge of a low-rise and stops. He can see the car. It's parked on the same side of the road about thirty feet to his right. The windows are gangsterglassed black, and he can just make out the shape of someone in the driver's seat. He pulls the gun from his waistband. He checks the safety and the magazine. It is slick with oil, glistening in the lamplight. Good to go. He holds it behind his back and saunters to the Mercedes' driver's window. He knocks with his left. Twice. No power to it. The window rolls down, slow as a drawbridge and before the word "Cuz" is out of Omen's mouth the gun is on him. Omen puts up his arm. He's quick. A knife would have glanced off it, but the 9-millimeter bullet is faster. It hits him in the elbow, scores a channel inside his upper arm and lodges in his chest. Blood begins to flow into his lungs. It knocks him backwards and sideways, sprawling across the driver and front passenger seats. The second bullet hits him in the forehead and it's good night Damien Noel Anderson. Blood and brains on the leather upholstery, black and gray in the darkened compartment under the halogen moon.

The spotter hears the shots. His babymother will be back soon and while he doesn't want to see her much, he wants to be on the street even less. He doesn't get up from the TV. He'll have to go down to Deptford to chuck his phone in the Thames later.

Germaine MacHeath walks back to meet the Prius at a stroll. He gets into the back, and the driver moves away on the electric, quieter than death. He makes a right and slides down to Beckenham before heading towards the Downham Estate. He drops his passenger off by the Co-op and drives away. The gun goes with him, stashed in a plastic bag under the passenger seat. It's going back to where it came from. MacHeath lets himself into a flat on a road of flats. He changes his clothes and showers, washing his hands and forearms with bleach and pumice stone. The flat has an old style coal fired stove in the living room. He lights it, and feeds his clothing and the pair of surgical gloves he was wearing into it. Once they are gone, he rings for a mini cab.

It is 7:00 and the first responders are on their way to Elfrida Crescent as the cab passes them on Bromley Road. Jermaine MacHeath checks his reflection in the sun visor's mirror. His white shirt looks crisp, and a good contrast with the sober charcoal gray Hugo Boss suit. He pulls his cuffs into line and leans back in the passenger seat.

The cab drops him off outside the Criterion. He hands twenty pounds to the driver and walks across the road as a plaster tiger on the roof snarls down. He steps onto the pavement. Behind plate glass, a girl with blonde hair buries her face in a menu and he can't be sure whether it's her. The menu slips slightly, and he is so intent on seeing her that he doesn't notice the three men who fall in on either side and behind until his legs are kicked away from under him and the pavement rushes up too fast. His hands are behind his back in cuffs and he lays face down, cheek against the paving stones, one man on his back and another on his legs. There is an instance of silence. Diners peer nervously and a teenager drops his bicycle and seeks shelter in a chicken shop. Germaine MacHeath sees combat boots as two more policemen jog towards where he is detained. There is a cut on his forehead that is bleeding into his right eye. The droplets itch as they flow, and he shakes his head. Another pair of shoes approaches at a stroll. The combat boots part to let them through. Not Prada. Jones the Bootmaker lace up brogues. Management shoes. They stop a couple of feet from his face and the man squats, bending low enough to look him in the eye. He tries not to flinch, but his eyes widen and this makes the policeman smile.

"Hello Germaine. Remember me?"

No reply.

"Germaine MacHeath. I am Detective Inspector John Peach from Tower Bridge Police Station. I'm arresting you for robbery and murder. You do not have to say anything, but it may harm your defence if you fail to mention something you later rely upon in court. Anything you say will be used as evidence."

It recites the script with an easy familiarity. The tone is conversational. John Peach reaches into the breast pocket of his coat and pulls out sealed plastic bag. A shell casing and a live round chime gently as gravity pulls them to the bottom corner.

"Recognise these, son?"

Something cold and damp turns over in the prone man's stomach.

"Found these at your dear old Mum's house down the road. Under a bed."

Anger. He strains against the handcuffs, forcing his head up enough to look the other man straight in the face.

"You put that there, you cunt."

"Of course you'd say that. I'd probably say the same if I was in your position. But it's not me you have to convince, Germaine. You have to convince 12 members of the public taken at random from the electoral role sitting in the Old Bailey. All I do is gather the evidence."

He jiggles the bag. Making the brass contents rise and circle like bees, silhouetted against the white plastic.

"If you're a good enough talker, fair play to you. Hard for a man with no legal income and a previous conviction for armed robbery, though."

Peach stands, his knees popping in the cold.

"Pick him up and put him in the van."

He leans against the bonnet of a police car and carefully writes something in a notebook, then turns and ambles to the restaurant. He picks up a menu, studies it, and then puts it in his pocket. It looks good.

Germaine MacHeath is carried bodily to the van. The three officers place him on a bench. He is not manhandled or beaten. They treat him with restraint. His pockets are searched. The bundle of notes, mobile phone and change they contain are meticulously cataloged. A dressing is applied to his head, and one of his captors dabs a tissue on to the blood on his face with hands that smell of leather and metal. They only speak to him to ask him whether he has anything sharp on him and to confirm their finds. He isn't taking part. Things are being done to him that are part of a system that has worked on many others, and will carry on once he's another number inside or back out on the street. It's as sterile as the antiseptic cream that stings his forehead.

Doors slam and lights dim. Blue light bounces off brick and concrete. The van pulls out and away.

Chapter 21

There are six men in the legal visits holding cell. It's a small room with a high ceiling, and the tiny rectangle of natural light far above barely takes the edge off the gloom. A long bulb hangs from a lopsided fitting, trickling weak amber light that is as thin as a lawyer's promise. The bench is narrow, forcing two of the men to stand. Germaine MacHeath sits with his legs apart. He is leaning forward with his elbows on his knees. His head is down, and he stares at the pattern of wear and cigarettes scars in the flooring. He ignores the occasional outburst of conversation around him.

The door bangs open and his name is shouted. A prison officer escorts him to a corridor of glass walled cubicles, stretching towards a desk. Another officer, another name check and he is directed to room number six. The man who waits for him is dressed in a suit that was expensive once. He stands and extends a hand. MacHeath shakes and sits, reflexively pulling the chair towards the table and finding that it is locked to the floor.

"Mr MacHeath."

"Mr Wilson"

The lawyer is the bearer of bad news to a dangerous man, and he takes on an undertaker's diffident solemnity. He's hoping that his client is realistic enough not to lose his temper and sour a day at work. He fans the papers out in front of him and starts his spiel.

"The charges of murder and robbery rely on three pieces of evidence. There's the handprint on the counter, the bullet casing and the live round found at your mother's address and the CCTV. You'll have to explain the first two more than the third, as all the film does is show what happened. The gunman is masked, and although there's nothing about his height and build that rules you out, it's really the prints and the ballistics that put you in the frame. All the CCTV does is corroborate it."

He pauses to rifle through a lever arch file.

"The bullet and the casing were found under the bed in the upstairs rear bedroom at 43 Beecroft Road by DI Peach during the search immediately before your arrest. You can see his statement here. The live round wouldn't be a huge problem in itself, although it is of the same caliber. It could have come from anywhere. The casing is more problematic. Now if we flick though a bit further to Deirdre Knowles' evidence, she's the forensic scientist who compares the casing with the two that were found at the Regent Street scene. This one's a real issue, because she says that the same weapon makes both the firing pin and rifling marks. That's the marks made by the bit that hits the bullet at the back when you pull the trigger and as it makes its way down the barrel when it's fired. We're going to have our own expert take a look at it, of course, but I don't anticipate that there'll be a total difference of opinion. I think that the best that we can hope for is some degree of less certainty."

MacHeath opens his mouth to speak. The lawyer holds up a hand. It trembles, but only slightly.

"It's easier if I set out the whole of the case before you give me your instructions, Mr MacHeath. You need to consider everything. Let's move on to the prints. It's a left palm mark on the glass top of the counter, with the fingers pointing at twelve o'clock. The prosecution say this means that the person was leaning over the counter at the time this was made. We'll get back to that in a moment. The comparison statement is more difficult. They're not allowed to say that two sets of fingerprints are the same any more. It's an opinion. They grade their conclusions on a scale from "no support" to "very strong support" for the idea that the prints were made by the same person. In this case, the level of support for the prints on the counter being made by you is described as "very strong". Once again, we're getting our own man to have a look at them. He's extremely good. But I don't expect that his report will be any kind of magic bullet. It's not unheard of for two experts to disagree completely, but it is very rare, and nothing you would want to bet the next thirty five years of your life on."

A half smile and a nod over the table. No angry response. An instant of silence, then Wilson coughs and carries on.

"The CCTV shows the man who shoots the shopkeeper leaning over the counter supporting himself with his left hand and pointing the gun with his right. This is unhelpful, because the prosecution will say that your fingerprints are in the same place as the robber's hand can be seen in on the footage. You can't identify anyone, but it's there and the jury are going to see it. It's up to you, Mr MacHeath. You have to decide whether we challenge this evidence on some basis other than its reliability."

Germaine MacHeath composes himself. This is a rehearsal. He pitches his voice low, and keeps it educated.

"I'm not denying I've been to the shop Mr Wilson. In fact, if you check the CCTV for a few days before you'll see me there with my girlfriend. She tried on a ring. That's where the prints come from. I can't remember leaning over the counter, but it's possible when I was paying or something."

Wilson makes a note, underlining a word as he goes. MacHeath tries to read it without him noticing, but can't decipher his handwriting. It's important to get feedback.

"And that bullet and that casing weren't found in my mother's house. They were planted. I wasn't even staying with my mum. Peach is angry because I am seeing his daughter. I don't know if it's a race thing, or because he's looked me up, seen my previous and decided that I'm not good enough for her. Either way, there's no way that that got into my mum's house without his help. I mean, I'm supposed to have robbed this shop, killed some man who works there and left a bullet and a casing under my bed. It's a joke. If I was going to do something like that, I'd leave the stuff at the scene and get rid of the gun. "

Wilson sighs. It's a tune he's heard before. Eighteen years of criminal defence and it doesn't get any better.

"I don't think that telling the jury that you are a far better criminal than the prosecution give you credit for is exactly helping your chances of acquittal. As for the rest of your account, it's very high risk. I'm not encouraging you to say anything that isn't true, but you have to be realistic. You run a trial on the basis that you have been fitted up and the judge's meter will be running right up until he sentences you to life with a tariff of at least thirty five years. It's a matter for you, and of course we'll try to get hold of the footage for the previous week, if it exists. The prosecution will have to disclose it. Can you prove this relationship?

The client is still; draped in silence as he thinks about Polly, about the hotels they stayed at, the meals they ate together. It was always the two of them. Together with the world shut out. Omen, the Turks and everything else were shadows that could never walk into the light that surrounded them. He shakes his head slowly.

"I took her out. I didn't take her home."

"Did you pay for things with plastic, Mr MacHeath? That would provide evidence we could use to support your account."

A more emphatic shake.

"Strictly cash."

"Pity. How about your phone records? Would they show any contact with her? You had a recently activated unregistered pay as you go on you when you were arrested, but we could access the call records with the phone company if you could remember your old number."

Germaine MacHeath thinks of the calls he has made and the connections that could be made from them.

"If I could remember the number, then would we have to give the police all the records, or just the ones that matter?"

The lawyer makes another note.

"I am afraid not, Mr MacHeath. Even if we served edited records, the police would be able to get the full document themselves once we gave them the number. It would be helpful in this case…"

He trails off, not wanting to finish the sentence. If the client admits to other crimes, he won't be able to represent him if he's charged and he pleads not guilty. Steven Wilson doesn't go where self interest fears to tread. He clears his throat.

"The real question is; will your girlfriend be willing to come to court? Without her, we can put the case to DI Peach but there's nothing to back it up. Unless you can remember the number, of course."

There is a polite knock on the door. A prison officer points to his watch and holds up five fingers. Wilson rustles and folds himself ready. Time to go. A handshake, a promise to book another visit and they part. His client walks back to the holding cell with his head down.

Chapter 22

The time display reads 5:30, but Ken McGuiness has already been awake for a while. It has been a long day. Operation Grandville is winding down, and he's probably back on tomorrow as duty SIO. Another day. It should be nothing to worry about, except that the datastick will come back with the morning post and what will he do with it then? He lies on his back and stares at the shadows on the ceiling. Thinking about the datastick starts him thinking about Sarah; the movement of her hair in the bathwater and her grey eyes turned into dead, painted colour in the steam. He goes through his route away from her flat again, mentally checking off each camera avoided and confirming that he had wiped the payphone's receiver. Far easier to worry about security than to work out where he can find the time to mourn her in secret. He thinks about the datastick and its secrets and he finds himself resenting her. He accepts that he brought it on himself. If he hadn't been sleeping with her. If he hadn't made that stupid "everyone matters" comment. Every "if" walks him round another circuit. The street lighting makes gothic shadows against the curtains, and he shivers, shifting closer to the empty half of the bed where his wife would sleep for comfort.

Moving patterns of light on the ceiling as a car passes. It is unusual. The road is suburban. It is not a cul de sac, but it's not a rat run either. Its residents are safely in their beds at this time, and prosperous enough not to work shifts. He lies quiet, rigid and listening. There is a scrape of rubber against stone as someone stumbles on the front path's uneven crazy paving. He's out of bed and pulling on tracksuit bottoms and a t-shirt before the first knock on the door.

He flicks on the porch light as he walks down the corridor. It is still dark, and the sudden brightness makes the two men on the doorstep blink and step back. They are still slightly off balance when McGuiness opens the door. The older of the two reaches in the inside pocket of his jacket and produces a warrant card.

"Detective Chief Inspector McGuiness?"

"Yes. What do you want?"

"Sergeant Gilmour and DC Milne from professional standards. Mr McGuiness, I am arresting you. You do not have to say anything, but it may harm your defence if you fail to mention anything that you rely on in court. Anything you do say will be given in evidence."

The younger of the two produces a set of handcuffs. McGuiness raises his hands into a boxer's guard and they stare at each other for a second. Gilmour raises his hands. Placating.

"Can we all be professional about this? You're coming with us, Mr McGuiness. I don't expect you to run away, because you don't have anywhere to run to. In the mean time, we're going to search your house while my Johnny come lately colleagues take you off to Colliers Wood."

Another car pulls up as he is speaking and three men and a woman get out. They walk towards the house unhurriedly.

"My wife's in hospital. She'll call me later."

He realises his mistake as soon as the words are out of his mouth. He wanted to sound like a senior police officer speaking to an inferior, but he is sure that the other man could hear the plea in his voice. He recognises it himself. There are innocent people, and they are going to find out all about me and I will be ruined in their eyes. Please don't break the news I have brought this down upon them. Let them sleep.

"You can't take any calls, Mr McGuiness. Get dressed. I will come with you to make sure you don't compromise the search."

McGuiness turns, and Gilmour follows him up the stairs. He stops at the bedroom door.

"Do you mind?"

The other man nods his head, slightly, and gestures to the handle. McGuiness opens the door and walks to the bedside. The landing light is on. He fumbles for clothing in the half light, then picks up a sweatshirt from a chair and puts it on.

"I'm going into the top drawer of the chest to get some socks, OK"

"Carry on, Chief Inspector."

The female officer arrives and stands in the doorway. He laces up his shoes, and is escorted out into one of the waiting cars, where he sits in the back, his face down. The door slams beside him, and the vehicle settles onto its suspension as the front seats are filled. Nobody speaks. The driver confirms that everyone is ready, and they are gone.

***

It's not uncomfortable, and it's pretty clean. The walls are whitewashed and graffiti free. There is a stainless steel toilet in one corner. It is neither blocked nor broken. There is a blue plastic mat on the shelf that passes for a bed. McGuiness sits with his back to the wall. He thinks.

Milne told the custody sergeant that he had been arrested for "misfeasance in public office." The charge meant behaving badly as a civil servant. It took in everything from financial corruption, through selling stories to the newspapers to tipping off criminals about ongoing investigations. He has never been tempted by money. The opportunity to sell on some piece of information to the papers had come up a few times, but he's been too cautious. He didn't trust journalists at the best of times, and he had always found the idea that they would go to prison rather than give up a source laughable. If they wanted to spend their precious time pouring over his bank account and calculating whether he could afford to take holidays or buy a new kitchen, it was theirs to waste.

It wouldn't be hard to connect him to Sarah. He wasn't paranoid enough to use a throw away, and his phone records would show multiple contacts with her landline and mobile. He was at her flat when she died, or at least shortly afterwards. He'd gone out of his way to lose any link with the call to the 999 operator. He'd be a suspect if he were investigating. At the very least a person of interest to the enquiry. Assuming there was an enquiry. There had been nothing on the TV or radio. He doesn't have the time to read newspapers, but he's pretty sure that someone would have mentioned a forensic scientist's suspicious death. Police like to gossip as much as anyone. Was it a suspicious death? Plenty of people die in stupid accidents at home. Electrocuting themselves with kettles, falling off ladders and drowning in baths. Not all of them were idiots. Some might even be educated, professional people. Yet it looked off. Wrong. Nothing she would do, and who drowns in a bath after a couple of spliffs and a glass of wine?

He finds himself on his feet. The cell is monitored. There are cameras on him, and he doesn't want to pace like a panicking suspect. He forces himself to sit down. Breathe.

What if the only reason for thinking that Sarah's death might have been suspicious is because of what was on the datastick? If that's true, it means that police killed her and the only thing keeping him safe is that they haven't found it. Not just him. Maxine, too. He can feel the back of his throat begin to close. If they found it in the search, what would they do? Kick him loose? They didn't have any evidence he'd committed a crime. His affair might break up his marriage, but cheating on your wife isn't criminal. They might tell her, just to teach him a lesson. Complaints were a vindictive bunch of bastards. Everyone said so. But there would be no point to it. If they wanted him to keep his mouth shut, then fucking over his life and leaving him with nothing to lose wasn't the way to go about it. Enlightened self interest, if you thought about it. If you thought about it long enough the whole thing sounded insane, something you might find on the bloody Internet next to a rant about how the CIA bombed the twin towers.

He pauses. Runs his fingers through his hair and breathes in and out. The lighting is unforgiving, and he has the beginnings of a headache. He wasn't going to ask Gilmour from Complaints if he minded watching him shower and shave, and he can smell himself, rank and biological over the background disinfectant. His stubble rasps against his chest as he hangs his head. He forces his mind back along unwelcome paths. If he wanted to keep a secret, he'd make sure that nobody would listen to whoever told it. That would mean making them into someone nobody would listen to. He looks around the cell, takes in the walls and the glass bricks, the stainless steel and plastic. It's not a big jump, when you think about it. Nobody listens to people in places like this, not anybody that matters. He is frightened to frame the next step, shaking his head slightly as it forms itself. What if they fitted him up? The story writes itself. Married man plays away. Girlfriend won't take "no" for an answer to her demand to leave the wife and start again. There's a lot to lose financially. Fuck. Everyone with a house in London was in that boat. Tempers fray. Words are exchanged and the faithless husband drowns her in the bath. He's a policeman, so he knows how to set it up to look like an accident. He's got some wild story, but where's the evidence?

He can't help himself. He's up on his feet and marching the cell. The long walk to nowhere. Forwards and back to where he started. No closer to a solution.

The wicket rattles and drops. McGuiness sees Gilmour's face, distorted by the glass. He sits, composing himself against the rising tide of panic.

"Come with us, Ken. You don't mind if we call you Ken, do you?"

"Would it matter if I did?"

He falls into step between them as they walk him through the custody suite. The interview room is small. Hardly room for the three of them to stand at the same time. There is a table, a stand for the machine that will record whatever is said and done onto 3 DVDs. There are four chairs. The Complaints sit on the recording side. McGuiness takes the vacant seat nearest to the wall. He leans and tries to look relaxed. Discs are unwrapped and put into the machine. There is the usual technical failure, but eventually, a high pitched electric drone tells them that it's good to go. Gilmour is taking the lead. He leans forwards, rests his forearms on the table and introduces himself.

"I am DS Gilmour from the Directorate of Professional Standards. The other officer present is.."

He gestures to his colleague.

"Detective Constable Alec Milne, also from Professional Standards."

"We are interviewing."

He makes eye contact.

"Please state your name for the tape."

"Detective Chief Inspector Kenneth McGuiness."

"Thank you. You have a right to speak to a solicitor, and that advice is free. You don't have a solicitor with you now, because you told the custody sergeant that you didn't want one. We can stop the tapes and facilitate you being legally represented at any time if you change your mind."

"I don't want a brief."

"Good. So you've nothing to hide. Tell us where you were three days ago. About nine o'clock."

McGuiness frowns.

"My daughter was born three days ago. I was at Kings Hospital with my wife. I left work and went straight there. Came straight home after they were both settled."

"Straight home. Are you sure about that?"

Eye contact. A pause. Gilmour nods to Milne, who takes a brown, A4 envelope out of a file. He opens it and spreads the contents face down on the table. Photographs.

"What do you want me to do? Pick a card?"

Milne turns the photos over. McGuiness sees his car and the traffic warden, a conversation, his arms out in a pleading gesture. A finger wagging in his face and him standing over the other man, a crash helmet caught in mid roll. The quality isn't great. The facial features could be anyone and there's only a partial registration. There's something else missing, but he can't put his finger on it. He feels an overwhelming longing for a cigarette.

"I am showing Inspector McGuiness a bundle of four stills from the King's College Hospital car park. Do you recognise anyone in these pictures?"

McGuiness picks them up, holds them in front of him and stares.

"Where were these taken again?"

These were taken in the car park outside Kings College Hospital, Inspector."

He looks at them again. They look like action photos. The angle of the camera is slightly upwards, making both men look tall. There is no time and date stamp.

"Are we going to get to watch the whole CCTV, or are you just going to ask me about a couple of stills?"

Gilmour deadpans. Milne fidgets. McGuiness continues.

"Because these look to me like they've been taken from a car, not from CCTV. The two men are on the same level as the photographer, if not slightly higher. There's no stamp, and if I was interviewing someone and I wanted to demonstrate that their car had been at the scene, I'd make sure that one of the pictures I showed them was the one from the car park cameras that shows them either entering or leaving. All car parks have a camera trained on the exit. It's how they catch people leaving without paying."

"You're not interviewing anyone. You're the one under arrest here."

It's a standard response. He's used it on solicitors in interviews himself. Don't get above yourself. We'll pick what you talk about. He's not playing.

"Yes. You don't have to answer anything. It's your interview. But it is on record, so I'll ask what I want to ask and you can answer what you want to answer. Up to you."

He doesn't leave any gap.

"Also, CCTV stills have a date and time stamp on each frame. None of these do. This isn't evidence that you've gathered from wherever you say it came from. These are surveillance photos. Was I under surveillance?"

"You need to stop messing around and tell us whether this is you hitting that traffic warden."

McGuiness ignores him. If he was being watched, he's probably fucked anyway. He might manage to walk away with a fine or some form of community service for hitting the traffic warden. There's the stress of his wife and child being hospitalised to consider, as well as his years of unblemished service. His career is over. He may stay in the Met. They've kept people who have done worse, but he can kiss any chance of promotion goodbye. But there's no reason for him to be watched, and no reason to be so shy about telling him if he was.

"Why don't you tell me if that's you?"

Milne jabs the picture three times as he speaks. He's leaning over the table. His complexion is mottled, and he extends his chin aggressively.

"Was I being watched?"

He doesn't look the man from Complaints in the eye. It's not a confrontation. An interview is the search for the truth, as they say.

"This is our interview, and I will ask the questions."

McGuiness is good at self control. Everyone says so. He struggles to hold down his laugh as Milne's face betrays the effort of turning embarrassment into anger.

"Do you want to try that one with the accent?"

Silence. McGuiness presses on.

"Who authorised surveillance on me? What offences do you think I have committed?"

"You don't get to question us. You're here to answer questions about an assault on a public servant by a serving police officer, Mr McGuiness."

"You cautioned me at the start of the interview. You told me that it would harm my defence if I failed to mention something I later relied on in court. I'm doing exactly that. If I go to court on this, and that's a very big if, I am going to rely on the fact that the only evidence that I have been shown comes from an unauthorised surveillance operation on a serving police officer. That's why I'm saying this. I'll repeat it for the benefit of the tape, shall I? Why was I being watched? What do you think I've done? Who authorised this?"

Milne struggles for eye contact, and this time McGuiness doesn't look away. Milne lets his eyes slide away, down to the table top. He picks up one of the photos and breathes out a yogic, "look how calm I am in the face of all of this" lung full of reconstituted air. The room is hot, and made hotter by the three of them. Faint dark rings are noticeable under his arms. They expand slowly towards a white tide line on the dark cotton. He holds the photo under McGuiness' nose. It is the one of the traffic warden falling.

"Are you saying this isn't you?"

"No comment"

McGuiness is calm. He doesn't feel the heat. He can't smell the sweat, fags and Maxpax coffee waft as the tabletop fan rotates towards him. He's somewhere high up, and he can see for miles. Silence is the best answer he can give now, and the best he could have got from Milne. He'd have said something if everything was in order. Not much, but enough to say, "shut up and move on".

Six more variations on "is this you?" and six more "no comments", later and they wrap up the interview. McGuiness is given a sheet of paper telling him that he has to make himself available for questioning on demand. He's not on bail, and that, he supposes, can be taken as a small victory. He buys a cup of coffee, and drinks it through a plastic lid as he walks to the tube station. It tastes of heat and it makes his stomach growl. It's 12:30, and the idea of going home, having a shower then going up the hospital is overwhelming, but he is on at two. Call of Duty, and all that. He gets a seat and leafs through a free paper looking for articles about battered traffic wardens and forensic scientists dead in suspicious circumstances until London Bridge. It passes the time and winds down the sense of dread a bit, and the first time he thinks about what the fact that he is under surveillance might actually mean is as he's crossing the road works on Lewisham roundabout.

The briefing room is packed. It's not exactly silent, but there isn't the rumble of pre-meeting gossip and banter. The air quivers like a dog being ordered to sit. Detective Superintendent Parry sits at the front of the room, his forearms on a table, and his large, square shoulders hunched almost to the level of his large square jaw. He sees McGuiness at the door and straightens up.

"Good of you to join us, Inspector McGuiness."

His voice is deep. Slightly rasping and without an identifiable accent. McGuiness weighs the inflection for a hint that his superior officer knows exactly what has delayed him, but finds nothing that couldn't be paranoia and caffeine. He walks to the front and sits down.

"Two nights ago police were called out to reports of a shooting in Elfrida Crescent in Catford. A man had been shot multiple times as he sat in his car outside a block of flats. DNA testing confirmed that the deceased was one Damien Noel Anderson, a person of interest to Operation Grandville. This identification has been confirmed by Mr Anderson's mother, who attended Greenwich Mortuary this morning."

He pauses to allow a wave of comment to spread and break.

"With this in mind, and given the pressure on Borough and divisional resources, the decision has been taken to scale down Grandville, with all but a skeleton staff under Chief Inspector McGuiness' command being redeployed to operations Hartfield and Jutland. Those staying with Grandville are DI Walsh, Sergeant Stevens, and DCs Welbourne, Kinch, Beddoes and Harrison. The rest of you are asked to report back to the pool, where you will be given your reallocation."

The new Grandville team sits in a semi circle in front of the table. So many seats have been vacated that they find themselves spaced as unevenly as Halloween lantern teeth and have to cluster to the front and centre.   Superintendent Parry continues in a more conversational tone. There is no need to raise his voice to be heard.

"Grandville has two priorities from here on in. Your first priority is to properly and positively identify the Western Way victim; your second is to find evidence connecting her to Damien Anderson. I know that Inspector McGuiness has a potential candidate for her. What's the current position?"

McGuiness nods to Stevens, who gives an "unaccustomed as I am to public speaking" cough.

"We're collecting Heather Buchan's parents from Gatwick later today. Unfortunately there are no family members on the database to give us a head start so I can't give any percentages that the Western Way victim is Heather, but I've spoken to the flat mates, and seen her Facebook page, so I don't think that there's any doubt."

Parry turns to McGuiness.

"That seems to be in hand, then. Ken, can you bring us up to date on the forensics?"

"The short answer is that there aren't any, or at least, the preliminary report says that they haven't been able to find a full DNA profile on any of the swabs that's anyone other than the victim's. There have been a number of different hits from various items at the scene-a can of coke and a few cigarette butts, but as it's a public place and a walk through from Plumstead Common station and the prison complex and Crown Court, it's hardly surprising. They've started to work their way through, and DC Welbourne's been checking for current whereabouts. Nobody comes across as viable. The DNA on the can links to someone who has been in prison since last Thursday, so it was probably his last piece of home comfort before his court date. A couple of the fag ends come back as people with previous. One's a female, aged in her 60's with a large extended family of frequent fliers. Another's a 17-year-old car thief. It's a work in progress, but I don't hold out much hope."

Parry's wipes a hand across his face, grating against his five o'clock shadow.

"You say they haven't been able to find a full profile?"

"No. They have managed to locate some of what they call cellular material, but it's a very weak trace. They haven't been able to separate it out enough to be able to say whether it's two or more people, or what sort of material it comes from. It is fair to say that the trace contains some of the Damien Anderson's features, but there isn't enough for them to give any sort of odds on it being someone else. I think that the nature of the crime itself strongly suggests the same person as Peckham Rye, but it would be dangerous for us to make that a solid assumption at this stage."

He takes a breath.

"We're still inside the seven day window for CCTV. What we need to find out is where she went before she ended up in the hands of whoever dumped her body on Western Way, and then thoroughly investigate the CCTV opportunities for sightings of Heather, and anyone talking to her or paying her any attention. The first port of call for that has to be the flatmates. I've reviewed the statements, and all we know is that she left her home for what I assume was a night out at about 8pm and was never seen again. I want to find out where she went, and who she was meeting. I'll distribute actions for all of you in an hour, if that's all right, Sir?"

He looks at Parry, who nods, and makes a note on the pad in front of him. McGuiness tries, but cannot read it without making it obvious what he's doing, so sits back and lets the senior officer take over.

"You can all get yourselves a cup of coffee, have a smoke or even get on with some work. Be back here in an hour and ready to put Grandville to bed. I'm not interested in easy solutions. If Anderson did do this, then whoever shot him has done the taxpayer a favour, but this enquiry needs to keep an open mind. Dismissed."

McGuiness is the last to leave. As he walks past the desk on his way out, his hand fastened around the cigarette packet in his pocket, he waits to be told to sit but it doesn't come. He takes the lift back down and joins the other pariahs in the car park. He thinks about CCTV, Damien Anderson and Heather Buchan. The morning seems like a different country.

Chapter 23

Germaine MacHeath sits on his bunk. He has a bundle of case papers in front of him and is pretending to read. He looks around the cell, taking in the damp staining at the corner of the window, the peeling paint and the grey, sandpapery flooring. His cellmate paces, pushing a mop in front of him. He has been doing this for three hours. It's annoying, but MacHeath has decided to let it slide. With all the filthy drug addicts and street drinkers in here, there are far worse options for a cellmate than an obsessive compulsive cleaner. He has to see Polly. He asked Danny to speak to her at Uni, but apparently she hadn't been seen for a few days. Write to her? The only address he can remember is her parents', and the chances of an obvious prison letter making it through are slim to none. He wonders whether he could send someone round to speak to her in person. The thought of the reception one of his crew would get at the front door almost makes him smile. But he is sure that she wants to see him. They have a connection. She said so. He needs her. Not just to beat the case. His skin jumps with pins and needles and he can feel her absence like an amputated limb. She is guarded behind walls, and Germaine MacHeath, unlikely freer of imprisoned girls, wonders whether he can free himself before the thorns grow too high and dense around her memory of him.

Someone is shouting through a cell window. A Scottish accent, stridently repeating, "Roxy, gie's a fag". There is a chorus telling the Scotsman to shut up, but he doesn't pause, his voice getting hoarse and more desperate as his long, nicotine free night behind a door ticks into its fifth hour. Germaine MacHeath rolls onto his side and tries to sleep. The rhythmic swoosh of a mop on the floor and the shouts don't prevent him. He's getting used to it. He's back in the hotel with Polly, her arms around him, her lips on his a future without walls and bars, where everything is optimism.

It's gone quiet. The shouters have shouted themselves into an uneasy silence and if sleep hasn't taken them, the threat of retaliation has kept them in check. Used to a wider bed, Germaine MacHeath rolls over and hits the cell wall with some force. He shakes his head, a red heat haze of pain fogging his vision. He squeezes his eyes shut and tries to force himself back into dreams. Floodlights, strip lighting and windows without curtains or blinds mean that it is never truly dark here. There are no sounds of cleaning. The bed opposite is empty, and he can see the mop leaning against the door. It slow strobes from light into shade and back again. Shadow where there is nothing to cast it. He is awake, sitting up quickly and looking around. It takes a moment for him to take it in, and then he is on his feet. There is a water pipe that runs across the top of the window. It is about eight feet off the floor. Tied to the pipe is a ragged rope made of torn up clothes and blankets. His cellmate hangs from a crude noose. His feet are about a foot from the floor. They aren't moving. It's hard to tell in indirect light, but MacHeath can see his face is dark, a purplish red somewhere between sunburn and a stroke. The bell is on the far end of the cell by the door. It is almost directly opposite the hanging man. He pauses, his feet struggling for purchase on the non-slip as he shimmies, unable to decide between calling for help or helping himself. Three steps at a run. He's by the bell. He pushes it three times, sharp and short, a half remembered distress call. Back to the window. He locks his arms around the hanging man's waist. The man is slight. He can't weigh more than ten stone. MacHeath is a big man, and strong with it, but the strain of lifting the dead weight makes his joints crack. He stands; his feet braced apart and he waits for the sound of running feet. Nothing. He can feel the other man's body heat, and a spread of moisture soaks through his t-shirt. He shouts.

"There's a man hung himself in here. Help."

Nothing. He shouts again, a fissure of panic sending the last word into pre pubescent falsetto.

Another inmate shouts. Then another. The wing is a cauldron of noise as the cries are taken up; echoes that leap from window to window like apes. His head is down, all his concentration is on keeping the rope slack. It's not easy. He has to balance the body while lifting it from the thighs. A slight shift to left or right leaves the man's upper torso supported by the rope. His face is against the man's stomach, and he can feel him getting colder. He wonders whether this is the point of death, and strains his eyes upwards to try to catch sight of the face, but his posture doesn't let him. He shouts again, one voice among many. He shouts again, his throat stripped and painful. His voice descends from a shout to a croak, and then to a whisper. By the time three prison officers run into the cell, 96 minutes have passed since he pushed the alarm. Two of them support the body. The third cuts the rope. They lay the body on the floor. One puts a mask on the face and another tries CPR. It's too late, and they know it. It's going through the motions, ticking off points in the flow chart so that the paperwork can look healthy. Cosmetic resuscitation.

They do not remove the body. A doctor is called, and a thin daylight has shuffled over Brixton by the time he arrives. The prison is overcrowded. Even a murderer like Germaine MacHeath cannot be expected to cohabit with the corpse of his cellmate, and he is left sitting in the association area while the prison creaks into life around him. He is subdued, and does not object when he is taken into the wing office. There, he is given a cup of tea, and a man in a suit asks whether he wants to see a counselor. He agrees. He is walked through to another wing. He asks about his belongings, and is told they will be brought to him. He is given a cell to himself. He sits on the bed and stares at the floor, following labyrinths in the lino. He is too exhausted to think, and cannot sleep. Eventually, he is provided with diazepam and fades to black.

***

DC Welbourne has put on his good suit and has taken the trouble not only to pick out a tie, but also to coordinate it with his shirt. His hair is gelled in a bed hair look that would have the unkinder members of the Grandville team making comments about boy bands. He parks the unmarked Ford Focus about a hundred yards from the house. There are a couple of black kids on bikes hanging around by the gates at Fordham Park, neither of them older than fourteen or fifteen. They both give him the hard eye and kiss their teeth with theatrical volume before cycling off. More show than menace. The area is on the up, so they say, but it's not exactly Blackheath, so he decides against putting a "police on call" notice in the windscreen. More chance of getting the tires slashed than getting a ticket.

It could have been CCTV and a day stuck in some council security office waiting for footage to download and watching commuters and tourists' resurrected nights. It could have been a trip to Gatwick to pick up the deceased's family, a death knock with a four-hour commute attached. Instead he is going to spend the day with three student girls. True, he has to take their statements about their missing flat mate, and true, the aftermath of said flatmates disappearance isn't exactly a singles evening, but all in all, the day looks good. He catches sight of his reflection and checks his hair.

There is a small flight of steps up to the door, and he takes them in two strides. The doorbell is broken, and he decides to tap the letterbox rather than to start the meeting with a copper's knock. Footsteps and voices inside, and the door opens a crack. Welbourne sees blonde hair and a blue eye outlined with heavy black eyeliner. He holds up his warrant card, giving her time to give it a proper check.

"Miss Salter? I'm DC Welbourne from the Serious Crime Directorate at Lewisham. I'd arranged to come round today to talk about Heather and take statements."

"Oh yes. Come in. Should I call you detective?"

"Simon is fine."

She sticks out a hand and they shake.

"I'm not Louise, I mean Miss Salter, although she's in. I'm Caz. Caroline Dooley."

She walks him through to the living room. There are two slightly dilapidated sofas grouped around a TV. There are posters on the walls; a couple of films, musicians and some proper art-the terracotta army and Klimt's "The Kiss". A mirror on the mantelpiece. The carpet is landlord corduroy brown, threadbare and partially covered with a rag rug. The room is clean, hoovered and dusted to an almost show house perfection. She points vaguely at the sofas and invites him to sit.

"Would you like a cup of tea?"

"Please. Milk and one, thanks"

She is wearing a long white skirt and a black pullover. He watches her take the two steps to the door. Not bad. She's out of the room for ten minutes, so Welbourne has a look around. There's no ashtray. The few books stacked on the floor are heavy duty, politics and history. Library stiffened covers and heavy on the footnotes. Nothing personal. A couple of girly glossies on the coffee table and a dog-eared copy of Pride and Prejudice on the arm of one of the sofas. He hears footsteps in the hallway and hastily takes his seat. She comes through the door backwards, a mug in each hand. She puts one down on the coffee table and sits on the other sofa. She smiles at him, a little nervously.

"So, Simon, are you going to shine lights into my eyes and hit me with a phone book?"

"You're probably alright for the moment, but I promise nothing. What I really need to know about is Heather."

"There's not a great deal to tell. We're not exactly friends. She was a bit, you know, religious, for me. Nice girl, but very, I don't know, committed. She'd go off to church every Sunday, and she didn't really mix. I mean, we like to go out as a group on Saturdays. Socialising. We work hard so we need a bit of release. Heather wasn't in to that. She'd go off and give sandwiches to tramps, or work in the food bank."

"She wasn't popular?"

The girl flinches. A guarded expression crosses her face. Welbourne can see her calculating whether she's become a suspect before she smiles again.

"I didn't dislike her. In fact, I'd say she was impossible to dislike. She was always friendly and very positive. You could always rely on Heather to organise the bills or help with an assignment. It's just she never really fitted in. We all like to be a bit of a family, but she did her own thing. Wasn't one of the girls."

It crosses Welbourne's mind that the nice young girl offering him tea could have killed her flat mate for not fitting in. It's not impossible. People have killed their own children for failing to live up to some ideal of family life. He shakes his head imperceptibly as he imagines himself trying to explain that theory to DI Walsh, or worse of all, to the governor. It's all been a bit of a waste of time. Sighing, he flips open his clipboard and finds a blank witness statement form. Another bit of unused material is on its way.

"Which church did she go to? Do you remember her saying anything about it?"

"Saint something's? I don't remember. It's over in Rotherhithe, near the Thames. I remember that she used to go on about how nice it was to go to the river and sit and think about things after she'd finished doing whatever it is they do."

"Did she say what sort of Church it was?"

"She was a Catholic, I think. She had one of those bead necklace things."

He starts to write the statement out, going through the biographical details at the start with her and moves on to everything she knows about her flat mate. He passes it to her when they are done. She smiles, signs and offers him another cup of tea, shouting up the stairs to her friends to come down and speak to him as she walks through to the kitchen. He watches her leave, and realises that all the smiles are just good manners. He's an official to her, something to be dealt with so she and her friends can get back to reading the books that are stacked around the room and going to nightclubs with other pretty girls and boys with A levels and names like Ethan. By the time he walks back to his car the sun is up, and he begins to feel uncomfortably warm.

Chapter 24

Germaine MacHeath has a single cell now, and the privacy can be good. Proper sleep without worrying whether his cellmate wants to get the voices to shut up for a minute by staving his head in with a chair leg is a definite plus. On the other hand, it's boring. He's behind a door for twenty three hours every day, and other than day time TV, there's nothing to take his mind off the bundle of case papers that sits on the desk in the corner by the window. He's read them, and read them again. They don't get any better. The fingerprint and the bullet casing. He has an answer to both of them, but he's a perceptive man. He saw his brief's face tense when he said he was being fitted up. The lawyer is not a fool. He's been around the block a few times. That's why he uses him. If he thinks that the case is dead in the water, then it's something he has to recognise. It's all down to Polly. The only thing standing between him and thirty five years behind a door is a policeman's daughter. He knows that Polly's father didn't find the shell casing at his mother's house. He's far too wary of her to bring that sort of trouble to her door. So not just a policeman's daughter, a corrupt policeman who is prepared to plant evidence to fit him up. He felt something move inside him when they were together. He wonders whether this was just him. Whether Polly was just playing him for a few good nights out and expensive presents. It simply cannot be true. He's been a user of women. It's almost the perks of the job for a drug dealer. Girls have thrown themselves at him, begging to be used. He knows the way users think, the calculations that they make and the bargains that this involves. He thinks back. She has never asked him for anything. He has given her everything freely. He shakes his head, and then remembers her body against his in the hotel room, the pressure of her hip against his thigh as she leant into him, the blue of her eyes as she stared into his, not flicking away but steady. Nothing to hide. He's written to her, asking her to visit, but the empty seat in the visits hall hasn't surprised him. Girls like Polly don't belong in jail. They shouldn't be pawed by gate screws or eye fucked by inmates. It would soil her somehow, and that's the last thing he wants. Sometimes he could swear he can feel that he is on her mind. It's like they are reaching out across London and joining hands. It's a bridge between them. He believes that it is as real as it is intense. He knows that she must be under pressure. Planting evidence on your daughter's boyfriend does indicate a certain level of parental disapproval. Prison talk about women ending relationships or playing away while their men are inside hisses in his ear when he's not distracted. He wants to see Polly. He wants to see her. He has to see her. He'd give anything to see her, but all he has are positive thoughts and hope. Short change.

It is 11am. It's two hours until feeding time and five until association. The prison is becalmed behind its doors, and Germaine MacHeath is lying on his bed reading. The print is small, and the window is dirty. Squinting and concentration have started a headache. Keys turn and the door opens. Two officers.

"MacHeath?"

"Yes"

"You've got a medical. Come with us."

It's about a ten minute walk. The officers bracket him, one behind and the other on his heels. They are silent, and wear expressions that don't encourage conversation. MacHeath keeps his head down. He's confused. He's not sick. His lawyer hasn't mentioned any psychiatrist or psychologist. It hasn't come up in their meetings, and he'd have been against the idea anyway. He's not guilty, not guilty but too crazy to be responsible. As far as he's concerned, things haven't reached that level of desperation yet. They cross a hub from C wing to the healthcare unit. There's no change in the décor. It may be called the hospital wing, but it shares the same green peeling walls. Nothing is bright white or shining, although a blanket of antiseptic has begun to fight a losing battle with the aromas of excrement and armpits as they march. They stop at a door. It isn't the standard half in half of metal and reinforced glass. It's wooden, an office or a storeroom, and looks as commonplace as it is out of place in the prison.

Lucy Yale doesn't look up as the three men enter. She appears engrossed in the file that is spread out on the desk. The two prison officers stand not quite to attention. Their hands are behind their backs, but their chins are up and they stare at a point somewhere north of the woman's head. It is easy to stare at someone who isn't looking at you, and Germaine MacHeath takes this advantage. It's hard to get a proper impression of her face. It's half hidden behind the paperwork she's studying and the light from the window behind her turns her into a hunched silhouette. She looks young, or at least she's slight. Long hair. Either white or light skinned mixed race. Her fingernails are well cared for and bright red.

Silence hangs, and there are better things for a prison officer to do than wait for some civilian to tell them their business. The taller of the two coughs.

"Prisoner E3223 MacHeath, Germaine for counseling appointment, miss."

She nods, puts the paper down and looks up. No smile. Nods her head.

"Thank you."

The taller officer executes an about turn that owes more to a well loved DVD of Full Metal Jacket than to basic training. She takes a few seconds before pointing to a chair and telling MacHeath to pull it over and sit. Although her expression remains impassive, MacHeath notices the slight roll of her eyes at the officers' departing backs.

"Mr MacHeath, my name is Lucy Yale. I'm a counselor. My job here is to help you process your feelings about the recent incident involving your cellmate. Can we start with a few personal details?

She ticks a form as he gives her his name; his date of birth and confirms that he was born in London. He can see her face now. She's dark. She could be Italian or Spanish. Quite good looking. Her mouth is slightly pursed as she concentrates, but he can see that she has full lips and that her mouth is unusually wide. She has thick eyebrows. Not part of his ideal woman template. She's young, but not that much younger than him. Late or mid twenties, he thinks. Nobody he'd pick out of a crowd, and certainly not someone suitable to be seen with. Pretty, but average pretty. He wonders whether this might explain why she looks vaguely familiar. She puts her pen down and looks at him.

"I'm going to ask you some questions about how you feel at the moment. It's in your interests to answer me honestly. I can't help you if you try to fake it one way or the other."

He nods. Not enthusiastically, but with what he hopes is depressed resignation.

"Yes Miss."

"It's a multiple choice. I need you to answer whether you strongly agree, agree, disagree or strongly disagree. Do you understand?"

A pause. Germaine MacHeath sighs then answers.

"Yes Miss."

"Do you feel tired all the time?"

He thinks about night in prison. The shouting. The ever present strip light.

"Strongly agree, Miss."

"Do you have problems concentrating?"

"Agree, Miss"

More questions. He notices that the same information is asked for in a number of different ways. Does he feel worthless? Nine questions later, does he feel like a failure? Strongly agree to both, naturally. He wonders whether this is an attempt to trip him up, a rehearsal for the sort of questioning he is going to get at his trial.

Finally, the questionnaire is completed. He has strongly agreed or agreed to most things, but disagreed that he can't think about anyone else, in a number of different permutations. She puts the pen down and looks at him. She remains as neutral as magnolia paint and he has to stop himself asking whether he has passed. He is not sure whether to meet her eyes. It doesn't seem consistent with the feelings of worthlessness and despair he has been agreeing with, but there is something about her that he can't pin down. It's like meeting someone who has lived next door to you in the past, someone who you passed every day without speaking. The silence is uncomfortable, and he cannot help himself.

"Is that it?"

"Is what "it", Mr MacHeath?"

"That. Thirty questions, well, sixteen if you don't count the ones that were basically the same thing dressed up in a slightly different way. You know, am I feeling guilty then is my conscience bothering me. Are you really going to tell me that you can work out whether I'm going to top myself on the basis of something I could have downloaded?"

She stares at him, and he meets her eyes for the first time.

"As I said when we first met, my role is to help you deal with what happened with your cell mate, but I'm sure you've worked out that it isn't all this is about."

He shrugs.

"Why am I here, then?"

"Why don't you tell me? You've shown that you're a man who likes to show off his intelligence."

"I think that the point of this isn't to make sure I'm OK for me. It's to see whether I need to be watched to stop me joining that poor bastard in the Brixton Prison bungee jumping club hall of fame."

"Very astute, Mr MacHeath. So no, although the questionnaire is part of the assessment, I'm afraid it's not over yet. You told me that you strongly disagreed with the statement that you don't think about other people. I'd like to explore that. Do you mean that you think about people generally, or did you have particular people in mind?"

He thinks for a moment.   He hasn't lasted as a criminal without a good instinct for survival, and there is something inside him that is telling him that Miss Yale could be helpful to him.

"If you mean "do I worry about everyone?" then, no. Obviously. But there are people I worry about, that I think about and that I want to be happy and safe. Isn't that true for everyone?"

She makes a note.

"So who is it that you think about?"

"My mum. She's devastated that I'm in here. She hasn't been to visit me. My little brother and…"

He pauses, his voice a little choked.

"My girlfriend. At least I thought she was my girlfriend but she hasn't been up here."

His voice trails off. He notices that Lucy Yale has raised her eyebrows slightly and made another note.

"What? Don't you believe I've got a girlfriend?"

He thinks he sees her mouth twitch. It could have been his imagination.

"I don't get the impression that commitment is your thing, Mr MacHeath."

"What makes you say that?"

"You're twenty nine years old. You are in prison waiting trial for murder. You have no visitors other than your brother and your legal team. Your file says that you don't have children. That's the sort of profile that's very common in here, but relatively rare among people who aren't in prison at your age. Doesn't exactly suggest someone with a history of stable relationships."

He shrugs.

"Lots of people have kids and end up in here. Not having kids doesn't mean that you're a bad person, or that you hate women, or anything like that. And people can decide not to visit someone in a place like this because they don't like being pawed by a low rent pervert in a nylon shirt pretending that picking some young girl for an intimate search is random."
His voice rises and he checks himself. She doesn't flinch. Another note is made, calmly, following which she looks up at him. Full eye contact. He notices that her eyes are different shades of brown, with one dark and one almost hazel. It is both familiar and strange. He dredges his mind, briefly. Nothing. He counts three seconds of silence before she looks down and scribbles something on her pad. When she speaks, her voice is completely calm.

"But you aren't "lots of people", are you? You're accused of shooting a shopkeeper during a robbery at a high-end jeweler. Even here, that makes you fairly special, doesn't it?"

"I don't think I'm special. It's easy for someone with a good job and an education to look down on someone like me."

"Are you saying that you came up hard, Germaine MacHeath? I thought your mum was a nurse and she owned her own place in Brockley."

She bites off the last word but it is too late. She puts her head down and seems to write, but she cannot sustain the pretense. He sits motionless, staring at her. It is never silent in this human warehouse. There is a subdued roar of voices, indistinct but ever present that makes true quiet as impossible as freedom, but both are oblivious to this as they stare at each other. Her face is blank, a retreat into deliberate professional dispassion.

"How do I know you, Lucy?"

She flinches slightly at the informality. She rearranges the papers in front of her and sits straight, reestablishing boundaries that are long broken with the studied body language of the official. But the dam is down and it's impossible to will the water back again.

"How do I know you?"

"Don't you remember?"

He dredges his memory, forcing his way through clouds of half remembered girls. He'd always been popular. Right from when he was about fourteen and started to show an interest and possibly even before that. Lots of girls, but not many girlfriends. He's always preferred to play the field. She leans forward and stares at him with her mismatched eyes. He studies her face, taking in the shape of her mouth and chin, her skin tone and her hair, trying to imagine her younger.

"Albany Centre. It was a party for a boy called Stephan."

A party in a community centre? He hasn't been to one of those for over ten years. Since he was able to go to real parties. Two were when he was a proper little kid; jelly, ice cream and party bags at the door when he left, so probably not one of those unless she's properly insane and has been holding a grudge ever since he pushed her out of the way during pass the fucking parcel. The last one. He can hardly remember, other than it was a bad time for him. His last night before he had to go to Court for sentencing for jacking some boy's phone. He'd been smoking weed and drinking all day to hide the fact that he was terrified of going to jail. He's ended up at some girl's house, then bailed at three am, his electronic tag going berserk all the way home. That girl?

"That was years ago."

"Twelve years ago."

"Were you…?"

"You walked me home and stayed for a while. You were all over the place. Happy and laughing one minute then silent the next. I couldn't work you out. You never contacted me, and I couldn't find you afterwards."

"You found out about me, though. How else did you know that my mum is a nurse?"

"You told me that. Don't you remember? You were explaining to me that you weren't just some black guy from an estate who was always in trouble."

He frowns. He can't remember much about it, and he is beginning to find the fact that she can somewhere between flattering and disturbing.

"Actually that's exactly what I couldn't do. Find you, that is. I did try. None of my friends knew you, and the people they knew who did weren't talking. It was only when I read your name on the file and saw your photo that I knew that you hadn't given me a false name."

He leans forward, his elbows on his knees and his head down. He looks conflicted, but there's only one question on his mind; how this can help him? The air hangs dead. Finally he raises his head. He's still leaning forward, and he looks her in the eyes. His voice is deliberately low when he speaks.

"You've got my record on your file, yeah? Check the dates."

He doesn't give her time to find the document.

"It was the night before I went to court. I'd already had my trial and I'd been bailed by a judge who told me that I was going to go inside when I came back. I was seventeen and shitting myself. I was basically a middle class boy who made a mistake and I was expecting to get raped in the showers. I'm sorry if I came across like a twat. I was really drunk and I was probably acting street for practice, you know. And the reason you couldn't find me is I was inside. I wish you had, because I was crying out for someone to visit me once I got shipped out."

"Not your only sentence, though. You've been in and out of trouble for the last 12 years. It says so in here."

He smiles with a craftsman's ruefulness.

"I'm not saying that you're wrong. But jail is like money, isn't it? It's a lot easier to get more once you've got a bit in the first place."

"I know what you're going to say, and no. I'm not claiming that I've been set up or sent down every time. But whenever there's been a doubt I've never had the benefit, you know? And now I'm in here for murder, and I really am being fitted up."

She makes a noise that is somewhere in between a snort and a cough. It's not sympathetic.

"I thought the police found your fingerprints on the shop counter and bullets from the murder weapon at your house?"

"Listen, Lucy. I know that you've heard what the prison officers say. "Everyone in here is innocent" and shit like that. I'm not saying that it isn't half true, but you're an intelligent woman. You've read about the system in order to work in it. Are you really saying that everyone who's ever been accused of a crime is guilty? Did you miss all those Irish blokes being released in the 90's?"

"You're not comparing yourself with the Guildford Four? Seriously?"

Although she's reading from the cynical "everyone's guilty and I know because I work with these scumbags" script, her voice is low and she lacks conviction. Something has changed, and there is an advantage to him here. He can't put his finger on what it might be, but he can definitely sense it. He mirrors her pose.

"No, I'm not saying that I've never committed a crime. You've seen my record and I'll admit that I did all of those crimes if it makes you happier. You know your history, so what I am saying is that I'm in the same boat as the men who got put away for murdering that paperboy, Carl Bridgewater. They were proper bad men, armed robbers and burglars. They were the sort of people who would shoot a witness, but they didn't."

His voice is soft and he leans further forward as he speaks, his hand making a slow advance across Ikea pine.

"I didn't shoot that man. I'm not claiming I've never robbed a shop or carried a gun. I've done things that aren't on my record. What I'm saying is that I accidentally pissed off someone I shouldn't, and by the time I realised this, it was too late and I was in here. I shagged a policeman's daughter. Not just any fed, a detective inspector on the Flying Squad. I even went round and had lasagna and red wine with the family before I knew who he was, for fuck's sake. I bought her a ring at the shop. That's why my print is on the counter. I made the fatal mistake of getting above myself. Black men with previous like mine definitely shouldn't look at girls like her. It's uppity, and there's nothing that a high ranking cop likes less than an uppity nigger fucking his pure, white girl."

She flinches. He wonders whether it is the crudeness or the content. His hand is almost next to hers and he imagines that he can feel her body heat. Her voice cracks slightly as she replies.

"But surely your lawyer can speak to her. There must be CCTV that would show you in the shop with her."

He almost laughs, but manages to catch himself. Not the time to look like he's taking the piss.

"The police control the evidence. It's their job. It should work out like you say, only in my case it won't. The DI investigating my case is her dad. The officer who says he found the bullets at my mum's house. That's her dad as well. The one who arrested me when I was on my way to meet her for an Indian. Well, you can guess who that was. My lawyer can ask for CCTV. It won't happen. It'll have been lost, or erased by the shop, or never existed in the first place. I've written to her, but she hasn't replied. My brief hasn't been able to get hold of her. She lives at home. Maybe she doesn't want to get involved. Maybe that's her decision not her dad's. She's my only hope of not spending the next thirty five years in a place like this, and she's under the control of the same person who controls every other hope I've got."

He's panting slightly when he finishes. It's a good performance, one that is helped by having more than a kernel of truth to it. He is almost surprised to see that his hand now covers hers. She does not pull away.

"Does she have a name?"

"Who"

"Your girlfriend. The policeman's daughter. You've said a lot about her, but you have never said her name."

"Polly. And I'm not sure if she's actually my girlfriend. She hasn't written or come to see me. She won't take my lawyer's calls. Sometimes I even think that she must have set me up to be arrested. I mean, nobody but her knew I'd be going to the restaurant at that time. They could have followed me, I suppose, but it keeps crossing my mind. It's driving me crazy. I have to know. Have to speak to her face to face. I'm desperate, Lucy. My life is literally slipping away from me and I'm stuck in here."

He feels her fingers link with his with a general's joy. It's great when a plan comes together.

"I could try to see her."

"There's no point."

"That's just defeatist, Germaine. "

"It's not. It's realistic. She's not going to talk to you. The only chance I have is if I could talk to her myself. I really thought that we had a connection, you know. I've got to get out of here to do that."

"No chance of that, though. Maybe you should give me the chance to help."

His mind is racing. Calculating. It might be a mistake, but he has so little to lose it's worth it.

"Lucy, I'm going to get out. They're working on the wall by the exercise yard. There's a scaffolding tower. I could get over. I'm going to turn myself in when I speak to her. Once I can actually have a chance at my trial that hasn't been fucked over by her fucking fed father. If you want to help me, I need a car. I've got outside exercise in two days. "

She takes his hand and puts it firmly back on the desk.

"There's no need for the lover man routine, Germaine. This won't cost you anything but money. Ten grand. You've got a social visit tomorrow. Sort it out then. You know ginger Mick?"

He nods. White boy. Part of the crew for the first robbery. Trustworthy, but obviously a man who keeps some very valuable cards close to his chest.

"Money to Mick, and there'll be a car waiting for you."

"What do you drive?"

She giggles.

"Me, I drive a Lexus. You won't be. I'll sort out something a little more modest."

There is a knock and the door opens. The two prison officers march back in at the double. They take up positions behind his chair. He gets to his feet, and as he does so she hands him a pamphlet. He glances at it. It is something about depression. He puts it into his back pocket. Later, when the sheer boredom of twenty three hour lock up causes him to need some diversion, he glances at it. Inside is a note. "Black Honda Accord. L728HYM Rosebery Road." He smiles to himself, takes the note and shreds it neatly.

Chapter 25

Ken McGuiness walks through Lewisham Market towards the police station. He has a paper bag in his right hand. The grease from his sausage roll has seeped through, making the paper almost see through. The pavement is busy, and he dodges into the gutter from time to time to avoid the few pedestrians too elderly or laden with shopping to get out of his way.

It's been a slow morning. He's read the statements that Welbourne took from Heather Buchan's flatmates, and he's none the wiser. He's reviewed the Jane Canavan file, and other than the twenty minutes he had to spend suppressing his horrors once he found out what "vagophilia" actually meant, it's been a waste of time. It's good to get out and feel the wind from passing busses on his face and the pavement under his feet. He was going to visit Maxine and the baby this afternoon. He'd even marked this in the diary, but he's decided that he'll go later. There is some CCTV of the Strand and Lincolns Inn Fields he wants to review, and it seems easier to get it out of the way first.

He leaves the lift and walks through the incident room. There's nobody about, which suits him, as he needs the limited quiet and solitude that an empty office brings to concentrate on what might amount to two hours worth of traffic and random passers by. He will eat his sausage roll at his desk, do what he has to do and be out of there by four at the latest. Should be at Kings by five. The blinds are down on the glass window in his office door. It disturbs him slightly. He cannot remember doing this, but he reassures himself that this might be because he is running a double murder enquiry while his wife and child are hospitalised.

He has his coat in one hand and his lunch in his teeth as he opens the door. There, crouched behind his desk with her hands in an open draw is Kath Stevens. It takes him a second to acknowledge what he is seeing. In this moment he is frozen. His mouth opens. He notices that she is wearing blue latex gloves. Her eyes are wide enough for there to be a complete frame of white around the iris. The sound of sausage roll hitting nylon carpet is deafening.

"Kath. What the fuck?"

He cannot complete the sentence. She stands, her arms crossed, hiding her gloves under her armpits and she hugs herself tightly as if she is trying to fold herself into nothing and disappear. She is completely still, and she reddens, the blood rising from her throat to her hairline like a theatre curtain.

"Are you searching my office?"

Her eyes begin to moisten and she starts to quiver. She opens her mouth, but says nothing.

"Sergeant, unless you are prepared to tell me exactly what's going on I'm going to arrest you and march you down to custody in fucking handcuffs."

She sinks back to the floor, head down and fetal, her shoulders shaking. He is sorry for her for a second, before he catches the wave of anger again and takes the three steps across the office at speed. He pulls her to her feet. They stand, his hands on both her upper arms like a lover. Her body is almost limp. He masters himself enough to stop himself shouting at her and uses a softer tone. He is aware that he sounds reasonable. Like a policeman talking to a volatile suspect not a colleague.

"What are you looking for?"

"A datastick"

Very. Sharp. Focus. Every blemish on her face. The line at which her makeup stops just above her jaw.

"What? Why?"

"I don't know what's on it. I had to look for it."

"Who told you to find it?"

"Complaints. A DC called Milne. He met me at court the other day."

"And you just went "OK DC Milne from Complaints. I'll just treat my superior officer I've worked with for five years like a fucking suspect because you asked so nicely" Did you? Fuck's sake, Kath, that's some commendable loyalty there."

She is weeping silently now, her body shaking and her face streaked with makeup and tears.

"I fucked up guv. It was the cash from the Docklands flat. I had a shitty day, a meeting with Beth's school before I came to work. I didn't have the money for the fees. They were going to kick her out, sneering at me and at her. I'd have to send her to Sedgehill. You know, the one where all the kids we lifted for the gang fight in the park where that kid was stabbed to death went. I couldn't see any way out. It's not like I have family who could help me out or anything. My Dad's dead and Mum is just a pensioner. There was so much money and I took just enough to sort out Beth's fees. I don't know what made me do it. I'm not trying to blame anyone else. I knew, know it's wrong. I even thought about putting it back, but by the time the money was in my bag and I was driving home it was too late. I'd fixed the search book. I'd fucked up and fucked myself. I spent weeks worrying about when it was all going to come on top, then I got the call to court."

"So did the defence bring this up, then?"

"That's the thing, guv. I went to court and waited outside like the notice said. It got to lunchtime and Milne came out of court. He asked me to go for a coffee with him. I told him to piss off at first. I thought he was trying to pull me, actually. Then he told me he was from Complaints. I almost wet myself there and then. I went to the café with him and he told me that I could make this all go away. Keep my job. Not go to court or to prison. Even keep the fucking money. All I had to do was find this datastick you had."

"But for god's sake. You could have told me. Asked for my help."

She looks at him, head on one side.

"I tried. In the car on the way to the Peckham Rye scene. You were so, I don't know, professional. Remote, I suppose. You gave me some management speak about only being there to present the evidence. You've never been exactly one of the lads, have you? When you said that I thought that if I told you what I was going through you'd nick me. This was before Milne spoke to me at court."

McGuiness flinches. He can vaguely remember the conversation, and his discarding what she was saying as her having an attack of the vapours about going to court. He is embarrassed by the memory of tuning her out and thinking about how he could square work and Maxine so he could get away to see Sarah. The realisation that this might not have been his finest hour sends him off balance, and he turns, shakes his head emphatically and paces. What would he have done if she had told him? Helped her fix the evidence so she could put the money back? Helped her get away with keeping the money. It's unthinkable. He'd have fucked his career, and probably joined her in the dock for good measure after she'd fucked it all up by leaving an audit trail of unexplained cash all the way to whatever hothouse her precious little snowflake who was too good for the local sink school went to. Shopped her himself? He reckons that this is more likely, although nobody likes someone who turns on their own, and Kath Stevens was on his team. Probably given her time to turn herself in. Wouldn't have changed anything, apart from not having someone he thought he could trust searching his office when he nipped out to the bakery. It's all about trust, and she's just shown them both that they haven't got any. The anger is back, righteous and roaring. He stands by the office door.

"Fuck off, Kath. I'll decide what I'm going to do and let you know when I'm good and ready. If you get to keep your job, if you get to stay out of prison, I can't work with you any more. I want your request for transfer on my desk when I'm back in tomorrow morning."

He starts to gather up his work. He will take it home after he has been to the hospital and deal with it there. The room is stifling. His hands feel slippery and he fumbles the CCTV discs into the file, almost dropping them and being infuriated by his own cack handedness. She is loitering by the door, waiting for him to leave.

"Guv"

He cuts her off.

"I have no fucking time for this. I actually have places to go and work to do, but even if I was on my way to have a fucking sauna, I wouldn't have time for a chat with you."

He puts the file under his arm and walks out of the office. As he crosses the incident room he turns. She is still standing by the door, stooped and skinny, like a child whose parents have forgotten to collect her from school.

"Oh, and sergeant."

She looks up.

"You can tell your mate Milne that he can fuck off as well. There is no fucking data stick. I haven't got what you were looking for."

He sits in his car hyperventilating until he is calm enough to drive.
The journey from work to the hospital has become a dismal pilgrimage. Each step and its attached emotion are repeated every day, and Ken McGuiness cannot bring himself to imagine a time in which it ends. The first bite of fear hits the back of his throat as he pulls into the car park like acid reflux. He looks around furtively before getting out of his car. The coast is clear. No traffic wardens roam waiting to convert an already disturbing day into a public shaming. From the car park he crosses a pedestrianised road into the main building. He buys two coffees from the concession. The lift goes to the seventh floor. He's relieved it's empty, as he's going to the sad girls' ward, and he does not enjoy the miserable company of those whose story is as depressing as his own.

The ward is in chaos. It always is. It is where the hospital houses women who are damaged by their pregnancy, and cannot go home because they, their babies or a combination of both are too sick. It also houses the damaged who happen to be pregnant while Social Services sort out the paperwork and ask the judge for permission to take the baby away. It's a combination he tries not to find incendiary, but Jesus, it is hard. Maxine is in a private room, off a corridor that runs along the ward. He tries not to look through the glass panels into the ward itself. The high wailing of a baby cuts through his attempts to ignore it like a drill. The infant is alone in a Perspex crib next to an empty bed decorated with partially deflated balloons. He begins to speculate involuntarily about whether the child's mother is down the pub, buying drugs or just nipped out to the toilet. It's easy to go down the road of resenting the unfairness of a world in which his child is confined to the Special Care Unit, while the feckless leave theirs to cry themselves to a fitful and solitary sleep. He knows this doesn't help. He doesn't want some crack head's daughter; he wants his daughter to be well and to come home. All this will do is piss him off and make sure that he argues with Maxine, who is a firm believer that his daughter can pick up negative emotions through the walls of her incubator.

She's not there, and he takes the lift back down along with an African man who clutches a cloth rabbit in both hands and avoids his eyes. The Special Care Unit smells of alcoholic hand cleaner and polish. His daughter is in a side room, one of six cots. It's closest to the window. The cot is empty, and there is a moment of frozen panic until he takes in the fact that Maxine is sitting in an armchair with the baby in her arms. It's not a true release. She's still wired up to the machinery that surrounds the cot, but it's progress.

"Can I hold her, love?"

She passes him the child without a word. He stands with his daughter clutched against his chest. He can feel her heart beat against his forearm. It is strong and regular. After a while he feels his wife's arm around his hips. They hold each other in silent relief as the sun ambles towards the horizon. Finally, a nurse tells him that he should put her back in the cot.

"We'll have to think of a name for her, Ken. And register the birth. The doctors told me that she could be out of here in a few days."

He swallows. He hadn't thought about a future after hospital. Visiting Max and the baby has been an oasis for him, and he finds himself wishing that nothing would change. There is a lot for him to sort out before he will feel comfortable about them both being somewhere less public. He puts on what he hopes is an enthusiastic face.

"Let's not be hasty. She's not even out of the incubator yet. You're right about naming her, though, and registering her. Have you thought of anything?"

They talk, but cannot agree until it is time for him to leave. He walks away leaving his wife and daughter safe from others in this fortress of white and brightness. They are free from all the harm of the outside world under the blank eyes of the CCTV.

It's about 6 o'clock and he's hungry. There's nothing at home but an empty fridge, and a takeaway doesn't appeal. He collects a slip from the ward manager and makes his way to the canteen. The place is busy. It's obviously some kind of shift change, and he looks around the press of surgical scrubs and white coats for a place to sit and eat. There, alone at a table in the corner, is the priest. McGuiness makes his way towards him.

"Do you mind if I sit down, Father?"

Father Anthony Mitchell pauses; his fork loaded with meat pie and chips half way between mouth and plate. He looks up. There are bags under the priest's eyes that hang over his cheekbones like storm clouds. The muscles in his face shake slightly, as if his welcoming smile comes at the cost of a huge physical effort.

"Of course, Chief Inspector. Are you here in your professional capacity or are you checking on our friend behind the counter to make sure she's not defrauding innocent customers?"

"Neither."

McGuiness considers telling him about Maxine and the baby. It's qualified good news today, and may not come across as an appeal for sympathy.

"I've a couple of family members in here."

"Ah, I'm sorry to hear that. I hope they're both on the mend. Are you on your way to visit them?"

"No. I'm on my way home to a stack of work, unfortunately. Are you here because the portions have improved?"

"Sadly not, although I am happy that they have. I have a parishioner to visit. They're quite an awkward character, so I thought that it would be prudent to fortify myself with some pie and chips before going up."

They eat in silence as McGuiness' mind shifts out of the world of antiseptic sprays and family back into that of work. He remembers reading something about the soup run Heather Buchan helped out on being linked to a church. Maybe Anthony Mitchell could help track this down. Worth asking, anyway, seeing as he was here.

"Father, perhaps you can help me with something?"

"I'll do my best."

"It's to do with a case I'm working on. Where's your parish, exactly? I'm embarrassed to admit that I lost the card that you gave me when we last ran into each other."

"I expect you had other things on your mind. It's St Stevens'. In Rotherhithe."

The witness hadn't been clear about the name of the church, but it was in the same area. Catholic, too.

"Is one of your parishioners a young woman called Heather Buchan? I'm afraid that I don't have a photo with me, but she's about 5'6". Strawberry blonde hair."

"I'm sorry Inspector, but I've only been in the parish for a few weeks. I haven't managed to commit the names of all my flock to memory quite yet."

McGuiness remembers the various priests who had been at his local church during his childhood. They had known everybody's names, and who was related to whom as well. It was part of the job.

"I have to say I'm surprised by that, Father. I mean, every parish priest I've known has seemed to know everybody from day one. Don't you have some kind of induction?"

Father Anthony sighs. It's always embarrassing to have to admit this, although he cannot help but be relieved that the policeman appears to be unaware of his, and he hates the word, fame.

"I don't have the greatest of memories, unfortunately. I had a very bad accident when I was a young man, and there are whole parts of my life that have stayed lost to me. I still have problems. I'm afraid I can get a bit confused at times."

McGuiness forks some chips, coats them liberally in brown sauce and considers as he chews. It's disappointing, if he was naïve enough to expect the first question to be answered with a positive ID and an account of a loner with a serious obsession with Heather Buchan. Things are never that easy.

"Where were you before St Stevens'? Were you in London?"

The priest smiles, slow and sad as a cortege.

"No Inspector. I came back to Britain very recently. I was in the DRC for many years."

"DRC?"

"Congo. A beautiful country."

"Wasn't, I mean, isn't there a civil war?"

"There is. A terrible, brutal conflict. But even among all the murder and horror there were people of great courage and nobility who tried to do good. I was lucky enough to work along side some of them."

"What brought you back here?"

"I suppose you could call it burn out. There was so much ugliness that I began to feel it corrupting me. It's not very fashionable to put it this way, but I started to think that my soul was becoming tainted by the violence, and that there was nothing that I or anyone else could do to stop it. Despair is a mortal sin, and it became a very stark choice between losing my faith or trying to fight on while my reasons for fighting were crumbling at the foundations."

The priest sighs, puts his knife and fork together and pushes himself back from the table.

"Now if you would excuse me Inspector, I have someone I need to visit before visiting hours end."

They stand. Father Anthony Mitchell extends a hand, and they shake.

"Just one last question, Father."

"I haven't heard that one since Colombo was on the telly."

McGuiness gives a half smile.

"He was a fine detective. They made us watch it at Hendon, you know. Which church locally does a soup run?"

"Oh we all do. Us, the Church of England. Even the local mosque occasionally weighs in the odd volunteer and can of Campbell's cream of mushroom."

"Do you set up at any particular place?"

"I haven't had the chance to join the volunteers yet, but I think that they go wherever they are needed. Central London has a particularly large population of homeless people at the moment, so it's usually up town. There's a regular pitch in Lincolns Inn Fields, though. They go every Saturday."

Chapter 26

The ward is quiet. It's dark now, and the overhead lighting has been dimmed. Relatives and friends cluster in pools of bedside lamplight, heads and conversation lowered. Father Anthony Mitchell makes his way to the nurses' station, but finds it deserted.

The ward is t-shaped, with a central corridor leading into two side wards where the afflicted are housed. There are a couple of small, private rooms on either side. He waits, tapping his foot and wondering whether he should try to attract someone's attention. It would be humiliating to come across as too demanding. As if his calling could compete with the tasks of the nurses and doctors who occasionally flit between the rooms at the top of the corridor. He checks his watch. It's quarter to seven. Visiting hours end at eight, and he really has to see Mrs Stone before then. He pauses, wondering whether he has to sign in before going further, then decides that this is a barrier he can ignore. He starts to walk up the ward. He finds Mrs Stone in the left hand ward and takes a seat beside her bed. She's asleep. He introduces himself to one of the nurses and clasps his hands. He's not actually at prayer, more considering what he will say when she wakes up and contemplating the events of the day.

"Father"

He looks up to see the nurse.

"I'm sorry to interrupt you, but your brother is on the phone. I told him you were busy, but he's very insistent that he talks to you."

It's an obvious mistake. There had been some talk about a young Franciscan coming to help him with his parochial duties as he finds his feet. Brother Michael Xavier. It must be him. No doubt he found out about the hospital visit from the diary. He must be keen. He wasn't expected for another couple of days. Father Anthony Mitchell thanks the nurse without correcting her and walks back to the nurses' station. It is still deserted. There is a receiver lying on the desk among the charts and files. He picks it up and holds it to his ear.

"Is that you, Father?"

"Yes. How can I help you?"

The man at the end of the line inhales and exhales, a bronchial drum rolling inside his chest.

"I want to unburden myself, Father."

The voice is familiar, and father Anthony remembers a smell of damp rot and ingrained tobacco. His face is suddenly hot, and the underwater thud of his pulse beats a strong, accelerating time in his temples. A white arc of pain forks across his forehead. He presses the bridge of his nose between his fingers. It is a partial relief.

"Who is this? Is that you, brother Michael?"

"Yes Father. It's your brother."

Father Anthony tries to speak, but finds that his throat is constricted and he can do nothing but grunt. He leans heavily against the counter. He is finding it increasingly hard to breathe. He slumps sideways into a waiting swivel chair. Darkness builds in the periphery of his vision, red embers glowing behind the wave of shadow. He is back in hell.

"I hadn't seen much of him for a while. It was a good thing, really. We were both living in her house, separate lives under the same roof, and I was still on the mini cabs. I got myself a better car. The Grenada wasn't reliable enough for the mileage, see. A silver Astra. New shape, well, new shape then anyway. Same as CID used to drive at the time.

Anyway, I was sitting in the kitchen having a fag and a cup of tea when in he came, whistling some tune that was always on the radio back then. I can still remember it, well, the chorus at least. "The only way is up for you and me" it went. He stands in the doorway, leaning against the frame and says to me,

"That's a nice new car you've got there. Fancy going for a drive?"

I didn't necessarily want to go out. I had a day off work and I was going to spend it watching the TV and maybe go to the local later, but he always managed to knock me off balance. It wasn't anything he did or said, necessarily, although he had done and said a good deal of things that would have knocked Mohammed Ali off his stride. There was something about the way he stood there looking at me, his half smile on his face and his eyes like patches of empty sky that made me feel like someone had walked over my grave, so I docked my fag, picked up my coat and out we went.

I started driving into the centre, and we cruised about for a bit. He was quiet on the way there, looking around and smiling and playing with the stereo. It was cassettes then, and he settled on Pink Floyd's "The Wall". We listened to that for a bit. I didn't object. It was my tape and my music, but when we got to the centre, he put on the radio and it was that bloody "Only Way is Up" song. He started drumming on the dashboard and singing along, but he only knew the chorus. So he's singing it again and again and it's getting on my nerves. I was glad when it ended and there was a bit of peace and quiet.

It was half five on a Friday afternoon and all the offices were kicking out. The streets were filled with secretaries, and he started playing the "would you?" game. There were lots of girls. Some were pretty. Others not so much. I was happy to go along with him. It seemed a normal thing, two brothers driving and chatting about girls in the sun. Nothing to worry about. I even started to take the mickey a bit. There was a girl waiting at a bus stop. She was tall, with dark hair and a bit of a Lady Di cut. She was wearing a green dress and bright red lipstick. Stunning. Like a model. He says to me, "I'd do her." I said to him that chance would be a fine thing. He didn't have any money and is clothes looked like he'd slept in them for a fortnight, so what would a girl who looked like she could have come off the cover of a magazine want with the likes of him? He laughs, and tells me that I'd be surprised. Shocked, more likely,

It was getting dark, and we got a burger from some greasy hole in Stokes Croft then parked up. He built a spliff and we smoked it. He had some vodka, too, but I didn't touch it. Not that I had any problem with drinking, or drink driving really, but I couldn't afford to lose my license. The hash was good. Not the usual soapy shit that was about back then, and I was feeling it when I started driving again. He put on some reggae, and I could feel the bass through the seats like a heartbeat. It made me nod my head and smile, and when I did he asked me what I was happy about.

"Nothing."

I told him. Nothing and everything. He says to me that it's good. How it should be, with two brothers spending time together. At this point we'd driven through Saint Pauls. There were drug dealers and whores out on the City Road. I pointed to one girl, and said to him that I betted that he could get her provided he had fifty quid in his pocket. He went all serious and said some people never have to pay; he was one of them and I shouldn't forget it. I laughed and told him I've never had to pay for diamonds and caviar either.

There's a roundabout at the bottom of St Pauls, and instead of going straight on to the motorway, I turned left. The street was dark. There were a couple of streetlights but there were patches between them that were proper ink. There were houses on both sides, with little front gardens and hedges, so even if there was any light from the windows, it never made it as far as the pavement. I slowed down so I could steer with my knees and roll a fag. There was nobody about and no other traffic when I saw her. She was sitting on a wall under one of the lampposts. She wasn't what you could call a stunner. She was short, and a bit on the skinny side. I didn't think that she was working, because she was dressed more like a punk than a brass, with ripped black tights and a red tartan miniskirt. Her hair was dreadlocks, like all the crusties had back then. I didn't like the look on a white girl, but even I though this one caught your attention, and I wondered what she was doing sitting on the wall all on her own doing nothing on a Friday night. I turned to him, and I said to him,

"How about her, then, Casanova? Do you reckon you could pull her?"

"Tenner says I could get her in the car."

I laughed, and he laughed too. I stopped the car and he got out. I was still laughing, and looking forward to seeing him sent away with his tail between his legs or, even better, get a slap round the face. He walked up to her and she stood up. She didn't back away or look frightened. I expect he was smiling, or saying something stupid, but I couldn't hear anything and his back was to me. He didn't even break step, just punched her in the face full force. She started to fall but he caught her by her hair and held her half up then punched her again twice. She went limp and he dragged her to the car like a kid with a toy. She wasn't moving. I froze. My hands were on the wheel and my mouth must have been open. I couldn't believe what he'd done. It was about 8 o'clock on a Friday in the middle of Bristol. I was waiting for someone to start screaming, or for the blue lights to go on behind us and for us to be arrested. He shoved her into the back and got in beside her. Drive, he said. Just fucking drive now. I should have told him to dump her, or to get out, or anything, but I put my foot on the floor and we were off to god knows where with a girl lying on the floor behind me and him breathing like he'd just done the hundred yard dash.

He told me to go to the lock up. I hadn't been there since the last time I told you about, Father, and I knew that it was bad news. I should have told him no, or even driven him and the poor girl to the police station. I could have got out of the car and left them to it, but I didn't. I could see her legs between the seats in my mirror, and I was getting a little bit turned on, even though she was out for the count. I thought that I couldn't turn him in. The last time sorted that out. Although I didn't kill that one, he'd probably say different then it was my word against his and we both know how that ends up. Both of us going down and me spending the rest of my life in some prison cell, and I wasn't innocent exactly, even if I hadn't done the murder. Whatever was going to happen was going to happen and there was no point in acting the hero.

The drive took about an hour, and all the time I was waiting to get pulled over. I stuck the taximeter on, and I suppose it must have looked like I was working and he was a customer, because nobody gave us a second glance. I parked up outside and he pulls her out of the back and caries her in like Dracula. He must have had the devil on his side because there wasn't a soul about. He dumped her on the floor and set about lighting candles and making tea.

"Go on. You can go first"

He said. So I did. She came round as I was getting her clothes off. He'd lit so many candles by then that the place looked like Halloween, and I was sure she got a good look at me because she stared at me and said one word, please. She sort of whispered it, so I hit her and she went out again. I don't usually like them to just lie there. I'm not a necrophiliac, but I was a bit freaked out. I started to imagine her looking at me through a two-way mirror or across a court, staring with her eyes wide open and her little voice whispering, "that's the one." I couldn't put it out of my mind enough to concentrate on the job in hand and I went all floppy. Had to roll off and pass her over to him. So there I was, sitting on a concrete floor with my dick in my hand wondering whether it was worth it as he fucked her and she whispered to him to let her go when he'd finished and shushing him like he was a kid having a nightmare.

She was a brave one. He finished. He got off her and he was pulling up his trousers when she was up and running. She almost made it to the door. I didn't think twice. I didn't think at all, to be honest. I picked up a tin of beans. It was full and it felt as heavy as a cricket ball in my hand. I threw it when she stopped running to open the door. It hit her on the head and down she went. I was on her, and I found my hands round her throat and I was squeezing and squeezing as she was bucking and thrashing underneath me. The harder she bucked, the harder I go and the harder I squeezed until she flopped for the last time and I came in my pants, falling on top of her. I watched her eyes go out like candles, lying there in the half light as my spunk got cold and my hard on collapsed.

"Nice shot"

He said.

"You'd best fuck off and clean yourself up. I'll sort things out from here. Leave us your car keys."

So I did as I was told. I straightened my clothes, and walked home. He was whistling that fucking song as I went. "The only way is up. For you and me."

Father Anthony opens his mouth. The confession has reached a point at which some form of intervention seems appropriate, but he cannot form the words. His mouth is dry and his head is pounding. Pain rushes and ebbs in waves. The man makes a sound that is somewhere between a laugh and a gurgle.

"Can God forgive us, Father? Can he forgive anyone who was there?"

He can smell pine needles and aniseed. He feels the laminate floor cool against his cheek and is conscious that he has wet himself. His legs move in short steps, scrabbling against the air for a purchase that they cannot find as he tries to run from the falling dark.

The ward cleaner finds him. It is not clear how long he has lain there, but the nurse who makes the first attempt to wake him notices that the damp patch around his groin is cold. An alarm blares and he is put onto a stretcher. He is surrounded by powder blue and white and he is taken to a place of safety.

Chapter 27

Brixton Prison. The door rattles and Germaine MacHeath is out. One hour's association. Outdoor exercise. He nods to the screw and makes his way down the metal staircase. There's a group of men formed up and ready to go. He joins the line. The man next to him is rolling a cigarette. He's a big man, bigger than MacHeath. His skin has an ashy tone and the whites of his eyes are yellow. MacHeath recognises him as a crack head, a punter and robber from Deptford or Lewisham. Can't place his name, but it's lucky he's in a place where names don't matter.

"Got a spare one of those, bruv?"

The man looks at him. It's a long look, and it's only the fact that his eyes are slightly unfocussed that stops it being a challenge.

"Shanks. What are you doing in here?"

"Remand, bruv."

The man hand over a packet of tobacco.

"You remember me, Shanks. Pirate. From Milton Court."

MacHeath nods, vaguely recalling an issue about robbing drug couriers that had to be sorted out.

"I know you. What you here for?"

"Waiting allocation. I got a twelve a few months back. Robbery and GBH."

"What did you rob?"

"Taxi drivers. Stabbed a couple of them. "

It's a drugs thing. Maximum violence for minimum returns and nothing but a half way house and thirty quid grant from probation to show for it after twelve years of hard time. MacHeath forces a rueful expression and shakes his head.

"Twelve years for that, mate? Fucking hell."

"You know it. I'm an innocent man, too."

They laugh, and the other man hands him a packet of Rizzla. The line begins to move. Two airlock doors and a gate and they are outdoors. The yard is small. It takes about 10 minutes to walk around it slowly. Some of the men take off at a run. Fitness freaks who spend their days doing press ups in their cells and dreaming of the day they can get out and have all the girls admire their prison muscles. MacHeath starts to walk. He's not in a hurry. Pirate falls into step with him. They light cigarettes and walk in silence.

There are buildings on three sides of the yard. Two are obvious cellblocks. Barred windows and the odd plastic bag of what he assumes is shit on the ground underneath them. It's revolting, but he can't say he blames anyone for not wanting to spend twenty-three hours locked up with their own filth. The third looks like some kind of admin building. It has proper windows and no bars. The perimeter wall covers the fourth, twenty feet of Victorian slab. In the corner between the two is a scaffolding tower. MacHeath looks up. A quick flick of the eyes. There are two prison officers supervising, and he doesn't want to attract attention. It's good news. None of the workmen are on the tower, and he is sure that he can step from it onto the top of the wall. He mentally paces the distance between the circuit and the foot of the tower. About five, he reckons. It's tight, but doable if the officers stay where they are, about a hundred yards away.

MacHeath can feel his muscles tense. It takes an effort of will to stop himself rolling his shoulders and stretching like an athlete. He looks at the man next to him and decides that he's no threat. He's a robber and drug user. Not the sort who would think that a few privileges for helping stop an escape were worth the damage to his rep on the yard. It occurs to him that he's also someone with nothing to lose. Twelve years behind a door and no money stashed for when he comes out. Strong, too, and it's harder to chase two men running than one.

"Do you want to get out of here?"

The other man looks at him without blinking, and nods. By this point they have almost done the full circuit. MacHeath starts to drift slightly off the beaten track towards the scaffolding. The foot of the tower is no more than three paces away, and he nudges the other man with his elbow.

"Follow me."

He breaks into a run. He's always been fast, and he is on the ladder and climbing full pelt, his arms and legs rising and falling like pistons before Pirate has made it to the bottom rung. A shout goes up from the other side of the exercise yard.

"Stop there, you men."

He ignores it, head down and focused on going up. He can hear his companion's breathing behind him. It sounds like a fat dog on a hot day. The scaffolding rocks and echoes as he reaches the first landing. He hurls himself across and onto the second ladder. Frantic whistles erupt and there is the sound of boots on concrete. He does not look back. He's about two thirds of the way up now, and the first of the prison officers has started to climb behind him, his colleagues a following swarm, all throwing themselves up the ladders. The tower begins to sway, as MacHeath reaches the top. He looks towards the wall. He halts, teetering on the balls of his feet. It must have been an accident of perspective. A trick of light and shadow caused by having to judge the distance in furtive glances from the circuit. The wall is a good eight feet away at least. It's too far to jump.

Germaine MacHeath's eyes fly backwards and forwards. Leaning against the railing are two planks. He picks one up, and pushes it out towards the top of the wall. It reaches. Just. It felt broad and solid when it was in his hands, but it looks as narrow as a high wire, shivering and insubstantial over the drop. Pirate reaches the platform and stands beside him, his body bent forward and his hands on his knees.

"Wait until I'm across, bruv, or we'll both fall."

The other man nods, and looks nervously down the ladder. The pursuit has reached the landing below them. MacHeath puts one foot on the plank. His weight makes it rise, and the far end shift away from the wall's edge. There is no way he can do it.

"Hold the end."

His voice has an edge of panic.

"Hold the fucking end. I'll do it for you at the other side."

The other man stoops and grabs the end of the plank. Germaine MacHeath steps out over the void. He does not look down. He crosses with two strides. His momentum almost pitches him over the wall, and for a moment he stands, his arms windmilling, oscillating backwards and forwards as he fights vertigo and gravity to gain his balance. He can see the backs of the buildings on Brixton hill, and the moving branches of trees. The car park is below him, and there is no sign of a reception committee, at least for the moment. There is a high-sided white van among the parked cars. It's the width of the pavement from the wall, about twenty yards on his left. He inhales deeply. Behind him, his fellow escapee is shouting for him to hold the plank, his voice increasingly overwhelmed by the sound of officers shouting for them both to surrender and lie down. Germaine MacHeath doesn't look round. He takes the wall at a run, gaining speed until he is almost opposite the van. He jumps.

His vision distorts as he falls. It's less than a second before he hits the van roof with both feet, his knees bent like he's seen paratroopers do in the war films he'd watched as a child. The force of the fall pitches him forwards, and he sprawls on the corrugated roof with the wind knocked out of him. He staggers to his feet and rolls down the windscreen, hitting the ground and running at full tilt towards the back of the prison. It's less than a minute since he started his climb, and he is not chased at first. Officers emerge from the gatehouse and set off after him as he rounds the corner into a residential street.

He's bet everything on Lucy Yale leaving her car. It's the gamble of a desperate man, but he wasn't locked down or refused exercise, so it's looking hopeful. She hasn't grassed him up at least. Long shots pay off sometimes. Ask Lee Harvey Oswald. He pounds up the road, his legs and arms pumping like Hussein Bolt, crossing diagonally and sprinting up towards Rosebery Road. He can't hear any pursuit, but his lungs and the sound of his footfalls are deafening. He scans for a black Honda frantically, knowing that it's only a matter of minutes, seconds even, before the air will be filled with the sound of sirens and helicopters. It's there. He offers Lucy Yale a prayer of thanks as he slips into the driver's seat and sees that the keys are in the ignition. He starts the car and drives off, heading towards Clapham Common. He wants to cheer, salute the air with his clenched fist and scream with the release of it all as he drives. He allows himself a brief smile as he turns onto the main road, heading west. Attracting attention would be stupid. He's a black man driving a car that's registered to a white girl, and he knows that a lot of police cars have automatic number plate recognition fitted. Could be a problem, but at that moment he doubts it. He's been luckier than a rich man's kid, and he'll ride this winning streak as far as he can. Time to celebrate when he's back in Lewisham, safe in the safe house and ready to plan his next move.

Chapter 28

The house is comfortable enough. There's a TV, a PlayStation with a couple of games, which he supposes would pass the time if you were into that. Two bedrooms. One even has a bed, although he slept in a sleeping bag downstairs last night, if you could call it sleep. Every slam of a car door in the street, every crackle or rustle of the stunted trees in the back gardens was the start of the police raid he didn't expect to survive. Germaine MacHeath sits in a shabby armchair. The TV is on, but the sound is muted. His own picture appears regularly, captioned with "believed armed and dangerous", "prison escape" and "public should not approach." It's fame at last, he supposes, and like all celebrities his main problem is that he is afraid to go out in case he is recognised.

He takes stock. He needs money, a car and possibly a passport, although that depends on what happens when he got the item that is number one on his wish list, a phone. He needs to contact Polly. He doesn't know where he stands, and he runs the possibilities through his head again and again.

She might not want to have anything to do with him. He thinks about her passion, and the way she looked into his eyes when they were together, and the warmth of these memories is so powerful that he feels himself raised above his surroundings. He smiles. He can't help himself. It lasts about a minute before he is dragged back to reality, to the threadbare lino, the dust and the curtained windows that blocked out prying eyes and natural light.

She may not want to get involved in the case no matter what she feels for him. He's found that this is not unusual. Even his own mother had refused to give him an alibi in the past, although unlike then the evidence he wanted from Polly would be true. He's not wedded to hanging about in London and fighting to clear his name anyway. You'd have to be as wet behind the ears and needy as a rescue puppy to put your faith in the system. That, or have the sort of life he'd hoped for when this all started and he met the Turks with Omen. He didn't own property, didn't have investments and wasn't that worried about being remembered as a criminal. He suspects that even his mother and brother would be hard pushed to think of him in any other way. Forget the bullshit he'd given Lucy Yale about turning himself in. It had sounded good, and he's sure he'd looked particularly sincere. He's heard that a female had been arrested on the TV, and he assumes that has to be her. She's been remanded in as well. That almost shocked him. People like that always got bail, didn't they? She's probably waiting in a cell somewhere, expecting him to turn himself in and row her out of trouble. She's out of luck, and should have known that from the start. He can't shake a mild unease. She'd helped him out in a big way and he'd probably ruined her life. It's too bad. There's nothing he can do about it that doesn't put him back in the noose, and there's be no point in escaping in the first place if that was what he had in mind. He tells himself that she'll only do a couple of years if she gets a guilty, and she's young enough to start over. He's got bigger things to worry about. He's already 90% decided that he's leaving. He's got his share of the robberies, and that's a good quarter of a million. That's enough to build on somewhere new. The States, maybe, or perhaps South America. He's been to Belize on holiday, and it looked like the sort of place where money stopped unwelcome questions in their tracks. There was a lot of dodgy looking people there, British and Yanks as well as the locals. Big drugs and money, so he heard. Worth a thought, anyway.

The main thing was to speak to Polly. He hoped that she'd come with him. No, hope didn't really enter into it. He knew that once he could speak to her, hold her and she felt the bond between them, she'd come. Even if she turned him down, he had to know. She was a thread that would pull him back to London and back into danger unless he saw her.

When he thinks it through, that's it. He needs a passport, a car and money. And a gun. He's not scared of prison. It's not as if he's never done time before, but he could feel the weight of thirty five years pressing in on him, the smell of cabbage, sweat and shit, the shouts and fights and the despair that seeped into every part of him like damp. He's not going back. Not to that. He'd rather die. Go out in a blaze of gangster glory. He needs to make contact. It's hard to reach out with no means of communicating. The people who know him, who he can trust not to turn him in for a reward or a favour, know about this place. It's too risky to go out, so he has to wait, hoping that someone will come.

Jumping at shadows and sudden noises like some terrified teenager in a horror film.

The knock comes in the evening. Three sharp raps and a slow one. MacHeath is on his way to the door when he stops. This is their chance to grab him off guard, gratefully opening the door to the armed police. He makes his way to the back of the house. The windows are filthy, covered in a thin film of grease and grime that turns the back garden sepia tone. It's not quite dark yet, and he strains his eyes, looking across the patchwork of garden fences and hedges, checking for a tell tale movement that would mean that the house was surrounded front and back. Nothing. He tells himself that this doesn't mean he's in the clear and arms himself with a kitchen knife. Not much good against a gun in the hands of a man licensed to use it, but it makes him feel slightly more secure. It could buy him a bit of space and time. Maybe.

He opens the door a crack. Standing on the second step is a figure in baggy motorcycle waterproofs and crash helmet. It is impossible to tell if it's male or female, let alone what he or she might look like. It nods at him and shrugs. He stands aside and follows into the living room. They stand facing each other.

"You Shanks?"

The voice is high pitched. It has a slight breathiness."

"Take the lid off."

The helmet is removed. Long braids frame a clear skinned face. Dark skinned and with large, white teeth. She doesn't look over fifteen.

"I'm Lissie. Alicia. Sugar's cousin."

"Where is he?"

"He can't make it. He's got feds all over him. Thought you wouldn't be too happy if he lead them straight to your door."

It made sense. Sugar was a good soldier. Loyal and intelligent. She takes her rucksack off and rummages inside, removing three white boxes.

"He says to give you these. They're pay as you go. They've got a couple of numbers programmed in already. He says not to use them here. They can track any calls and they'll come for you if they do. There's some walking around money too. For cigarettes, food and stuff. There's clothes in there too. I checked and it's all proper. Named gear, you know. Nothing off the market."

She hands the boxes, and an envelope over. He checks the cash. It feels like about two grand. Helpful, but he'll need a lot more if Belize is going to happen.

"So what am I supposed to do with them? I can hardly go for a wander, can I?"

"That's what the bike's for."

She takes off the waterproofs. It's like watching a Russian doll disassemble itself. She is tiny, slim and drowned by the clothes. She lays them on the sofa.

"He says to tell you that it's registered to a bloke called Solomon Olumbi. It's taxed, insured, tested and 100% not stolen, so you ain't going to get pulled over for some lame bullshit traffic beef. Clothes and lid should fit you."

She grins.

"I could practically spin that around while I was wearing it. You got a big head, mate. The bike's parked up outside. It's a blue and black Aprilla. Just 50cc but it goes like fuck. That's why I took it here. No chance of any car following through the traffic."

"So do I call Sugar?"

"No. His number's on one of the phones, but he says not to use it unless you have to. There were two CID cars parked outside his house this afternoon, and he don't see that ending anytime soon. Anything you want to say to him, say to me and I'll pass it on."

"I need a couple of things. Someone has to speak to my brother, Danny. I need a number from him. It's for Polly. He'll know who I mean. Also, tell Sugar I want my share of the money for the last two jobs. Either in cash or travellers cheques. And a book."

"What book?"

"A passport."

"OK. I'll tell him. Listen. I've got places to be, and just an Oyster Card to travel on, so I'm off. One of the numbers in the phones is mine. Call me if you want. I'll be round tomorrow anyway."

She slips out of the door before he has opened it fully, and is gone. Germaine MacHeath walks to the kitchen, opens a tin of baked beans and prepares for another evening in front of the TV. Things are moving on, and he is happy to be on his way somewhere, even if he's been reduced to the status of passenger.

He takes the bike out the following morning. The waterproofs fit him reasonably well, although they are a little tight around the crotch and armpits. The helmet is slightly too big, but will do. It's been a while since he's ridden. He's been a car driver since he was seventeen and old enough to drive something better than a moped. He drives up to Bromley, then back towards Dartford along suburban roads before coming back to the safe house through Welling and Woolwich. He enjoys it. The rush of air and the blur of the road under his wheels are a contrast to the three paces by two that have defined his life since his arrest. He passes three police cars there and back. None gives him a second glance.

She's waiting for him when he returns, sitting on the wall outside the house. She's dressed like a school kid, a white shirt, dark blue blazer and blue miniskirt. She's carrying a holdall slung across her shoulder. She watches him back the moped into the curb and stands up as he dismounts.

"All right, big man?"

He doesn't reply. He doesn't take his helmet off until they are both inside and the door is closed.   She puts the bag down and throws herself into an armchair.

"Got your money. Sugs says that he's going to need four photos but he can sort you out a book."

She reaches into her pocket and pulls out a crumpled piece of paper.

"I went and saw your brother at college. He is fit, boy. I could have stayed with him all day, but things to do. He went and spoke to some white girl and this is the number. Can't tell you if it's the one you want, though."

He takes the paper, folds it and puts it away. Just touching it makes his nerves twitch. He is light headed, like smoking a cigarette after quitting for a week.

"Listen, Lissie, I need one more thing. Ask Sugar to get me a gun."

She stares at him, big eyes and cigarette smoke.

"What do you need a gun for? Seriously. Who are you going to shoot in here?"

"That's not your problem, is it? Tell your cousin what I said."

She nods.

"I need a car. Nothing flash, but reliable. Ferry tickets, too. Not Dover or Portsmouth, they'll be well locked down. Somewhere low budget. Newhaven or something. Two days time."

"Laters. See you tomorrow."

She lets herself out. He counts the money when she's gone. It is just shy of two hundred thousand. Not all he's owed. He reckons that Sugar would tell him that sorting him out cost him, and that it was only fair. Couldn't argue with that, although seventy grand seemed a bit steep. It's what he would have done, and he's resigned. It even helps a bit. You don't have to be grateful to someone you're paying.

The next day he takes the bike to Dartford Heath. He parks in a car park that caters for the golf and dogging crowd. It is secluded and small, with a good view down the road in each direction. He checks carefully before taking off his crash helmet. There's nobody around. Birds are flying in and out of the tree line behind him, and every movement makes him flinch and double take. He sees everything with exaggerated clarity, hears every sound from the crack of a braking twig through to the roll of traffic on the dual carriageway. It is not this hyper awareness that makes his fingers shake as he types the number on the piece of paper into the phone.

Polly Peach is bored. She'd been frightened at first, when she heard that Germaine had escaped, but looking back on it this had been caused more by her father's total overreaction than by anything that she thought her former boyfriend might do to her. She hates it when her father says that he knows best, and more so when it is such obvious nonsense. She's sure that Germaine is long gone by now. He's been out of jail for two days, and he was so intelligent. Not in a passes exams way, admittedly, but he was someone who knew how the world worked. He'd really impressed her when he talked about making deals, making money and the ways that he'd avoided being ripped off. Surely Germaine would see the sense in getting the hell out of London? It seemed obvious to her. In his shoes, she'd have been on the first plane out and you wouldn't have seen her for dust. No way would she be looking for her ex. It would be flattering, though. Germaine loving her so much that he'd risk everything to see her. Like something out of a film.

She yawns. She's stretched out on the sofa in a pair of jogging bottoms and a sweatshirt. The TV is on in the background, but there's nothing to watch. She's seen Gilmour Girls before, and she chose it because its familiarity was comforting. She feels a bit on edge, although she can't explain why.

There are textbooks open all around her, but she hasn't given them a second look for days. The house is full of policemen, and studying is the only excuse that she could think of that lets her have bit of privacy. Not even her father could argue about her spending time on her precious education. She checks her phone. It's habit not necessity. She's not allowed to speak to any of her friends in case it interferes with the operation. She grimaces and imagines heavy air quotes as she thinks the word. It sounds unpleasant. Painful, even. The sort of thing that someone else did to you for your own good but you still had to sign a piece of paper saying that you were cool with it just in case it all went wrong. And she had. Signed her consent, that is. She regrets it now. She worries that two days without speaking to anyone has left her seriously out of the loop, and that's nowhere Polly Peach belongs.

She goes over the instructions her father gave her. Instructions? Fuck it. Orders. That's what they were. If he calls be pleased to hear from him. She has to admit that will be easy enough. The memory of the time they spent together in that hotel isn't one she wants to dwell on when there are three cops in her kitchen (four if you include her dad). She'd rather liked being a gangster's moll even if she hadn't exactly realised that was what she was at the time, and Germaine was good looking enough. He had a nice body, too, but that was only to be expected. Black guys worked out and showed their muscles more.

It had been exciting the first time the phone rang. It brought that cold liquid sense of fear and anticipation, only to let her down by being a salesman touting PPI recovery. She'd screamed at him to fuck off, then hung up. Her father hadn't been happy about her language. He saw it as her letting him down in front of the other police. As if she hadn't heard them chatting in the other room and swearing every other word. He was such a massive hypocrite, her dad, and a sexist, too. Like it would be a problem if she were a boy. Still, she'd kept her cool for the next couple of calls. Two of these had been from friends, and the other someone wanting her to take a consumer survey. She'd suggested blocking all numbers apart from Germaine's, but they'd told her that he was pretty unlikely to call her from the number she had, as that phone would be long gone. She'd blushed and sulked. There was really nothing worse than being patronised when you knew that you'd said something stupid.

The phone rings up a private number. Polly waits for the ruck from the kitchen before answering. She's calm.

"Hello"

"Polly?"

She mouths a frantic "it's him" as she points.

"Germaine?"

"Yes, it's me. Are you good to talk?"

"It's fine. Where are you? Are you OK?"

"I'm not far, Pol. I really need to see you."

"I've thought about nothing else since I heard. Can I come to you?"

"Not a good idea now. Let's meet tomorrow."

"OK. I'm in Brockley for a photo shoot. Some college thing. We could meet at 2?"

"Sounds good"

"Do you know the café in Hillyfields Park?"

"Top of the hill? Yes. I know it."

"See you then, lover."

The line is dead. Her father puts a hand on her shoulder and tells her he is proud. One of the other officers takes her phone, and all four of them disappear into the other room for the sort of furtive conversation that she is not allowed to overhear. The noise of feet fills the hallway, and then her father comes back. He is alone.

"OK Polly. I want to run through the procedure for tomorrow. You will wait for MacHeath outside the café on the top of the hill at Hillyfields Park from 1pm. There will be police officers watching you, so you'll be perfectly safe. All you need to do is get up when you see him, hold your arms out for a hug and say "Germane". We'll do the rest."

She has heard her father speak like this before, standing in the kitchen and speaking in that measured way into his mobile phone that let the other person know that he was in charge. You can't grow up as a copper's daughter and be totally insulated; however much he may have thought that nobody could hear him. The tension around her eyes retreats and she almost smiles, before tears begin to flow. Her father puts his arms around her.

"You're being very brave, love. It'll soon be over,"

Polly Peach sobs into his shoulder. She knows she can be brave, but it doesn't feel like courage. She doesn't want to think about it. She sniffs, breaks away from him and goes to make herself a cup of coffee.

Chapter 29

Germaine MacHeath opens the bin he has found at the edge of the car park. It has a heavy, self-closing lid and has been put there for the convenience of dog walkers who have been forced to tidy up after their pets. He takes out a bag and, holding it at arms length, drops in the mobile phone. He reties it and puts it back. He's sure that the call isn't going to make its way onto any policeman's radar, but there are other calls he'll have to make and he doesn't want to leave Polly's number in a place that will get her into trouble. He puts the crash helmet back on and rides home.

Lissie calls round in the late afternoon. She has another holdall. The shoebox inside is heavy, and he does not need to take the contents out in front of her to know that it's what he asked for.

"Someone will drop a car off tonight. You don't have to know who or when. It'll be parked outside."

She hands him a key

"Just click the alarm when you come out of the door and you're good. There are ferry tickets in the box. It's…"

She screws up her face as she tries to remember the unfamiliar names

"Newhaven to Dieppe."

She smiles as it comes to her, and for a moment she looks like a schoolgirl who has answered the question successfully.

"Oh, yeah. And I need to take your photo for the passport."

She produces a digital camera and a green sheet from the holdall.

"You have to get a kitchen chair. I've got to hang this in the doorway and take your photo in front of it, so it looks like a photo booth. The GPS is switched off, so it won't show where it was taken. Just in case."

As he submits to her organising, he realises that this is a symptom. Sugar is stepping up. Leading. The world is moving on around him and all he can do is sit in a safe house and wait to be helped. After she's done, she sprawls in an armchair and lights a spliff. She takes two pulls and passes it to him.

"Listen Lissie. I need you to do something for me. If I give you some cash, can you do some shopping for me?"

"Sure. I can go to the Co-op and pick you up some food if you want."

"It's more than that."

He counts out three thousand pounds.

"I need you to go and buy me a ring. Something nice, but not too ghetto. A diamond and gold."

"Nice. How big?"

"Come here."

She walks over and stands in front of him. He takes her hand, lacing his fingers through hers. He tries to remember how Polly's hand felt in his, its weight and how wide he had to span his fingers. The memory makes him smile. When he looks up, she is staring at him.

"If it fits you, then it's good."

He tries to take his hand away, but she holds it for a second. Her grip is fierce, and she smiles down at him.

"Do you want to go upstairs?"

He realises that he knows nothing about her. She looks young, but she could be any age between fifteen and twenty. It's been a while, and it might take his mind off jumping whenever anyone walks past the house.

'How old are you, Lissie?"

"Sixteen"

He's seeing Polly tomorrow, and he can't get her out of his head. Anyway she's a mate's cousin, and he can't afford to piss Sugar off.

"Thanks, Lissie, but I can't."

"Don't you like girls?"

"I'm not in the mood. There's things we both need to be doing."

She shrugs.

"Your loss. I'll be back in the morning."

He sleeps uneasily that night and wakes early to the darkness of the blackout blinds. He smokes, a mixture of cigarettes and weed, but neither manages to dial back the tension. He notices that his fingers are shaking as he lights up. His mouth is the sort of desert dry that no amount of tea, coffee and water can shake off.

Lissie arrives as the TV is changing programs. It's 11 o'clock. She drops off a jewelry box, which he puts in the inside pocket of his jacket. She doesn't chuck herself down in the chair or smoke, but stands by the door.

"Good luck, mate"

She puts out her arms and he is struck by how childlike she looks. He embraces her.

"Thanks for everything, Lissie. And stay safe, eh."

He lets go of her, and she leaves. He waits at the door to watch her, but she doesn't look back. She ambles up the road with her gangster roll, holdall slung over one shoulder and he wonders whether she is going back to school.

One o'clock. He has shaved, and put on a shirt. He pulls his jacket on, takes a breath then walks out the front door. It's the same suburban street, empty except for a man walking on the other side of the road with his dog. Neither spares him a second look. He raises the car key and presses the fob. A black Punto blinks back at him. He resists the temptation to look around him before getting in. The engine starts first time.

Hillyfields Park is a green hill. He used to play football there as a kid from time to time, the local lads from the Turnham Estate and his Lewisham team fighting their postcode battles within barely noticed rules. He parks the car in a side street opposite the girls' school and walks uphill.

The café is at the top. Polly sits outside at a table, a cooling cup of cappuccino unattended in front of her. There are people around; some joggers, dog walkers and a few who look like office workers who have come into the park to eat lunch. Nobody stands out. She's played "spot the cop" for half an hour and has given up. She could almost believe that she is there for a genuine date. The café itself is deserted. It's design, not accident. Although nobody said this to her, she knows this is to keep members of the public out of the way, and it's almost exciting to be part of the team. Not enough to make her consider following her father into the job, but good enough to keep her interested.

Germaine MacHeath reaches the top of the hill with a smile on his face. Her blonde hair is unmistakable. He has been drawn towards it from the moment he has been able to see her. He walks past the tennis and basketball courts towards her. She stands and opens her arms. The sun is on her like a spotlight, and the leggings and sweatshirt she wears hug her figure, emphasising the narrowness of her waist and the symmetry of her shoulders. She is the most beautiful thing he has ever seen, and he quickens his pace to walk towards her.

A jogger stops as she stands. He reaches into his rucksack and pulls something out, concealing it inside his hooded sweatshirt. He'd been running slowly, aimlessly crossing and recrossing the paths on that side of the hill. He walks towards the café deliberately, his arm dropping to his side as he approaches. A man in a suit stops eating his packed lunch and stands. He puts his hand under his jacket as he walks. A woman carrying a dog lead emerges from behind the café. Others stand and converge, leaving their lunchtime lethargy behind them as they draw firearms.

Germaine MacHeath has eyes only for his Polly. He wonders whether it's a manners thing that keeps her behind the table. He thought that she would come and meet him when she stood, rather than let him do all the work. It's not enough to dampen his mood. He's heard someone say that they were so happy their heart was singing, and thought that this was bullshit at the time, but if his heart isn't singing as he walks towards her arms, it's certainly laying down a decent rhythm track. He decides that he will not embrace her immediately. He will give her the ring first. He is so fixated on the decreasing distance that he doesn't register the shouts of, "Stop. Armed Police. Germaine MacHeath. Lie on the floor with your hands behind your head. Now."

MacHeath's hand is inside the pocket, reaching around for the jewelry box. The pocket is deep, and he can't lay his hand on it immediately. The shouting breaks through his barrier of happy thoughts and he spins round, his face a contorted rictus of shock.

The first officer sees him spin. Face him. Hand in pocket.

"Gun. Gun. Gun."

The first shot takes MacHeath in the chest. He slumps, but does not fall. He tries to take his hand out of his pocket but the pain has locked his muscles, turning hand to fist and catching him as he struggles to pull it free against the friction of lining and the overwhelming pain. The second shot takes him in the upper chest, severing the aorta and he is down. He barely hears the sounds of running or the crackle of radios. His eyes roll, trying to find Polly among the branches that wave high above him. He is dead before the air ambulance lands.

The news takes a couple of hours to filter through. There are a few reports of a man being shot by police in Lewisham Borough, but Barbara MacHeath doesn't really listen to them. The radio is on. She's intent on finishing the staff rota for the next week and it's more background than information. She registers the report, kisses her teeth and shakes her head. As far as she can see, the police are always shooting people. She has just finalised her work, and decided how she would explain the bad news to those on at the weekend when the doorbell rings.

There is a man and a woman at the door. He's middle aged and white. She's black, young and slim. Both are wearing suits, but she can tell CID at a glance. It's not entirely down to her older son's lifestyle. Years at the accident and emergency coalface have brought her into contact with more police than most criminals, professional or otherwise. There have been a lot of them around since her older son escaped from prison. She doesn't like it, but she's a law abiding person. A nurse. A Christian. She does her best to smile at them.

"Can I help you?"

"Can we come in, Mrs MacHeath?"

She turns and walks back into the house leaving the door open. The man and woman look at each other, shrug and follow. She goes to the kitchen and sits. The woman stands by the sink and the man takes the seat opposite her.

"I haven't seen Germaine and he hasn't contacted me. I don't know why you think anything has changed since your colleagues spoke to me yesterday."

The man extends a hand to her. She cannot stop herself shaking it, even though she has lost patience with professional politeness.

"Mrs MacHeath. My name is Alistair Richardson. I'm a Detective Superintendent."

She doesn't respond. She's not impressed by rank, but polite enough not to say so. The introduction hangs in the air before he continues.

"My colleague is Detective Constable Sue Goulding. Would you like a cup of tea? Sue, make Mrs MacHeath a cuppa, will you?"

She doesn't respond. She's seen this scene in the waiting area at work many times. The senior police officer, the solemn faces. The offer of refreshments removes any doubt. It seems so unfair. One of her sons is dead. A cup is put in front of her, and she finds herself raising it to her lips. It is insufferably hot.

"I am sorry to have to be the one to tell you that your son Germaine died this afternoon."

She shivers, suddenly cold. Her mouth opens. It was so unfair. They said lightning didn't strike twice, but first Damien and now Germaine. She is almost angry with herself as she realises that her own grief will mean she cannot help her friend. She fights against her desire to cry. Not in front of these people. Never. She manages a question.

"How?"

Superintendent Richardson shifts in his seat. He runs his finger under his collar.

"He was shot by police. There will be a full enquiry. The Independent Police Complaints Commission has been notified, and their staff will be investigating in due course."

"Why? Why did they shoot him?"

"My understanding is that he drew a gun on officers during an attempt to arrest him."

She doesn't move. There's nothing to say. She's always feared that it would end like this. She has no illusions about her son. Every time the police came to her door she'd tried to prepare herself for bad news. She realises that this is impossible now. Nothing can prepare you. The grief is raw, and she has to fight to control herself. She will not break down in front of these people. Her eyes fill and she makes no attempt to blot her tears. She sits without speaking, sipping her too hot tea. Eventually the officer breaks the silence.

"Can we call anyone? A family member? A friend?"

The burn on her lips revives her enough to write down two numbers; her oldest friend and her pastor. The female officer leaves, phone out and paper held in front of her. Barbara MacHeath remains completely still. Neither of them speaks. They wait out the minutes to the hum of the fridge.

Chapter 30

Chief Superintendent Whiting finds himself in that particular mix of fear and fury that comes with being ultimately responsible for a situation he didn't create and which is obviously, completely out of control. He was the commanding officer of Lewisham Police Station, not the bloody commissioner. It wasn't even a divisional operation, for Christ's sake. He's been told that the Commissioner will ring him shortly, and the Press Office will be in touch, but so far he's been on his own. A crowd has started to form in front of the police station a couple of hours ago, and he is sure that he has seen a couple of film cameras among them. He holds a copy of the Evening Standard. The headline is "Cops shoot armed gangster in park." He glares at Detective Inspector Peach of the Flying Squad across his desk.

"Well. Was he armed or wasn't he?"

"The officers believed he was, Sir."

"That's not the fucking question that I asked, Inspector, and you know it. Did he have a gun on him or didn't he?"

"We did recover a gun, Sir."

Superintendent Whiting manages to repress a smile.

"Thank God for that. Where was it?"

"In his car."

"Hold on. This happened in Hillyfields, didn't it? Are you saying he drove into the park?"

Inspector Peach looks sheepish.

"No, Sir. It was parked on a side road."

"A side road?"

He slams the paper down in front of him.

"Who is responsible for this, then? You have no idea how badly this is going to play out. Do you remember when that man was shot at Stockwell tube station? Someone had the bright idea to tell the press that he'd vaulted the barrier and was wearing a fucking puffa jacket. The CCTV showed this was a lie. So now, because of this horseshit, you are going to look like a liar when you say that this was a well planned operation. The officer that shot this man will look like a liar when he says that he thought that the suspect had a gun and was a danger to himself and the public."

"I don't know, Sir. There were reporters at the scene, and maybe they overheard something and got the wrong end of the stick."

"You'd better hope that's true, Inspector, because if it turns out to be a leak from your team I absolutely guarantee you that there will be no closing ranks to protect you. We all have to think of the Service's reputation."

Chief Superintendent Whitehead gestures to the window.

"What am I going to say to them?"

It's a rhetorical question. He doesn't expect Peach to reply, and he fully intends to ignore anything he might suggest anyway. He slumps in his chair and hopes that this is as bad as the day is going to get. He stares at the telephone, waiting for a call.

***

Barbara MacHeath's home is full. She hasn't had so many people there for years, not since her Danny passed his exams and got into university. The atmosphere inside is solemn. She sits in the kitchen with Country, Pastor Campbell and five or so older people she knows from church. A mixture of her sons' friends and her neighbours are spread out around the house. There were people she didn't recognise when she last went to the bathroom. Copies of the Evening Standard are everywhere, and are being discussed angrily. There is a rumour that Germaine hadn't had a gun on him when he was shot. Apparently someone overheard the police talking in Hillyfields before the area was cleared. She's confused. If Germaine pulled a gun on the police she would mourn him. He was still her son whatever he had done. It was different if he hadn't. The police had no cause to shoot him if he didn't threaten them, even if he had killed someone and escaped from prison. It was just wrong.

Pastor Campbell is a small, thin man. His Jamaican accent is light, bleached out by many years of living in London.

"We should ask them. The youth are getting angry, and it may be about nothing at all. We should go down to the police station together and ask to speak to the man in charge. He'll have to tell us whether Germaine had a gun. You're his mother. You have a right to know. It's in their interests to tell the truth."

He stands up and graciously bends to help Barbara out of her chair, despite the fact that she could pick him up under one arm. She rises and they plough through the crowd to the front door. She stops for a moment. The street is filled with people, most of them young. Some of them may be Germaine's friends. She doesn't want to stereotype anybody, but there is an element that looks extremely thuggish. The majority are just normal people. Her neighbours. People she recognises from work. Pastor Campbell stands on the low wall in front of the house. He holds up both hands dramatically.

"Ladies and Gentlemen. We are going to march to Lewisham Police Station in order to ask the police exactly what happened to Mrs MacHeath's son. I know that emotions are running high for some of you. Many of you are Germaine's friends and family. You may be right to be angry. What we need is information. This is not a protest. If any of you chose to come with us, then it will be to support the MacHeath family. I ask you all to behave with dignity and restraint. We cannot allow the police to portray this community as a bunch of thugs."

With that, he hops down from the wall and takes Barbara's arm. Country takes her place by her friend's side and they start to walk towards the centre of Lewisham. The crowd outside the house undulates like a wave, and then falls in behind them. It grows as they walk. By the time they reach the Police Station the streets are filled with people.

The crowd that is already there is smaller. It is also younger and more vocal. Many wear blue bandanas. Not all by any means. It contains a large proportion of the bored and curious. It has been threatening enough to alarm the duty inspector into deploying two vans of TSG, the public order unit. These are parked on the wide curb outside the station door. The smaller group is subsumed into the larger one that arrives with Barbara and Pastor Campbell, who leave the comfort of anonymity and approach the police lines. An officer in full riot gear stands in front of them.

"Go back and go about your business."

Pastor Campbell draws himself to his full height. He is staring the policeman in the chest.

"My good sir. The lady standing next to me is the mother of the young man who was shot earlier today. We are not here for trouble. We just want an answer to one question."

"What's the question?"

"Did the young man who was shot have a gun on him or didn't he?"

The officer turns and leaves the two middle aged figures standing between the police lines and the crowd. He speaks to a sergeant, who goes inside.

Superintendent Whiting is still waiting for a call when the news arrives. He's looked out of the window a couple of times, and has seen the crowd and the cameras.   It doesn't look good.   The phone ringing sounds like salvation and he snatches the receiver from the cradle. The contents of the call kill any euphoria immediately. He sits at his desk wondering what to do and listening to the noise outside. He picks up the phone and dials. Engaged. He breathes deeply, forcing down panic and remembering his own advice. Saying anything that can come back to bite him as a lie would be fatal. It is actually worse that he knows where the gun was, and he almost regrets asking the question. He stands, walks to the window and looks out. The crowd is huge, blocking the road outside the police station and backing up into the market on the one side and onto the roundabout on the other. It's peaceful at the moment, but he knows that if he were to go out there and accept that the police shot an unarmed man that will change. If he goes out and repeats the Evening Standard line, it might defuse things. Who knows? Maybe they'll all hang about for a bit until everyone gets bored and goes home. Fine for today, but in however many week's time, he'll be remembered as the senior officer who was filmed passing on false information. A fool at best, and possibly a liar. Not exactly career ending, but the sort of thing that would stick him at Chief Superintendent until he retires. The best option is to say nothing. It's absolutely clear. There is no point in meeting the mother and her religious friend. Without any recording, they could say that he said anything. Far better to batten down the hatches and let whatever is going on outside blow over of its own accord. He makes a call.

The TSG sergeant is standing by the van looking at the crowd. It doesn't look exactly ugly, but he's a ten year veteran. He's policed demonstrations before, and he knows how quickly this can change. Barbara MacHeath and Pastor Campbell stand about ten feet away from him. They are silent. Her hands are clasped in front of her and her head is bowed. He mirrors her stance, and the policeman cannot deny that they look dignified. His radio crackles into life. He puts it to his ear and listens. He looks up at the glass front of the building behind him, looking for someone to appeal to and mentally cursing the chain of command. He disconnects the radio. He crosses the distance in a few strides. He's a tall man, and his training has been to project confidence. He leans towards Barbara MacHeath and speaks to her. His voice is low. It's not overheard. The nature of the message is obvious, as she slumps. She allows herself to be lead away by Pastor Campbell, who walks her to her friend. There is a collective intake of breath from the crowd as the two bereaved mothers embrace and try to overcome their own grief enough to comfort each other.

Pastor Campbell knows the danger. He shares the anger he can see on people's faces. It's not necessarily against the police, and certainly not against the sergeant who has just spoken to Barbara. He was polite, and it was obvious he was just passing on a message. He feels he should try to calm things down. He is still in front of the crowd and he opens his arms wide enough to be nailed to a cross.

"Friends. The policeman who just spoke to Mrs MacHeath passed on the message that the officer in charge of this police station will not speak to her."

Shouts start. Nobody is chanting. It's all individual anger. A bottle arcs over the crowd and smashes. Splinters and shards burst across paving stones. More shouting. Another crash from further up the market as the front window of TK Max goes in. It's near enough for the sergeant to see figures leaping in through the hole and fanning out inside. More bottles. The sergeant speaks into the radio urgently. Shields are taken out of the van as the TSG kit up and form a line in front of the police station. This isn't a demonstration. Not even an angry one. More bottles. More shop windows are put through. It's a mob. It's a riot. Fire starts in broken shops. Lewisham begins to burn.

Chapter 31

Ken McGuiness phoned in sick. It's a first for him. He's always been actually ill when he has done this in the past. The thought of going to work today was too much for him. He doesn't want to face Kath Stevens. He's not sure what he'd do, and he cannot think of what the right thing to do is, either. He can hardly have a go at her. The reason she's got to go is tied into things that neither of them wants to be common knowledge. He has realised that people will jump to the conclusion that they had been having an affair and in typical Met form, she had to be the one to go when it ended. Unfair, but the truth is worse, and he acknowledges that he will have to ride this one out. But not now. It's too close, and the small act of cowardice of not going to work seems the lesser of two evils.

He has spent the morning at the hospital, and has returned home with the news that Maxine and the baby are coming home either tomorrow or the day after. Max reckoned that they had to register her in six days, and he cannot think of a single name he'd want to saddle his daughter with. It had been a frustrating conversation. He was reduced to knocking back her wilder suggestions and promising to think about those that were neither too new age or too Wuthering Heights. He's pretty sure she's wrong about the timescale as well, but it's an argument he can't be bothered to have. Not when the possibility that his daughter will end up being called Rosebud is there to argue about.

He cannot bring himself to spend the rest of the day on the sofa. He doesn't really drink, or at least, he hasn't reached the point where a bottle and daytime TV is a good afternoon for him. He tries to read a book, but finds that he cannot concentrate. The characters and their lives are too unreal. Eventually he gives up. He picks up the Jane Canavan and Heather Buchan file and sits at the kitchen table.

He reads, then gets up and fetches some blank paper. It occurs to him that there has to be a starting point that the same person murdered both women. He corrects himself. The same person was involved in both women's murder. The DNA and the crimes themselves are too close to be a coincidence, but the rapist and the murderer could have been two separate people. Unlikely, but possible. He takes a pen and writes.

Two columns. What the two victims had in common and what separates them. The second is easier. Jane Canavan was in her early fifties. Heather Buchan was nineteen. Jane was a manager at a charity. A person of responsibility and, he supposes, of some power even if that would have been restricted to a pretty small kingdom. Heather was a student. At nineteen she had never come to police attention. According to her flatmates she'd been an idealist. Couldn't say that for Jane. He's worked with people like her. They didn't last long in the force, thank god, but they were there. He remembers a sergeant he had worked with when he was still in uniform who thought of female victims of domestic violence as his personal harem. Even at nineteen, Jane couldn't say she'd never been nicked. Arson was an odd crime for a young girl. It pointed towards a disturbed child, a dysfunctional family background, and there was nothing that suggested that from Stevens and Welbourne's statements. Moira Drinkwater's account of Jane Canavan's life in Wales was a bit of an eye opener, too. He wonders where she managed to dig up the technical term for it. Their bodies had been dumped ten miles apart. Peckham and Plumstead. Jane's was almost concealed. Heather's displayed for everyone to find. A statement?

He shuts his eyes, trying to distill the case down to a question that will point a way to the solution. Eventually he leans forward and writes;

"What does a volatile, manipulative vagophile in her fifties have in common with a nineteen year old, idealistic Catholic student?"

He reads the flatmates' statements again. He reviews the CCTV, credit card and oyster card usage reports on Jane Canavan, silently cursing that Heather Buchan hadn't bothered to register her card and make tracing her last movements possible. Out at Waterloo and never seen again. The CCTV showed someone who might have been her walking back over Blackfriars Bridge. Heading North. Heather had helped out on the soup run. It was where she had been going the night she disappeared. She'd gone to a Catholic Church in Rotherhithe or Bermondsey.

He pauses. He remembers his conversation with Father Anthony Mitchell. The priest didn't recognise Heather. Then again, all he was asked to identify was a name, and he's only been in post for a few days. He did say that his church wasn't the only one involved in the soup run. According to him, everyone chipped in including other faiths. It followed that anyone who was involved in handing out food to the homeless and who went to church in that area would be part of the same crew.

He stands. His thoughts are on overdrive. The soup run went all over, wherever there was a need. They catered to homeless people. Jane Canavan had an interest in the homeless as well. Even though she hadn't been exactly altruistic. It was the only point at which their lives even possibly converged. The alternative was that a predator whose habits were entirely random took them both. Also possible, but this made investigation an exercise in waiting for whoever this was to make a mistake, like the Yorkshire Ripper being stopped on suspicion and being caught ditching his knife and claw hammer or Ian Brady frightening one of his accomplices so much that he went to the police. The problem with this scenario is that a lot of people were likely to die before the lucky break.

If the link was an interest in London's homeless population, then the next question was how the victim and perpetrator came together. Moira Drinkwater described Jane as a heavy drinker. Her credit card showed that she had bought two bottles of wine in a riverside pub after leaving Waterloo. He'd assumed that she'd been drinking with someone, possibly her killer, but that wasn't automatically right. He could imagine volatile, angry Jane, her professional life getting more out of control, consoling herself with a proper drink after working late. You seek solace when you're drunk and feeling down. It's human nature. The sort of solace Jane had looked for in the past was easily available on the South Bank and Central London. She'd been walking north over Blackfriars Bridge in the last possible sighting. It's busy there, and he couldn't imagine a well dressed middle aged woman openly soliciting the homeless without attracting someone's attention.

He gets up, goes into the garden and smokes a cigarette. The question nags at him. Where could Jane Canavan have gone? He flicks the butt over the garden wall. He remembers the conversation at the hospital with the priest as he watches its trajectory. The soup run has a regular Saturday night slot at Lincoln's Inn Fields. Heather Buchan left her home to work as a volunteer. Blackfriars Bridge to Lincoln's Inn Fields is about a five minute walk. Well heeled volunteers staffed charities. Jane Canavan wouldn't have got a second look chatting to the clientele in the way that she would have if she had tried to pick up dossers on the Strand or the South Bank. Here was a place where the victims' paths crossed.

It all came back to Father Anthony Mitchell. He was involved with the soup run, and he could get access to the records. He could confirm that Heather was working in Lincoln's Inn Fields, or at least where she was volunteering on the night of her disappearance. It occurs to him that a list of all the volunteers would be helpful. They might be witnesses. It was even possible that one of them was the person he was looking for. Not all volunteers were do gooders. Some of them were people who had been helped and wanted to give something back. Someone like that could slip under Heather's radar and still be "street" enough for Jane.

The man he was after would be older. Middle aged at least. He'd been active in the 1980's. He didn't think Sarah's information was wrong, just dangerous. The thirty year gap in the offences was a concern. The truth was that murderers have their ordinary lives as well as anyone else. He could have been sick, or in prison. It would be worth checking a list of the volunteers against the PNC. Anyone who had been sentenced to a long time in the early nineties and who had just been released was worth a look. He slaps his forehead. Sick, in prison or overseas and carrying on his project somewhere else. He wracks his memory. Hadn't Anthony Mitchell told him he had come back to the UK a few days before Jane Canavan's death? Congo was the sort of place where you could probably literally get away with murder. Who would notice a couple more corpses among the thousands? He laughs out loud. It's a ridiculous idea. Besides, it would take serious physical strength to overpower either Jane or Heather. Jane had been tall, raw boned. She wasn't young, but she was a forceful character, someone who had no problems in asserting herself. Heather may have been smaller and slighter, but she was young and fit, and probably fighting for her life. He'd met Anthony Mitchell a couple of times, and if he had to use one word to describe him it would be frail. Besides, all the evidence was that he was a man who put himself in danger to help people. Kath Stevens had showed him the video on line, and it was impressive. Not the sort of man who exploited and murdered women for personal gratification. The two didn't fit at all. Still, worth finding out where he had been on both dates. Better to positively rule something out than have it come back to bite you.

He's on his feet and searching for his coat before the thought has finished forming. He's out of the house seconds later. He wonders whether he should call this in, but decides that his sickie would make this awkward. He gets into his car and starts to drive.

Chapter 32

Father Anthony Mitchell discharges himself from hospital that evening. He's been prodded about, poked and scanned, but he has learned nothing new. A portion of his brain was damaged by a skull fracture. Occasionally this leads to him having seizures. They're not regular at the moment. The last one was some years ago. He's been told that they will get more frequent as he gets older. It's not an encouraging thought, and he shivers as he stands outside the hospital waiting for his mini cab.

The heating in the car is stifling, and he finds himself drifting into a waking dream. He's suddenly conscious that the car has stopped. It's Peckham, and traffic is backed up towards Camberwell Green as far as the art college. The radio is on, and he is sure that he hears the announcer say something about widespread rioting.

"What's going on? Why have we stopped?"

The driver is Eastern European. He's a solidly built man with a greying crew cut. He speaks respectfully, aware of his passenger's clerical collar.

"I'm sorry, Father. It has all gone crazy. The radio said that Lewisham is on fire. All the shops have been broken into and people are taking things. Something is happening up ahead by the library. It's probably the same. I'll try to work around it and get you home."

The car pulls rapidly onto the opposite carriageway and executes an elaborate turn. They drive uphill towards East Dulwich.

"I'll try to go through Greenwich. I think New Cross will be the same. Too many black boys fighting in the street there."

The car navigates its way through to Peckham Rye, and passes the park on its way towards Brockley before heading towards Deptford Bridge. As they reach Blackheath Hill, Father Anthony notices a crowd in the street ahead. They are walking towards Lewisham Town Centre. The car slows, and for a moment it looks like the crowd will stop them. People stare into the car at the priest and the taxi driver, but nobody tries to block their progress. The faces around him are of all races. They are all young and they look excited, energised. There's no obvious anger or chanting. They clear the crowd and are at Deptford Bridge. Father Anthony notices that the Tesco Metro's windows have been put through. A sad collection of shattered and depleted display items hangs half into the street. There is nobody around. The car slows at the junction, and he looks up towards New Cross. He can see streetlights and the orange shimmer of fire in the middle distance. What is missing from the scene comes to him. He would have expected there to be policemen everywhere.

"What's happened to the police?"

The driver clears his throat in a perfect cocktail of derision and contempt.

"Police? They ran away. They protect police stations and let these people get on with it. It's disgusting. I think we'll be OK from here. There's nothing for them to steal on Lower Road."

The rest of the journey passes without any contact with either policemen or rioters. The cab pulls up outside the parochial house and Father Anthony looks up at St Steven's silhouette. The steeple looks solid, reaching to the heavens and unchanged. He pays the driver and stands on the threshold to watch him drive away.

Once inside he boils the kettle. There is no milk in the fridge so he makes do with black coffee. He sits. He's too tired to read so he puts on the TV. Scenes of riot scroll across the screen. Lewisham, Peckham, Tottenham. London seems to have gone mad. He watches burning buildings and surging crowds with disbelief. The coffee gives him a burst of energy and he decides to go and have a look to see whether anywhere close by has been affected. The street is quiet. There are no pedestrians, and the houses have a hunched appearance. He imagines his neighbours watching the same images and deciding to lock and bar the doors and windows, sitting in fearful hope that the situation would be brought under control. He can see an unmistakable glare on the horizon. He thinks it's coming from New Cross, and wonders what has been set alight. He's cold. He takes a parting glance at

St Steven's intending to go back into the parochial house and believes that he can see lights inside. He doesn't trust his eyes at first. It could be a reflection of streetlights. An optical illusion, even, but the more he looks the less any other explanation applies.

Father Anthony goes and checks the diary. He tells himself that it's probably some activity he's forgotten about after his collapse at the hospital. Maybe the diocese has arranged for another priest to take communion? The page is empty. He decides that he will investigate. After all, it's not as if there is anything in the church that is worth stealing, and he thinks that a few disaffected youths are unlikely to be violent.

The doors are open. Not wide, but unlocked. He pushes the right hand one cautiously. He knows that it's important not to alarm whoever is in there. It swings open, the hinges oiled and slick. The church is lit with candles that build walls of light and shadow that disorientate him. He reaches for the light switch. Nothing. He flicks it up and down; hope giving way to acceptance. The fuses must be gone. His eyes have become accustomed to the light, and he sees that the candles have been arranged so that they create a pathway towards the foot of the bell tower. He swallows. Hard. It's almost a mockery of ritual, a sacrilege. How dare someone come into this place of sanctuary and ridicule it? He starts to walk towards the stairs. The candles are all around him now, leading the way and marking his retreat like landing lights. The church is usually cold, but the sheer number of flames has made it warm. He reaches the bell tower. The stone stairs curve to the right. There are two candles on each, a path that winds upwards. Father Anthony follows, each step echoing uncomfortably loudly off the stone.

He is out of breath when he reaches the head of the stairs and stops, leaning against the wall to recover. The bell platform is a wooden walkway that circumnavigates the tower. There is a small window on each wall, covered with shutters that could do with both repair and repainting. It is brightly lit and hot, a moist blast that comes from the three paraffin heaters and two gas fires that have been arranged around the far side. Candles stand on every surface. He tries counting how many, but is distracted by the sight of the young woman who is handcuffed to the railing, her hands behind her back and her legs bent underneath her.

She is naked, save for a silver slash of gaffer tape that binds around her lower face. It's obvious that he has to do something, and he takes a step towards her.

"Hello, Craig."

The voice is harsh, forced over vocal chords by phlegm saturated lungs. Father Anthony looks up. There is a figure in the far corner.

"What? I'm not Craig. I'm the priest of this parish and I must ask you not to profane God's house. Let this girl go and leave."

His voice sounds weak. The other man laughs.

"I know what you are calling yourself now. I've seen you on TV playing the hero with all the darkies. But I know you, big brother, and I know what you are isn't what you pretend to be."

Father Anthony feels the perspiration running down his nose. He can only stammer ineffectually as the man continues.

"We've been having a few trips down memory lane, Craig. I hope you've enjoyed them. It's time for the last installment, so stay still and listen. I'm not going to bore you with how we got her, but we had her tied and ready in our special place. She was a big girl. Not just fat, although she was certainly that too, but tall and broad with it. Taller than you, anyway, and she took a bit of putting to sleep to get her there. I went first, and then you had a go. Afterwards, I decided to get a bit artistic. I cut her open like a fish and I couldn't believe my eyes. She wasn't just a fat girl; she had a baby inside her. I started to laugh. I couldn't help it. I had been down the Spa earlier to buy some cans and they were doing a two for the price of one. I could never resist a bargain, and there we were again. Two for the price of one.

I called you over. I mean, I had to show you this. It was amazing. It looked like a little alien once I'd got through the fat and meat and I could see it properly. Its face was squashed against the bag, and its eyes were open. I wondered whether I was the first and last thing it would ever see, and it made me feel sort of spiritual. Powerful. Like God. You wouldn't come. I called you again and again, but you stuck over by the chairs, sitting and smoking and ignoring me. It pissed me right off, so I took the knife and slit open the little bag it was in. I pulled the thing out and held it up. I shouted to you, "Fuck me, Craig. You're an uncle!"

It was only a joke. Poor taste, I grant you, but there's no excuse for rudeness and you were bloody rude. You started screaming at me about us being damned, and that we were going to hell. I tried to calm you down. I went over to you. I was planning on giving you a bit of reassurance. You know, hug it out and get on with the fun. I didn't like it when you were upset then. I know you did a lot for me in the beginning. I still had the thing in my hand and you were like a vampire with a crucifix, screaming to get it away from you, and how we were the devil and we were going to burn. I couldn't help but laugh. I mean, I'm only human and there were you, a rapist and a murderer, going on about one unborn kid like it was the be all and end all of anything. It was fucking funny, if you'll pardon my French. You didn't like that at all. I was right next to you. I had nothing but trying to calm you down in mind, and you hit me. Bang. Just like that. Straight in the jaw. I was bigger than you by then. You always were a bit of a squirt. But it caught me by surprise and down I went. You ran out and I followed you once I'd got myself together. I chased you down to the ring road. It was the middle of the night and there was nobody about. I was a bit chary of being seen running around covered in blood but I had to stop you. You left me no choice. I was going to try and persuade you to come back and stab you if you wouldn't, but it worked out far better than that. You were just running out of the estate and onto the dual carriageway when I shouted at you to stop and come home. You looked back but you didn't stop running then wham. The lorry hit you. Even I was shocked. I mean, what a bastard. There's no way he could have missed that because I was a hundred yards away and it was loud. I waited until I was sure that nobody was coming then I checked on you. I must admit that I thought you were a gonner. You were all at an angle, with a dent in your head that made it look like an Easter egg with a bite out of it. Nothing for me to do. So I went back, tidied up a bit then went home.

You were on the news the next day. In a coma after a hit and run and nobody knew who you were. It went on for the best part of a year. I even went to see you. I nicked a white coat and walked through the ward. Saw you lying there with tubes sticking out of you and the breath machine gasping on beside you and I didn't stay. You didn't look like you were going to pop your clogs any time soon, and I thought that it might be a good idea to either finish the job or make myself scarce for a bit. There were just too many people about in the hospital for plan A. You hear about it, see it in films, one bit of air in the blood and it's goodnight Vienna, but it's harder than you might think. I got beside you, and I even tried to get the thing that was putting something into your arm open, but no joy and I almost had to run when a whole gaggle of doctors and nurses showed up for a look at you. It was a close one. I nearly shat myself. There's a reason why the people who get away with killing people in hospital are always medics.

So it was back to plan B. I went and got myself a job up in London. Just building site stuff at first. Fetching and carrying and making the tea, but the boss liked me and I went to college. Once that was done I went off to Saudi, building oil refineries. Nice job to get into. Lot of work about. I've been all over the world, Craig, I mean it. You wouldn't believe the places I've seen and the people and things I've done. I'd forgotten about you, forgotten I even had a brother when there you were all over the telly. A priest. A bloody fucking hero. My big brother Craig. I decided to come and see you. I've had a great time in London. Hiding out among the dossers isn't exactly the Ritz, true, but it's easy not being noticed when you are one of the invisible men. It suits me fine. I even did a couple while I've been waiting. One stupid cunt even tried to get me pissed. Can you believe that?

I started to talk to you, but you didn't recognise my voice. I was going to just come up and say hello, but you didn't know me at all. You didn't seem to know yourself, so I told you your story to jog your memory. And here we are. Two brothers. Together again like family should be. I think we should do her, and then get back to our magical adventure. What do you say, Craig?"

He walks around the back of the bell platform. As he leaves the shadows, Father Anthony sees he has a knife in his right hand. The candle flames turn the blade molten, and he looks at the man's face for the first time. He's bald. Younger looking than he had expected from the voice, but with the lines and crevasses of the long term smoker and drinker that turn his face into a chiaroscuro. The left side of his face is puckered and white, a moonscape of scarring from his cheekbone to his jaw. His lips are pulled back into a bad tooth smile and he nods towards the priest as he takes another step. It's a greeting and an invitation. The girl struggles frantically and futilely as he bends down beside her.

"Do you want to go first, or shall I?"

Father Anthony feels as if he is not in command of his body. This is not the first time, and there is a familiarity in this lightness and purpose. He crosses to the other man and stands.

"Let her go."

"Oh come on Craig. It's just rude to refuse a gift and we both know what happened last time you were rude to me."

His arms extend towards the other man. He is not consciously ordering them to do so, but the action is right and good. The man straightens to face him.

"Calm the fuck down Craig. You can either fuck her and kill her with me or watch while I do, then we'll burn your stupid toy God house down and get on with our lives."

He can feel the toweling of the man's hooded sweatshirt knotted beneath his hands as he pulls him away from the girl. He has the brief advantage of surprise, and has him off balance for long enough to pull his head down and scream into his face.

"I'm not Craig. My name is Father Anthony Mitchell."

He is off balance and his momentum pulls the other man after him as he crashes against the rail and the window slats, desperately trying not to fall. A candle goes over. Then another. The floor is saturated with wax and paraffin and flames begin to eat at the rail and the floor with delicate licks. Fear gives him purpose. He must save himself and save the girl. Nothing else matters. He pulls his chin into his chest and fights as the fire spreads.

***

Ken McGuiness parks outside the parochial house and is concerned that the door is wide open. He rings the bell, knocks and finally gives up waiting and walks in. He is worried that he will find the priest collapsed or worse, but the house is empty and dark. Reluctantly, and irritated that his mission seems to have been frustrated, he shuts the door behind him and walks to his car. He is about to sit when he notices flames and smoke pouring from the church tower.

He goes to investigate. It's his job. There might be lives at risk. He calls in as he walks across the road. The 999 operator answers on the third ring. He introduces himself and tells her that there is a serious fire at St Steven's Catholic Church in Rotherhithe. He requests assistance and is told that there is unprecedented demand on the system and while it is on its way, it may be some time. He doesn't stop to ask, and sets off to the church.

He is relieved to find the nave deserted. He sees the candle path and wonders whether it's kids mucking about or actual Satanists. He checks the sanctuary quickly, and is about to leave when he hears shouts from the tower. There is someone up there. He knows that rescue may be impossible. The fire might be too powerful for him to do anything. It would be a dereliction of duty not to try. He follows the candles to the bottom of the stairs then takes them at a run.

The top of the stairs is an inferno. The flames have overwhelmed the far side of the platform completely. He can barely see the two men, and has to strain his eyes against the smoke and glare. They are surrounded in fire, arms around each other and still struggling. He takes a step in their direction. His instinct is to separate them, but the heat is too intense and he is driven back to the staircase. They are howling, the words lost in the roar of the flames and the ticking and popping of the wood turning black, red and white around them as they lurch backwards and forwards across the flooring. They pinball against the rail and the walls until the rotting and burning shutters give way and they are gone. Ken McGuiness stares at the night sky. The through draft intensifies and the flames pull towards the space with renewed strength. It is only now that he sees the girl. He runs to her, alarmed by the shift and squeal of the platform under his feet. He tries to pull her to her feet, but she is restrained. He sees the handcuffs and instinctively reaches for his back pocket for the key, but there is nothing there for him to find. The flames are rising as he takes one bracelet in each hand and pulls with all his strength, hoping that the chain or the upright will give. Nothing. It is getting harder to breathe. He stands, takes one step back and kicks the wooden post with all his strength and it breaks. He picks the girl up, puts her over his shoulder in a fireman's lift and runs. He staggers slightly under her weight as he reaches the bottom of the stairs and his momentum takes him half way up the aisle before he regains his balance. He carries her outside and swallows air like water as the cold of the night covers them both.

The first camera flash is like an explosion, and he wonders behind pinwheels whether he is hallucinating or has inhaled enough smoke to cause him some serious damage. He recognises the second, and is aware suddenly that he is carrying a naked woman. He puts up his left hand to hide her, realises that this looks worse and drops it again. More flashes and shouts. A paramedic arrives and covers them both with a blanket. He allows himself to be escorted to an ambulance. He only lets go of her once they are both inside and the doors have closed.

Chapter 33

The press was attracted to a burning church. It summed up the depravity of the mob, something that every editor, every chief constable and every politician was keen to push, and not without good reason. Three people died, although none of them in Lewisham. What had started as a dignified protest turned into two nights of violence and looting. The rights and wrongs of Germaine MacHeath's shooting got lost among the pictures of burning shops and kids with handfuls of trainers jumping in and out through the smashed window of a Sports Direct. A virtuous circle of the great and the good surrounded all of the possible misgivings about an unarmed man being killed in a public park. The riot had become a symbol. There was no agreement about precisely what it symbolised, but the best thing about symbols is that they fit every size. Callous consumerism and disenfranchisement came in for equal stick, and both went on as if nothing had happened once all the talking had stopped.

The Metropolitan Police did not do well. They brought the riot under control by the third day, but however much the Commissioner appeared in front of the media to praise the bravery and dedication of his officers, the fact remained that the Met had run. They had stood by while the mob destroyed, stole and generally ran amuck. Lines of officers stood protecting police stations while churches burned. The headlines were unforgiving.

One exception was Ken McGuiness, or "Hero Cop Chief Inspector McGuiness of the Murder Squad" as the headlines went. He had, after all, saved an innocent and attractive young woman from both a fire and a serial killer, and you don't get more heroic than that. Cheryl Lane, the young woman in question, was interviewed at length and was enthusiastically grateful to both the priest and the policeman. It was universally acknowledged that they were both the sort of people that had won the Second World War, the 1966 world cup and probably the battles of Trafalgar, Waterloo and Agincourt. The press was humane enough to resist the temptation not to pixelate the photographs of Cheryl's rescue. If she remembered anything of what had been said between the priest and his brother, she chose to keep it to herself.

The hero cop in question was kept in for observation when he arrived at Kings College Hospital. Smoke inhalation and shock are both potentially serious, and for eight hours he sleeps under the same roof as his wife and daughter. He discharges himself early the following morning.

***

It's eight o'clock, and the morning rush hour is just getting into full swing. The air at the lights at Camberwell Green is a blue grey particulate soup. Walking is a soft waterboarding. Ken McGuiness sits in a Turkish café. It's too early for the crowd fuelling up before professional duty or personal misfortune takes them to the nearby court, and the early morning builders and posties are already at work. The place is deserted apart from him. He nurses a cup and waits for Martin Bright.

He is still not sure that this is the right move. He could have just sent the datastick to him. He'd even gone as far as putting it in a jiffy bag, before realising that if he were Bright he'd want to meet the person handing it over. He's heard too many old school comments about looking into people's eyes to know whether they are lying, and they're all bullshit. A good liar will always fool you, eye contact or no eye contact, but when he puts himself in Bright's shoes he knows he'd want it to be face to face. There are times when the strictly rational isn't enough. He was right, too. All setting this up had taken was a call to Martin Bright's secretary with a request for a call back and a number. It had been returned within twenty minutes.

The door opens, and Deputy Commissioner Martin Bright enters. He is wearing a red tracksuit top. He obviously thinks that he blends with the locals, but he looks diminished without the blue serge and silver frogging. He is tall, and thin with it, although he has a presence that suggests that he is wiry not willowy. He has blond hair fading from a widow's peak. His skin is pale rather than pallid and his eyebrows and eyelashes are translucent. It makes his face look raw. McGuiness' first thoughts are of chemotherapy and creatures that live without natural light. His nose is aquiline, bisecting a thin lipped mouth and lining up with a cleft chin. He puts out his hand and McGuiness stands to shake. Bright's grip is aggressively firm. His fingers are long and tapered. Jack Frost or the Stockwell Strangler.

"Inspector"

"Sir"

They sit, and Bright waves over the proprietor. More coffee. McGuiness slides an envelope across the table, which is pocketed without comment. Both men drink. More silence. Both waiting for the other to fill it. Both trained interrogators. Both recognise the trick.

"You've read it."

"Yes."

"I assume that you're not about to get on your white charger as we're sitting here."

"Correct."

"What do you want?"

McGuiness has asked himself the same thing. To be left alone? To make sure that his family are safe? Saying this out loud risks showing weakness, and he cannot see a trace of pity in the other man's face. What would Bright say if the tables were turned?

"I want an assurance that this episode won't affect my career."

A smile. Cold charity.

"I read your file. An able and ambitious officer. I think we understand each other. You can pick up your family, Inspector. Nothing arising from this will be recorded."

Bright stands. Another handshake.

"Before you go, Sir, do you know what happened to Sarah Reed?"

"A tragic accident."

"A convenient one for you, Sir, if I may say so."

He stares into Bright's eyes now. They widen. The pupils contract.

"It was an accident, Inspector."

Ken McGuiness decides to leave it. He has somewhere to be, and people who rely on him. Not the time.

"I never suggested anything else, Sir."

He watches the other man leave. He's tied to Sarah's memory by chains of his own making. It sounded true, and the man didn't look like a liar. But what do liars look like?

***

McGuiness makes it back to the Special Care Baby Unit in time to witness his wife and daughter being discharged. He and Maxine walk out through the glass foyer. She holds their daughter in her arms and he has his arm around her. It reminds him of the old nuclear survival leaflet that had done the rounds when they were both students. Protect and survive. He'd certainly done the first. He was hopeful about the second. Hero cops are hard to set up, sack or prosecute, and the force needs all the good press it can find at the moment. It wouldn't help Deputy Commissioner Bright to bring down the one face on the Met that had stood up and personified the Total Policing motto. He is sure that the DNA tests that are being done on the corpse of the man who had fallen from the tower with Father Anthony will match the partial profile extracted from Jane Canavan and Heather Buchan, and he has decided to let sleeping dogs lie. How could he not? His future looks bright, so to speak, and he can't see how anyone could possibly gain from any other course of action. He has kept a copy of the datastick. Not in the house, naturally. There are safety deposit boxes for that sort of thing. It's insurance.

Maxine turns her head as they leave and looks up at him. He kisses her. It seems like the right moment.

"How about Finola, Love? It was my mum's name. You could shorten it to Fin. Cute enough for this little girl? What do you think?"

Maxine nods. He kisses her again and they walk down concrete steps together.

Behind and seven floors above them Father Anthony Mitchell lies surrounded by the silence of machines. No devils haunt his dreams as he drifts towards the event horizon. To the pure, white light of perfect peace.

Printed in Great Britain
by Amazon

44098853R00137